I0591402

THE CORRECTION

JOHN HAZEN

Black Rose Writing | Texas

©2021 by John Hazen
All rights reserved. No part of this book may be reproduced, stored in a
retrieval system or transmitted in any form or by any means without the
prior written permission of the publishers, except by a reviewer who may
quote brief passages in a review to be printed in a newspaper, magazine
or journal.

The author grants the final approval for this literary material.

First printing

This is a work of fiction. Names, characters, businesses, places, events, and
incidents are either the products of the author's imagination or used in a
fictitious manner. Any resemblance to actual persons, living or dead, or
actual events is purely coincidental.

ISBN: 978-1-68433-762-0
PUBLISHED BY BLACK ROSE WRITING
www.blackrosewriting.com

Printed in the United States of America
Suggested Retail Price (SRP) $18.95

The Correction is printed in Garamond

*As a planet-friendly publisher, Black Rose Writing does its best to eliminate
unnecessary waste to reduce paper usage and energy costs, while never
compromising the reading experience. As a result, the final word count vs. page count
may not meet common expectations.

To Lynn, my rock, with whom we've never needed a Correction.

THE
CORRECTION

1

My parents disowned me sixty-seven years ago today. Or did I disown them? I think it was a little of both.

They disowned me for not continuing the family business. As the first-born, it was my obligation, my duty, my solemn responsibility to not only continue the business but also to ensure that my firstborn heir took on the mantle.

No, we aren't in the mob or anything as untoward or unsavory as that. In fact, we're the antithesis of the mob. We attempt to do good. The reason we take the actions we do is solely for the betterment of others, never ourselves. Our "family business" has had a much more profound—and usually positive—impact on the world and its history than any mob ever could.

The obvious question to be asked is why I would forsake my responsibility. I would have to be very selfish or very insensitive to turn my back on a venture that does this much good. Perhaps I possessed both of these qualities, but they had nothing to do with my decision. I'll get to my reasons all in good time.

During the first couple years of my outcast status, I considered reaching out to my parents to see if we could get back together. I missed them. Then I would remember what my father did to me and that my mother stood behind him. I could never forgive them. If I received so much as a hint of an apology for what they did to me, we would have let bygones be bygones. I received no outreach or olive branch. In their minds, I was the transgressor, the one who was turning his back on eight-hundred years of family tradition. I should make the outreach and beg forgiveness.

I got a message from my mother saying she was divorcing my father. She had just learned of something he had done many years earlier that she found unforgivable. As soon as she became aware of it, she packed her bags and left. Since the business I was forsaking was on my father's side of the family, not hers, she was willing to re-establish contact with me. I thought it rather hypocritical that she was outraged at my father for something he did to offend her but was blind to his sin against me, even though the sin resulted in the death of my son. I didn't return her call.

I was thirty-two when they disowned me. Now that I am approaching the century mark, I think it is time that I tell my story. I do this even though I betray the trust of my family and my ancestors, a trust they closely guarded for nearly a millennium.

First, let me take some time to describe the conditions my parents demanded I meet. They were very simple. All I had to do was to marry and to have a child that grew to adulthood. Sounds reasonable, doesn't it? It should be, except that I had to marry a woman of their choosing, someone the family could "groom". It could not be someone I fell in love with, especially if she was one of "them".

I apologize for being so scattered, but I am ninety-nine years old. Scattered is what we do, but I assure you that my mind is sharp. My body has been failing me of late, but don't let me digress into a litany of my aches and pain. I have so much to say and I'm afraid I'll run out of time before I get a chance to say it. I'm also scattered because I'm afraid that, if I blurt out the truth right up front, I'll lose you as an audience. You won't believe anything else I have to say. You would think: "Poor demented, old dotard."

So, I beg your indulgence as I provide a series of examples. As I mentioned, I am violating a trust that goes back eight hundred years, so it's probably best to return to the beginning. I'll go back to when my ancestor discovered that he had a gift—or more precisely, a power—that he passed down to subsequent generations. This power is known as The Correction.

2

October 7, 1264–Warwick Castle, Warwick, England

Francis Wentworth and his apprentice, Joseph Spencer, struggled as they wheeled into place the scaffold and pulley system that suspended an enormous grey-streaked freestone. The timbers in the scaffold creaked under the great weight. Francis hoped the ropes holding the stone wouldn't snap. He had spent three months carving, shaping and polishing. It would be the focal point of the altar in the castle's newly renovated chapel, but not if it fell and cracked before they got it in place.

Francis, a skilled master mason and sculptor, had only been working on this job for four months. He was hoping this piece would enhance his standing. It would be a centerpiece, over which the priest could conduct all the sacraments, that would be on display for centuries.

The foreman of the castle renovation, Edward Carpenter, was a tough but fair boss that Francis wanted to impress to secure long-term employment on this job. The exquisite carvings on the stone would make a favorable impression, he believed. But he had to put it in place without damaging it.

Once they suspended the stone over the exact spot they wanted it, he told Joseph to turn the screws on the pulley to lower it into place. As it slowly dropped, Francis made necessary adjustments. Once it was down, there was no moving it. He trusted that Joseph could lower it with care and finesse. His apprentice had only been with him for a month, but Francis found him to be conscientious and a quick learner.

Francis made a final adjustment to the pulley. The rope strained, but it held on. They lowered the stone the rest of the way and it settled into place with a thud. Francis gazed upon the piece with satisfaction.

It was late evening and Francis dismissed Joseph so he could head home to his young wife. Francis would stick around for another couple hours to do some finishing and polishing before he went home to his wife and daughter.

He had just begun the work when he heard a shuffling noise behind him. He turned around but saw nothing, so he concentrated once again on his task. A short time later, he heard the noise again.

"Joseph, I thought I told you to go," he called out without looking up. "You head on home now."

Minutes later, he heard the sound once again. This time he stood and turned around. Dusk had fallen and he squinted as he looked out into the darkening chapel.

"Now you're getting me angry. Whoever's there, show yourself!"

He grabbed a candlestick, lit the wick and walked in the direction of the sound. After ten feet, the image of a person became apparent. It was an old man with white hair and a long flowing beard. Stooped over, he stumbled along with the help of a wobbly cane.

"Old man, you shouldn't be here."

The man said nothing. When he was close enough for recognition, he raised his head and looked Francis in the eye. Francis stepped back in fear.

"Grandpa? Grandpa Michael? It can't be."

Michael Wentworth, Francis's grandfather and the man who taught him masonry, had died ten years earlier. Francis himself had found the old man dead on the floor of his shop. The old man's heart had simply given out.

Grandpa Michael continued to look Francis in the eye. The old man stared at Francis for a few seconds and then spoke.

"I know where I need to be, Francis. It's here."

"Here? Why are you here?"

The old man ignored his questions. Instead, he issued a command to his grandson.

"Go to the cathedral."

"What cathedral?"

The man said nothing in response.

"What cathedral? Salisbury?"

The Cathedral Church of the Blessed Virgin Mary in Salisbury naturally popped into Francis's mind. He had worked there for ten years performing finishing masonry work inside the cathedral. There was still much construction and finishing work left at the cathedral, but the fundamental sections—the nave, the transept and the choir—were completed. There would be a lull in construction for a few years as the elders replenished the coffers to pay for the completion. Francis could not afford to wait until the work started up once more. He had a wife and daughter to care for. He had to move on. His preference would have been to move to London to work on the construction of Westminster Abbey, but his inquiries about employment went unanswered. When a friend told him they were looking for skilled masons for the renovation of a castle in Warwick, a hundred miles north of Salisbury, he applied and was accepted.

Now, an old man who appeared to be his grandfather but could not possibly be, was telling him to return to a cathedral, which Francis interpreted to be the one in Salisbury. He gave no explanation why Francis should go there or what he should do once he got there.

Francis called out once again, but the old man did not respond. He turned and walked away, leaving through the door. Francis chased after him.

"What cathedral? Grandpa, please stop and talk to me. You can't be suggesting I go back to Salisbury. That's a two-day trip. Stop, old man. Talk to me."

When Francis reached the door, he looked to his left. His grandfather was not there. Francis searched in all directions but the old man had disappeared. He should have easily overtaken the cane-walking gentleman, but he couldn't find him. He turned around and went back in the opposite direction in case his eyes had played games on him. They hadn't. The old man was not there, either.

Francis gathered up his hat and coat and departed the chapel, leaving his tools where he had dropped them when Grandpa Michael appeared. He walked out into the crisp autumn weather and headed towards home.

He opened his front door and his ten-year-old daughter, Emily, ran into his arms. He picked up the blond-haired, lithe girl and hugged her tight as she giggled in delight. Martha, his wife, trailed along. She had on her apron for preparing dinner.

"You look like you saw a ghost, Francis," she remarked in her voice, in which remained a hint of brogue from her Irish forebearers.

Francis put Emily down and patted her behind as she went off to play. Staring at her running away, he responded to his wife.

"I did. I saw a ghost."

Martha laughed, thinking he was joking. Her laughter subsided when she saw by his face that he was deadly serious.

"Whose ghost?" she asked.

"My Grandpa, Grandpa Michael. He came to me when I was finishing up at the castle."

Martha sat down. She was both more religious and more superstitious than her husband. She could believe that a ghost, especially that of Francis's grandfather, appeared to him. It was definitely not out of the realm of possibility in her way of thinking.

"Did he say anything to you?"

"Yes, he told me to go to the cathedral?"

"The cathedral? Salisbury Cathedral?"

"He did not say, but I think so. It has to be."

"What are you going to do?"

"I can't leave you and Emily. I can't leave my job. It's at least a two-day trip in each direction."

"Emily and I will be fine for a week. You just finished the baptismal font. Show it to your boss tomorrow. He'll love it. You know he will. You already have ideas for your next project. Tell him about it, but that you need to visit the quarry to select a suitable stone. The quarry's just north of Salisbury, correct?"

"That's right. You're brilliant, woman! Are you sure you'll be okay?"

"Of course, we will. God is speaking to you. You must go."

• • •

Three days later, Francis walked into Salisbury Cathedral. It was one of the largest religious structures in all of England, let alone the world. Its magnificence filled its congregants with the power of God every single day. When the choir was singing or the monks were doing their chants, the sounds echoed throughout the nave, lifting the entire cathedral to heaven. It wasn't just the music that did this, the cathedral and everything about it had a majesty. Francis knew he had contributed to that majesty.

He knew it was wrong for him to take pride in his work. His efforts went toward the glorification of God. That—and the sizable salary he received as a skilled artisan—should have been enough for him, but he couldn't help himself. Whenever he walked into the vestibule and then the sanctuary, he noticed the pride that filled his chest when he observed the tiny details in the stone that his hands had produced.

On this day, however, he was not at Salisbury Cathedral to admire his handiwork. Not being a religious man, was he not there to pray. He attended the consecration of the Cathedral and then services on Christmas and Easter with his wife and daughter, but that was the extent of his religious fervor. Francis would never state it out loud but he was ambivalent about the existence of God. When cholera decimated Salisbury two years earlier, he and his family were spared, but friends who lived on both sides lost children to the insidious disease. He felt blessed, but he wasn't sure that it was any God that blessed him. He wondered what kind of God would take two children.

Why was he here? He was told to come. It was a Tuesday, so there were no services going on. He arrived at the Cathedral at eight in the morning and took a seat on the aisle about halfway down. There were only two other people, an elderly couple sitting toward the rear, in the massive sanctuary. Were they the reason he was here? He didn't know either the man or the woman and they paid him no mind. So, he sat there quietly.

Fifteen minutes stretched into a half-hour which stretched into an hour which stretched into two hours. As he was approaching the third hour, he decided he was being ridiculous. Nobody else had entered. The old couple had left a long time ago. A young bearded priest entered the sanctuary, and piously performed his daily sacraments at the altar. Francis examined the earnest cleric as he went through his rituals. There was nothing out of the ordinary. He rose from the pew to leave. As he turned to head up the aisle, he bumped hard into a man who was about Francis's age and build. Francis stumbled and lost his balance. The man stopped and helped him up.

"Please forgive me," he said as he offered a hand, "I can be such an oaf."

Francis accepted the man's help and stood up.

"No harm, sir. You seem to be in quite a hurry to pray."

"I am. I'm late for work, but I come to the cathedral every day to pray for my father."

"Every day?"

"Yes."

"Is he sick?"

"Not as far as I know. I see him occasionally, but we have not spoken in five years."

"Why not?"

"It was something I said. I wish I could take it back, but I can't. I really have to pray now."

"Do you mind if I sit with you while you pray? My name is Francis Wentworth."

"Suit yourself. I am Richard Marsh."

Francis followed Richard to his spot and sat beside him. Richard knelt and closed his eyes in prayer for fifteen minutes. He sat back in his pew for another minute and then got up to leave. Francis got up with him. As they left the pew, they both crossed themselves and headed toward the exit.

"May I walk with you as you head back to work?"

"If you like. I'm working on a house about a mile from here. I am a carpenter by trade."

"I'm a mason. I worked on this cathedral for ten years, but now I live in Warwick."

"Where's that?"

"A two-day ride to the north."

They walked along in silence. Francis sensed he was there to help improve Richard's strained relations with his father, but he had no clue what. He probed.

"Tell me about your father."

"He's also a carpenter. He taught me the trade. We were inseparable for most of my life, but then I said something that I wished I could take back the second it left my mouth."

"What did you say?"

"To be honest, I don't exactly remember. It was in a moment of anger. My mother had passed away a few months earlier. I did not grasp how distraught he was. I didn't feel he was treating a client fairly. His work had slipped. I complained to him. He answered me back and it escalated. After that, he broke off all contact with me. I tried apologizing many times, but it always fell on deaf ears. We live in the same city, so it's impossible to avoid each other entirely, but he never acknowledges me. If we're approaching each other on the street, he walks to the other side. We had always argued, sometime heatedly, but we always had my mother there to knock our heads together and bring us to our senses. Without her there, the things we said festered. God, I miss her, but I miss my father, too."

They stopped in front of a sturdy yet undistinguished house. Richard looked at it longingly.

"This is my father's house. We built it together. I always go by here after my visit to the cathedral even though it is out of my way. I hope one day he will look out and see me. His heart will soften and he'll come out to me. We'll embrace and all will be forgiven. It will never happen. My only solace is that my daily prayers will protect him and keep him safe. Maybe my prayers will be answered and someday we'll come back together. What I wouldn't give to return to that moment and not say what I said. I can't do that, can I?"

Francis looked upon his newfound friend.

"I guess you can't."

Francis put his hand on Richard's shoulder and then spoke one more time.

"Then again, maybe you can."

Richard turned and looked him in the eye. The next instant, Richard disappeared. He simply vanished. Francis couldn't believe his eyes. He felt a little dizzy, but the feeling passed as quickly as it came.

He stumbled back to the cathedral. The same priest that he had seen earlier was still there.

"Excuse me, Father."

"Yes?"

"I was here a short time ago with another man. Have you happened to see him?"

"I saw you here earlier, but you were alone."

"I see. Do you know Richard Marsh? He says he comes here every day to pray for his father."

"I know a Richard Marsh. He's a carpenter, I believe. But he doesn't come here every day. He attends services pretty much every Sunday, but no other days. He's often with his father, also named Richard. His mother passed about five years ago. They sit in that pew, right over there."

"Together?"

"Why wouldn't they sit together?"

"No reason. Thank you, Father."

Francis went to the house Richard had pointed out as his father's. He stood outside and gazed into the front window. Sitting there was Richard and an older man Francis assumed to be his father. Francis contemplated knocking on the front door, but he thought better of it. He knew why his grandfather sent him on this journey. He didn't need to know anything more.

3

Francis climbed onto his wagon and prodded the horse forward. Although he was looking forward to heading home to his wife and daughter, his mind was swirling. He had trouble believing any of this. Maybe Richard Marsh never existed. Maybe he never returned to Salisbury Cathedral. Maybe it was all a dream. He hoped he would wake up soon to find himself laying beside his dear Martha. But it didn't happen. The dream continued as the horse clopped its way down the road.

It wasn't until he was well along that he remembered the quarry. He was already several miles past the turnoff and contemplated not turning around. He could say he stopped there, and they had no stone that was suitable for the purpose, but he didn't want to get caught in a lie. So, he turned the wagon around and headed back.

It was already mid-afternoon. While there still would be daylight, he knew from experience that selecting the perfect stone was an arduous task requiring time. Starting this late would carry him into the dark night. He contemplated pulling over and setting up camp for the night so he could get to the quarry first thing the next morning. He talked himself out of doing this, however, knowing it would only delay reuniting with his family.

As he approached the quarry, he noticed a block of freestone around his size sitting in the middle of the courtyard. As he approached, the superb quality of the stone became evident. His experience told him he could make it come alive. The stone's subtle striations were calling out to him. He practically salivated as he looked over the flawless specimen.

He resigned himself to the fact that, given its location in the courtyard, it was most likely spoken for. A purchaser would arrive any moment to pick it up. But it wouldn't hurt to ask.

As he brought the wagon to a stop, Aldred Fitzgerald, the quarry foreman, emerged from the warehouse office. Francis had become friendly with Aldred during his time at the cathedral. They were kindred spirits with a shared appreciation for a fine piece of rock. The quarry did very well in providing all manner of stone during the construction.

"Francis, is that you? I thought you moved far away from these parts."

"Hello, Al. Yes, I've moved far away, to Warwick, north of here."

"Well, it's great to see you, I must say. What brings you here?"

"I need a sizable piece of high-grade stone for an altar-piece for the chapel at the castle I'm working at. The quarries up our way are all very inferior compared to what you offer. That piece in the middle of your courtyard caught my eye."

"It's a beauty, isn't it? I actually thought of you when we mined it. There aren't many people left in these parts who appreciate true quality."

"I assumed it's sold already. It looks like it's ready for someone to pick it up."

"It was spoken for, but I just got word today that the buyer is backing out. Are you interested?"

"Yes! I'll send payment to you when I get back."

"You're good for it. I'll get my men to load it on your wagon. It's heavy, but your horse can handle it if you take it slow. It's going to take a while, so why don't you come home with me. My wife can make us a nice dinner and then you'll stay the night and get a start first thing in the morning."

Francis was about to give his regrets, saying he wanted to get back home as soon as possible, but then he reconsidered. It would take some time for the men to place the heavy stone in his wagon without cracking it. Then he would not be heading out until dark. He would have to stop soon anyway. Also, he didn't want to offend his friend.

"Sounds good, Al. Lead the way."

The first thing the next morning he was on the road with his new purchase. Because of the weight of the marble, his progress was very slow. He would have to add at least one additional day to the trip. Any faster, he could burn out his horse. This gave him time to contemplate the happenings of the preceding days.

The more he thought about Richard, the more unbelievable the entire scenario became. In fact, the circumstances were so outlandish that, by the time he arrived home in Warwick, Francis had convinced himself that it was all a dream. Richard and his father were merely figments of his imagination.

As Francis pulled the wagon up to the front door, he heard his wife call out. "Em, your daddy's home!"

Martha rushed out the door and ran to her husband. He dismounted and gave her a big hug and kiss.

"Well, what did you discover? What did Grampa Michael want you to do?"

"It was nothing. A waste of time, although I did pick up this magnificent piece of freestone at the quarry. It was like it was waiting there, just for me."

Martha eyed him curiously. Francis could tell that she didn't believe he was telling her the entire truth about the trip. At that moment, Emily flew around the side of the house and jumped into his arms.

"Well," Martha said, "You're just in time for dinner. Get yourself cleaned up some and then we can eat."

They all sat at the table and, once Martha said grace, they all dug into the lamb stew she had prepared. Francis was trying to figure out the best way to tell his wife that he hadn't been entirely truthful when Emily spoke up.

"Daddy, did you bring back the stone Grandpa Michael left for you?"

Francis and Martha looked at each other, dumbstruck.

"How do you know Grandpa Michael?" Francis asked. There was no way she could know him. Grandpa Michael had died a week before Emily was born.

"He visits me when I play in the back."

"And you talk with him?"

"Yes, he said you were helping a man and his daddy. You helped them, so Grandpa Michael gave you the stone."

Francis sat in stunned silence for a minute, gazing at his daughter as she continued eating. Then he slowly turned to Martha and told her the truth about the cathedral, Richard and his father, the stone. Everything.

"I thought it all a dream," he remarked. "No one can disappear like he did, only to find them with a different life than when you left them, can they?"

Martha said nothing. She reached over and took her husband's hand.

"Emmy dear. You must tell us everything Grandpa Michael said to you. Tell us every word that you can remember."

4

Present Day

Can I attest that this story is the God's honest truth? Probably not. As with any lore handed down orally over the course of eight hundred years, time has obscured, forgotten, embellished and altered pieces of this story. We do not know what happened to Richard. We do not know if Richard even existed.

Neither do we know for a documented fact that Francis Wentworth existed, but I was raised on the belief that he did. Furthermore, I believe that I am his direct descendant, through a line of first-born children, starting with Emily. As such, I am blessed with this special—for lack of a better word—power.

5

Francis tried out his newly discovered abilities numerous times in Warwick. He would talk with people and find out if they had made one decision or took one action they regretted and wanted a chance to do over. After placing his hand on their shoulders, their wishes were granted. He was amazed every time.

His subjects, and everyone else, were entirely oblivious. Their old pasts simply evaporated away. They were filled with a set of fresh, new memories. He'd see the person afterwards and, in each case, that person was leading a happier and more productive life than they had before. The person had no recollection of the previous life, nor did anyone else. Francis was the only person aware of what had happened, or so he believed.

This went on for two weeks before he made a big mistake. It was an unintended error, but it was a mistake.

Joseph Amesbury was a laborer who lived a couple streets away from the Wentworths. Francis and Martha had a casual acquaintance with him and his family. Emily often played with their daughter, Jane. Joseph's situation was much like that of Richard Marsh. He and his father had had an argument and they hadn't spoken with each other in twelve years. The situation was so similar to Richard's that Francis had no problem springing into action. He granted Joseph the ability to take back what he said and thus repair the relationship with his father.

That same afternoon, Francis ran into Joseph as he walked down the street with his father. They appeared to be the on the best of terms. Francis went home, extremely satisfied with himself over another job well done.

Emily came up to Francis when he arrived at home.

"Daddy, I was playing with Jane, a friend of mine, when she disappeared."

"Disappeared?"

"Yes, we were running together. I turned to say something to her, but she wasn't there."

"Nobody can just disappear, honey," he said, knowing full well that it was possible for someone to just disappear.

"She did. I went over to her house to see if she ran home. A woman who was not her mother answered the door. She said there was no Jane living there."

An eerie feeling came over Francis.

"Em, what is Jane's last name?"

"Amesbury."

"Oh my God," Francis screamed. "What have I done?"

Martha rushed in. Flour from kneading dough covered her hands.

"Francis, what is it? What's wrong?"

"Martha, do you know Emily's friend, Jane Amesbury? She's got dark long hair, about Emily's height and build."

"No, I don't think I know her."

Francis knew for a fact that Martha knew the girl. Jane had been to their house a number of times. Martha also knew Joseph and his wife, Maria.

"Martha, I'm trying to remember the name of Joseph Amesbury's wife. I think it's Maria."

"No, it's Lucy."

"You're sure about that?"

"Of course I'm sure, Francis. What is going on?"

He knew exactly what had happened. He had made it possible for Joseph and his father to reconcile, but he had altered other events in Joseph's past. Somehow, staying close to his father resulted in Joseph and Maria never meeting. As a result, Jane was never born. Francis sat Martha down and explained the situation, or at least his understanding of the situation, to her. He told her it was almost as if he had killed Jane. He snuffed her out of existence. She was a memory only to Emily and him.

"Martha, I'll never use my gift again. It's too dangerous to continue."

"Francis, God gave this gift, and one does not refuse God's gifts."

"I'll think about it."

"Francis, it would appear that you are not the only one who has this gift."

"Who else has it?"

"Emily."

"Emily?"

"Why is it I can't remember either Jane or Maria, but Emily can? She's just like you. She can see not only the present, but also the Corrections."

"I hadn't really thought about that."

"You owe it to her to continue to learn about your talent and then to teach your daughter to use it wisely. You need to be careful about who you help. If someone has children, you must back away and not help them. Also, I'm convinced this is a gift from God, so you need to only help people who are looking to do good. It can't be used to help someone who cheats or looks for revenge. Reuniting with a father is a noble goal, but someone who is looking to amass a fortune because he can go back and change the past is not."

"You're very wise, my dear."

"Yes, I am, aren't I? The first thing we need to do is to put our daughter's heart and mind at rest. We have to explain to her about her gift and about Jane's disappearance. This must be quite confusing and frightening to her."

Emily grew up knowing that she had the gift. Francis taught her to use her gift wisely, that Corrections should only be for those who she believes will use their second chance wisely. They should use it to mend relations with people. They should use it to live fuller lives than they are currently leading.

She was also taught to not talk about her gift to anybody. She shouldn't even tell people she knew and trusted. If the truth became known, she could not prove it. Once she helped people with a Correction, they had no memory of their previous lives. Nor did anybody else. If she told somebody, they wouldn't believe her. They couldn't believe her. People who heard her would either think she was not of sound mind or that the devil possessed her. Neither of these possibilities would work out well for her. She could spend the rest of her days in an asylum or they could kill her. It was best to perform her Corrections with no fanfare. She would remain quiet. It was a time of rampant superstition and ignorance. If she told someone that she could send people back in time to correct mistakes, it could get her severely punished, including being burned at the stake for heresy and blasphemy.

She could not even tell her two younger brothers, Mark and Luke. Francis and Martha could tell from an early age that neither boy had the gift. Emily was the sole child who could make Corrections. Neither should she lord it over them that she had this power and they didn't. Francis was of the belief that one should not glory in God's gifts, but in what you do with those gifts.

When she was eighteen, Emily met a nice young man, a carpenter, who asked Francis for his daughter's hand in marriage. He agreed, and they were wed. It didn't take long before she was pregnant with her first child. As time went on, her size and other symptoms showed she was to expect delivery of twins. She contacted a local midwife to help once the time came.

Her delivery was difficult and Emily almost died, but she was strong and ultimately pulled through. In later years, she wondered if the gift would have vanished forever if she had perished.

The midwife had delivered two healthy boys, Francis and Michael. Emily was eager to see if one of them had inherited her gift, just like she had. However, she knew she couldn't rush it. The boys had to be mature enough to accept the awesome responsibility that comes with every Correction. Unfortunately, Francis had passed away from influenza just before the boys were born. She missed him terribly, but she also missed having him around to indoctrinate the boys, if in fact they had the gift. She was on her own.

Although she could only wait for the boys to grow before educating them about their ability to perform Corrections, she could observe them when she performed one. She remembered when she was young and she would periodically have these strange feelings. These weren't the same as the normal feelings boys and girls go through as they enter puberty. These were sensations of something odd happening in the world. It wasn't until much later that she could correlate these feelings with the times that her father performed a Correction. Now she was hoping to do the same with one or more of her sons.

She observed them through their first five years and detected nothing out of the ordinary. She was resigned that the gift stopped with her when she got the confirmation she was looking for.

Their neighbor, William Chester, was repairing tiles on the roof that had loosened over time. His wife, Annette, had asked him to look after their five-year-old son, Mathias, while she was at the market. To monitor him, he had the boy play with a wooden toy in front of the house. As William worked, a heavy ceramic tile broke loose and slid off the roof. Before he could grab it, the tile went hurtling down. He screamed, but it was too late. The tile struck Mathias in the head, rendering him unconscious immediately.

William bypassed the ladder as he jumped from the roof. He picked up the inert boy and carried him inside and placed him on his bed. He ran out the door to get the physician. By the time they returned, Mathias was dead.

Mathias had often played with Frances and Michael. They cried when they learned of his death. In their youthful naivete, they couldn't quite comprehend how someone their age was there one day and gone the next.

William and Annette were very private people. They weren't antagonistic towards their neighbors, but neither did they embrace them. Therefore, Emily's work was cut out for her as she attempted to figure out a way to perform a Correction. She made up a pot of lamb stew and walked over to the Chester house. Annette answered the door.

"Hello, Mrs. Chester. I know it's a tough time for you, and I wanted to offer our deepest sympathies. At times like this, it's hard to do even the most basic things, so I made you a pot of lamb stew."

"Thank you so much. Won't you please come in?"

"Yes, that would be nice."

Annette took the pot as she led Emily into the modest house. When they walked in, they found William sitting in a straight-back chair. He was staring on into space, his teeth clenched.

"Look who's here, love. It's Emily Freeman, our neighbor. She brought some lovely stew for dinner. It smells delicious. Emily, why don't you have a seat while I put this in the kitchen."

Emily sat down beside William. She could practically feel his self-pity and his self-loathing.

"Mr. Chester, Mathias was a good friend to my boys, Frances and Michael. They played together all the time. My boys wanted me to tell you they're very sorry."

He looked over at Emily. His eyes bespoke defeat and sorrow. "Thank your boys for me. I've seen them around. They are good boys."

"Yes, they are. Mr. Chester, you can't go on blaming yourself for Mathias's death."

"But I am responsible for his death. Nobody but me. I'll carry that around with me all my life."

"Is that what Mathias would want you to do? Blame yourself?"

"Who are you to come in here like this and tell me what I should be feeling?"

"I don't mean to offend you, Mr. Chester. If you could have anything in the world, what would it be?"

"What are you saying?"

"If you could make one wish in the entire world, what would it be?"

"I wish I never went up on that roof. I wish I never had Mathias outside with me on that day."

Emily leaned over and put her hand on his shoulder. He disappeared. She found herself in her own home, listening to the sounds of her two boys in the yard between their houses, playing with Mathias. She walked out the door and saw Annette walking along, carrying a straw basket full of produce from the market. Instead of her usual avoidance and lack of communication, Annette let out a hearty hello to Emily. "Beautiful day, isn't it?" "Very beautiful," Emily responded.

I have often theorized that, although the subjects of the Corrections are not aware of their previous reality, a bit of the Correction may seep through. There was no way that she realized that life had been restored to her son, but deep inside her she knew that something momentous had happened. She was appreciative and joyful, as was her husband.

Emily went inside her house to prepare dinner. She'd only begun chopping her vegetables when the boys walked in. They looked confused and concerned. Emily asked them if something was wrong. They were reticent to say anything, but Francis spoke up. He was always the more talkative of the two and would be the one to speak up for both of them.

"Mama, we thought Mathias was dead, but then today he is alive. We don't understand."

Emily looked down on the twins.

"Michael, you thought that Mathias was dead, too?"

Michael nodded his head. Both boys stared at the floor, looking like they had done something wrong. Emily got down on her knees.

"Come here, you two."

They trudged over to her. She snatched them both and enveloped them in a bear hug as she kissed their cheeks.

"I love you both so much. There is nothing wrong with you. In fact, it proves to me how special you are. I can't tell you right now what happened. I will tell you when you're older but right now I want to tell you that there is nothing wrong with you. Nothing at all. Do you understand?"

They both nodded, but she did not convince them. Emily was still holding on to them.

"If there's something wrong with you, you won't be ticklish. Let's see."

She started tickling the sides of each boy. Soon they were squealing with laughter and struggling to get free, but Emily held tight for a minute and then let them go. As she watched them run off, she felt happy that she was able to pass her gift on to the next generation. Both of them would carry it on. Little did she know that, by passing her gift on to twins, and other twins who were subsequently firstborns in the family, she would impact my life centuries later.

6

1493 to 1532–Warwick, England and London, England

Francis and Emily had codified most of the rules that would guide subsequent generations in performing Corrections. They established the basic tenets: do nothing that would endanger children and do nothing purely for monetary or personal gain. Family members of future generations would adopt additional rules, like do nothing that could significantly alter history.

Most of us down through the ages have strived to follow these rules simply because they make sense. However, there is no known punishment for those who stray from the rules. As Abraham Lincoln once said, "Law without enforcement is just good advice." As such, it would only be natural that, over the course of eight hundred years, there would be a few that would skirt the rules or would ignore them outright.

One such rule-breaker was Thomas Acton. Thomas was born in Warwick, where his family had lived for centuries. At seventeen, steeped in the lore of Corrections, he set off to find his fame and fortune. He was keenly aware that he would not achieve fame and fortune in Warwick, so he made the one hundred mile trip southeast to London.

He found London intoxicating. The sights, the smells, the sounds all around him stimulated all his senses. He wanted to be a part of it all, but he also wanted to be above it all. His parents had attempted to apprentice him to a local mason, but Thomas found that boring. He thought he could do much more with his life.

He didn't have any specific skills, except that he could read and write and he was adept with numbers. Considering the poor literacy rate in England during this period and the vast majority of those who could read and write were concentrated in the upper classes, Thomas was indeed a rarity. He also had a certain charm and an ability to get people, especially women, to do his bidding. He hoped these abilities would make him a desirable commodity. He also believed he could use one other talent to great advantage: his ability to perform Corrections.

Despite years of his father drumming the rules and restrictions concerning Corrections into his head, Thomas felt no inhibitions in how he could use his gift. Corrections could be—and should be—put to monetary advantage. If a great tenor could put his gift to use and then get paid for it, why couldn't he do the same thing?

He became especially excited about the possibilities once he discovered that it was possible for him to perform a Self-Correction. Either nobody before him had ever attempted a Self-Correction or, if someone had thought about them, they deemed them unethical and wrong. This would fall into the area of using the gift for a personal advantage, not to help the lives of others. Thomas did not see a Self-Correction this way. He saw it as putting his gift to the maximum advantage possible.

Once he arrived in London, he put his limited funds toward the purchase of a passable suit at a clothier. It wasn't the highest style suit, but neither was it something that would get laughed at either. His immediate aim was to land himself a rich woman who would take care of him until he secured employment. He would try out different opening lines on rich women to see what worked and what didn't. He would tell them how beautiful they were and then gauge their reactions to determine his next course of action. If they slapped him in the face, he would say he wished he hadn't said that, touch his own shoulder and find himself face to face with the same woman. Because of the Self-Correction, she would have no memory of his previous slight. Then he would try a new line to see if that one worked. Eventually, he'd get a smile on her face. He knew he was in.

He took up with a few women, and they contributed monetarily to his cause, but he soon found them boring and insipid, so he would move on to a new woman. Then he met Lady Antonia Frazier. She was a rich, cultured widow ten years his senior. He felt an immediate connection with her. She felt the same toward him because he won her over on the first try without the need to perform any Self-Corrections.

He became Lady Antonia's constant companion and, because of her connections to society, he soon found himself with entrée to the finest salons in all of London. This gave him access to the richest and most powerful men in all of England. He devised a way to ingratiate himself to the nobles.

There were men of the upper classes who spent their days formulating schemes to undermine or discredit a noble who was close to the King. If they were successful, the noble would fall out of favor and the one who orchestrated the coup would be raised up to fill the vacuum. If they were unsuccessful, they would lose their heads, but the rewards of being in favor with the King was definitely worth the risk.

Thomas's plan was simple. He would approach as many nobles as he could at various functions and talk with them. He would exchange pleasantries and spout a few innocuous inanities before excusing himself. Over the course of the next week or month, he would chart the statuses of the nobles he'd spoken with. Thomas would then pounce when Lady Antonia advised him of a new intrigue or scandal in the court involving one of those nobles.

He would perform a Self-Correction, saying something like, "I wish at the gala on April 20, 1495 I had advised Lord Exbury to keep a close eye on Will Fallon. I wish to tell him that Fallon will spread some libelous gossip about him that will make its way to the King, causing Exbury to fall out of favor." Francis would then touch his own shoulder, causing him to perform the Correction. He'd black out for a second and then come back to the present time. He'd remember giving Lord Exbury the advice, but he wouldn't be too sure of the repercussions.

He would then go to Lady Antonia and ask her the latest news about Lord Exbury. She, of course, would know the latest about Will Fallon's attempt to libel the Lord that the King's Guard had headed off before the news could do any damage to Exbury's reputation. Fallon was now being held in the Tower of London, awaiting his fate. Thomas would smile, knowing that the information he gave to Lord Exbury was vital.

Thomas realized that only a small portion of these prognostications would work out for his benefit. The members of the nobility were very selfish and self-centered. They did not readily welcome newcomers into their ranks, no matter how useful that person may have been. However, with each of these Self-Corrections, his reputation was further enhanced. All he needed was one nobleman to recall that he got the information that saved his life and position from Thomas.

Thomas also had to be ready for the possibility that his attempt at prophecy might backfire. He may say something about a person based on information that he or Lady Antonia had misheard or misconstrued. He could end up in the Tower for spreading scandalous lies. In cases like these, he would do what he called a Correcting Self-Correction. He would go back and wish that he had spouted the inanities that he had originally made to the noble. In that case, everything would revert back to what it was and nobody would be the wiser. On the times when he had to do this, keeping his various realities straight was difficult.

Thomas wanted to climb the ranks, but he could afford to be patient. He was young and well-situated with Lady Antonia. In fact, he found that he was falling in love with her. She cemented this love when she came to him one day and told him she was pregnant. He did the right thing by offering to marry her. She politely declined for various political and social reasons, but she told him she was happy to be carrying his child as she had fallen in love with him as well.

On May 28, 1495, Priscilla Frazier-Acton was born. Thomas would have preferred to father a son to carry on the name and the Correction legacy, but once he saw her, he fell in love. He knew he had to redouble his efforts to ingratiate himself with London's aristocracy in order to secure a place in society for his daughter.

Over the next fourteen years, Thomas was the aide to six different nobles as he moved his way up the ladder. In two of the cases, he left the noble's employment not because he wanted to but because the nobles were convicted of treason and executed at the Tower. Thomas avoided the same fate through skillful applications of Self-Corrections.

His big break—and his first career stability—came when he met Richard Foxe, the powerful cleric and a top advisor to the newly coronated King Henry VIII. Using a Self-Correction, Thomas was able to provide information that a group of men was plotting to overthrow the King. When Lady Antonia first heard about the plot, the men had already been arrested based on a tip provided by William Tyndale. (Tyndale ironically would flee England years later after opposing Henry's marriage annulment.) However, at the time that Thomas spoke to Foxe, nobody knew of the plot. Thomas could go back in time, give Foxe the information, and Foxe would be the one to save the King.

This time, Thomas's Self-Correction worked out exactly as planned. Foxe remembered Thomas and sent for him. He was curious about where Thomas got his information, but he didn't press when Thomas obfuscated. He had heard of Thomas's reputation and was eager to hire him.

For the next two years, Foxe—and therefore also Thomas—was at the pinnacle of power both politically and ecclesiastically. Foxe acted as Henry VIII's chief confidante and advisor. Thomas was the busiest he'd ever been in his life, and he was loving it. Foxe gave him assignments, and he rushed off to complete them. Thomas attended an occasional meeting that Foxe had with the King. Foxe was brilliant, and it thrilled Thomas to be in the presence of that brilliance.

All the while, Priscilla was growing into a proper young lady.

In 1511, Thomas Wolsey made his meteoric rise to become the King's primary advisor. As a result, Richard Foxe found himself on the outside. He was no longer in the circle closest to Henry. He accepted his demotion with grace and class.

Richard explained to Thomas Acton that he would no longer be the power he formerly was. For the rest of his life, he would focus on his episcopal duties as a cleric. He was going to take the lead in reforming what he had viewed as a corrupt clergy. He also had ideas about starting a new school at Oxford University, Corpus Christi College. Foxe was well aware of Thomas's thirst for the limelight and his predilection for glomming on to the next highest noble in the court. He believed Thomas would not rest until he was the personal advisor to the King himself.

Knowing of his protégé's thirst for notoriety, Richard told Thomas that he would understand if he wanted to work now for Wolsey. Thomas fooled him by stating he wanted to continue working for Foxe. He told him that the past few years had been the most satisfying of his life. He wanted to stay in Foxe's employ, if the Bishop would have him.

Thomas immersed himself in Foxe's work. He actually found it restful to be away from the intrigue of the royal court. For three years he continued doing this work, enjoying every minute. He found that Richard's faith was infectious as well. He was starting to believe in anything other than himself for the first time in his life.

Then, one day, there was a knock on his door. It was the King's guard. They were there with a warrant for his arrest. The warrant had been issued based on statements he had made six years earlier where he impugned the character of

Rufus Argyle, a close confidante to Wolsey. Thomas remembered the statements he'd made to Sir Thomas More, secretary and personal adviser to King Henry VIII. Thomas Acton had advised More that Argyle was planning to convene a meeting of noblemen to mount a coup against the king.

Of course, the news that Thomas gave More came from actual events that would happen in the future. In actuality, the plot was thwarted long before they got to the King. Argyle and six other noblemen were beheaded. However, Thomas went to More with enough details of the attempted coup—the time and place that the coup would occur, the methods they would use and other details— that made the information extremely credible. More took it seriously and, as a result, he got credit for thwarting the coup.

In this new reality, however, Wolsey shielded Argyle. The other men were executed, but ironically, Argyle was spared. Then, when Wolsey came back into a position of power, Argyle came with him. He uncovered that Thomas was the one who advised More, and he was now taking revenge. Thomas found it rather ironic that he had, through his Correction, saved Argyle's life, but naturally, Argyle did not know this and now he aimed to take Thomas's life.

They placed Thomas in the Tower pending his fate. Richard Foxe appealed on his behalf, but since Foxe was no longer in power, his appeal fell on deaf ears. Thomas was sitting in his cell reading his Bible when the lock on his door noisily unlatched. When the door opened, Priscilla was standing there.

Thomas's daughter had grown into a raven-haired beauty. At nineteen, she was engaged to marry Wendell Stapleton, a young gentleman who worked in the shipping trade. Thomas liked him very much and thought he would love and take care of his daughter. Thomas and Priscilla embraced as she walked in.

"I'm so happy they let you see me one last time, my love. How's your mother doing?"

"Not well, Father. The consumption has made her very weak. The physicians have prepared me for the worst."

"Tell her I love her."

"Father, why don't you do a Correction and get yourself out of here so you can tell her yourself."

"I wish I could. I've been wrong my entire life. Working with Richard Foxe has opened my eyes. I have used Corrections for my advancement and profit and lost sight of everything my father told me. He said that Corrections are for the betterment of others. They are to give people a second chance to change their lives for the better. I have been selfish. I have taught you to be selfish. Promise me you will only perform Corrections to help others. Promise me."

"I will, Father. But can't you do this one selfish Correction, just for us, and then start your resolution tomorrow?"

Thomas laughed. "You are a clever one, my darling girl, but it doesn't work that way. I have to start right now to be a father you can be proud of. I want to be a person I can be proud of."

"But I am proud of you, father."

"See, it's working already."

She smiled in spite of herself.

"Priscilla, I need you to escape to the countryside. Take your mother, if she is up to it. These people are vindictive and brutal. They may not stop at me. They may try to kill you as well. It is important that you live, that you perform Corrections that will cancel out mine. It's important that you keep the line going and that you use your gift to improve the lives of others."

"I will, father."

There was a knock and a key fitting into the latch. It was time for her to go. It was the last time she ever saw her father, a father of whom she was proud.

7

May 26, 1723–Whitchurch, England

George Allenwood, my ever-so-great grandfather, crossed the ocean to the New World. I once figured out how many greats away from me he was, but that was many years ago and, though my mind is still sharp, I've had to jettison much minutia to keep storage space in my mind to remember the big things.

George wasn't fleeing oppression or anything like that. He was a Methodist, but after an initial period of violence against Methodists, the sect had more or less gained general acceptance. He left simply to find his fame and fortune. Stories of the rawness of the New World filled him with wonder and a pioneer spirit.

He also needed to find a wife. He was in his mid-twenties and had an obligation to produce an heir to his gift. Not having yet found an appropriate mate, perhaps a woman from the colonies would be more to his liking.

He got himself a ticket to cross the Atlantic on the HM Empress, a merchant ship, out of Portsmouth. The ship was scheduled to leave on June 22nd at eight o'clock in the morning. He had nothing keeping him in his little hamlet of Whitchurch, so he traveled two hours and arrived in Portsmouth on June 19th.

He went for lunch at The Fatted Calf, a pub near the port. The waitress came over to take his order. George looked up at the face of an angel framed by a mass of curly straw blond hair. She had sky-blue eyes, but a black shiner surrounded her left eye.

"That must have hurt," he offered.

"I walked into a door," was her curt response. "What can I get you?"

George knew in an instant she was lying. "Your doors really need to have greater respect for someone so lovely as you. I'll have a beer and the shepherd's pie."

A smile couldn't help but curl her lips before she retreated to put in his order. When she returned with his lunch, George spoke up. "I'm George, George Allenwood."

"I'm Alice Hopkins, it's nice to meet you."

"Believe me, the pleasure is all mine." This time, her smile lingered a little longer.

When George got up to leave, Alice said, "I hope to see you again."

"You most assuredly will," was his response. Over the next two days, he ate every meal at The Fatted Calf and talked with Alice more and more. Finally, at dinner on the night before he was to sail, he made his pitch.

"Alice, tomorrow morning I am sailing for America to start a new life. Will you join me in that new life? I'm not a man of vast means, but I'm not a pauper. I can't promise you a world of luxury. It may even be a very hard life. But one thing I can promise you. You will never walk into another door again as long as I am around."

"I can't just up and leave."

"Why not? You said you have no family left. You're not married. The man you have been seeing is a sailor, so you don't see him for six months of the year. I'm sure this pub can find someone else to take your place."

"I can't. I just can't."

"Well, I went down to the shipping office and purchased a second fare, just in case I could convince you to accompany me. You would have your own cabin. I will ensure your safety. If you feel you have to stay, I will be sad, but I will understand. The ship, the HM Empress, leaves from Pier 6 at eight tomorrow morning." With that, George stood up and exited the pub.

The next morning, George arrived at Pier 6 at seven-thirty. He stood on the dock until about five minutes to eight and then turned to head up the gangplank onto the ship. Halfway up the ramp, he heard his name called out. His face transformed into its biggest smile ever. He dropped his duffel and ran to Alice, who was struggling with a valise of her own. He gave her a big hug and grabbed her bag as they hurried to the ship.

The ship captain, Ambrose Dunmore, greeted them as they came onboard. He then had a crew member show them to their cabins. This boat would be their home for approximately seven weeks.

Luckily, George had purchased first-class tickets so they would be sharing their meals with the captain and first mate. Even with their upgraded accommodations, they knew they were going to lead a rugged life over the upcoming weeks, and probably over the rest of their lives. George kept looking at Alice to gauge her mood and reaction to her situation. To his relief, Alice not only didn't mind the inconveniences, she appeared to be thriving in this environment.

Passengers on the Empress were expected to pitch in and help the crew whenever and wherever they were able. The captain did not think women, as the 'weaker sex', would do as much. He definitely did not require them to partake in any purely physical labor. George was therefore amazed when he came up from his cabin to the main deck and saw Alice pulling on a rope along with six sailors as they raised the topsail. The sailors were singing a rather bawdy song. Instead of being offended or embarrassed, she was joining in, learning the words as she went along.

George grabbed the rope right behind her and started to pull along with the rest. Alice looked back at him and smiled sweetly. George had been nearly certain that he and Alice would end up as husband and wife. Now he was certain of it.

After finally raising and securing the sail, the sailors all congratulated George and Alice for their pluck, but mostly they were enamored with Alice. She was officially a 'member of the crew' now. After that, there was nothing she would not try. George would occasionally point out that a task might be beyond her physical capabilities. Sometimes she would listen to him, sometimes not.

One evening, George was on deck gazing at a steadily reddening sky as the sun set. Alice walked up beside him. She put her hand in his.

"There's an old saying," he said while still staring at the setting sun. "It goes: 'Red sky at night, sailor's delight; red sky at morning, sailors take warning.' It's supposed to refer to the weather, but I think it's much more. I'm staring at this beauty with you by my side and I can't be any more delighted or content."

"George, I don't know how to thank you for all this. If you had not come along, I would have lived out my days in Portsmouth, having no idea what I can do and what I can't do. I would have been unhappy every single day of my life.

I don't think I'll be happy every single day, nobody can be, but now I can at least try. Does that make any sense to you?"

"It does. It really does. I knew from the second I saw you that you could be much more than a waitress in a pub."

"I do have one question of you. Why haven't you asked me to marry you?"

"It would be quite presumptuous of me, wouldn't it? I've only known you a few short weeks."

"I am giving you liberty to presume, sir. In fact, I will die of sorrow if you didn't ask for my hand."

"And the rest of you, I hope."

She laughed and then kissed him tenderly. "I hope that answers your question."

"Alice Hopkins, would you give me the ultimate joy of being my wife for the rest of our days?"

"I will, George Allenwood. With all my heart, I will."

Captain Dunmore apologized that he wasn't authorized to perform the ceremony himself. He said it was a myth that a sea captain could perform these services. However, one of other passengers, Caleb Partridge, announced out of the blue that he was an Anglican minister and he would be happy to perform the ceremony, even though George was an "accursed Methodist". He said it with a smile, so George assumed he was kidding. Even if he wasn't, George didn't want to wait until they got to America to wed Alice. He wanted her then and there.

Reverend Partridge conducted the ceremony the next day with the entire crew and all the passengers in attendance. Afterwards, the Captain threw a big party for the newlyweds. As the party wound down, Dunmore chatted with George.

"Thank you for having this party for us, Captain," George said.

"We don't get many of these shindigs on our ship. It's nice to have something good like this on-board every once in a while."

"Are you feeling well? You seem out of sorts."

"It's my wife. She's been ill, very ill. I won't be back to England for months. She might be gone by then. I never should have left her."

"Would another captain have been able to pilot this boat?"

"Yes, I have a friend, Andrew Pinsgry, who's in port right now. He would have switched with me with no problem. I wished I had stayed back with Emma and asked Captain Pinsgry to take my place."

George considered for only a moment. The reason he asked about an alternate captain was purely selfish. If there were no options and Captain Dunmore had stayed behind, the ship would not have sailed. George never would have met Alice, let alone marry her. Since another captain was available to take over, George felt confident that his path would continue unchanged. There was a chance Captain Pinsgry would not want a woman on board. Some captains were still old-fashioned and thought a woman on a ship was bad luck.

George would proceed with this Correction even if the ship didn't sail. Alice was the woman he loved. She had an abusive boyfriend and he was the only one who could save her. He would track her down and win her over, no matter how many times it took.

He put his hand on Dunmore's shoulder. Like that, the captain disappeared. In his place was a different captain, Andrew Pinsgry. Everything else was exactly the same. Alice was across the deck, talking with the first mate but looking over at George with love and devotion in her eyes. He looked back, feeling like he was the luckiest man on earth.

8

Let me tell you about one of my most successful Corrections. The year was 1941, so I was twenty-years-old. I was in my, for lack of a better word, itinerant stage. At this point in my life, I wandered around America, looking for people to help. I had taken a job as an encyclopedia salesman, which provided me with ample opportunities to travel and meet people.

From a very early age, my father drummed into me that by far the two best places to find people who needed the help I could provide were churches and bars. I was in a small town in northwestern New Jersey. It was Sunday morning, so I thought I'd drop into the quaint Methodist Church located right off the town square.

A young woman was in her wheelchair in the front of the church. She was near an older woman I took to be her mother, seated in a pew. It was obviously an old church and, despite some improvements made over the years, it had not been designed with the handicapped in mind. As a result, the young woman was extremely conspicuous to the entire congregation. She looked like this was her usual spot each Sunday. She may have been resigned to it, but she did not appear happy. She gave off a certain melancholy air that made her an unmistakable candidate for my help.

The trick is often figuring out the best way of insinuating myself so I can help in a way that does not come off too strong or pushy. This is more of an art than a science. Often I've found that the entry point is to focus on a feature or some other characteristic that is totally incongruous with the makeup of the person. I catch them off guard and they lower their defenses for a split second. Then I can slip in through the breach.

After the service, she appeared depressed, downtrodden and unapproachable as her mother wheeled her out of the church. Her mother's expression was no less woebegone. I was at a loss on how to approach, but then I saw a fresh orchid pinned to the lapel of the younger woman's jacket.

"Excuse me, but I couldn't help but be taken with the beautiful flower on your lapel. It's an orchid, correct? I'm guessing it's a member of the *Cattleya* genus. Am I correct?"

I knew I was correct. As an encyclopedia salesman, I sampled my product and learned things. But I still had to phrase my observation in a way that left the person with whom I was speaking feel that they were the expert, not me.

After I said this, I detected looks of surprise on their faces. What man knows the names of flowers, never mind their Latin names? But after the looks of surprise receded, I detected hints of a smile from both mother and daughter. The smiles disappeared as the women advised me I was correct, thanked me and hurried on their way home. I knew I had them. It was just a matter of time before they opened up to me. I just had to be patient.

I also knew I had something I didn't normally have. I had an ally, the mother. Usually when I zero in on a person who I think could use my help, they are solitary figures. I rarely get an assistant. The mother would help me lower her daughter's defenses.

After the church service, I went back to my hotel, The Wayfarer. It was a quaint bed-and-breakfast a block away from the church. The B & B was owned and operated by friendly gray-haired women named Wendy Tate. She was in the downstairs parlor, reading a book when I walked in.

"Hello, Mr. Vance. Welcome back. How was the church service?"

I didn't recall telling Mrs. Tate where I'd been, but I figured the proprietor of an establishment in a small town like this had a way of knowing these things.

"Inspiring. It reminded me of the story Will Rogers once told about Calvin Coolidge. Old Silent Cal arrived home from church one day and his wife asked him how the service was. 'Fine,' was Cal's response. 'What was the sermon about?' she asked. 'Sin,' he responded. 'What did the preacher say about sin?' 'He's agin it.' "

Wendy Tate burst into laughter. I'm not sure if she found it all that funny or whether she felt obliged to laugh at her lodgers' jokes, no matter how lame the humor may be.

"Good book?" I asked.

"Mildly diverting. Perfect reading for a lazy Sunday afternoon."

"I'm always on the lookout for a good read, so let me know if it's worth my while. Oh, is there a local florist around? I'd like one that carries orchids."

"Then you should go to Calabrese Greenhouse and Florist. It's about a mile east on this road. They have an array of flowers and I'm sure they carry orchids. They won't be open today, though."

"Thank you. I'll try them."

The next morning after breakfast (Mrs. Tate set out a magnificent breakfast, I must say.), I headed down the road to the Calabrese Florist. It was a crisp and cool autumn day, making for a very enjoyable stroll. I reached the establishment in about fifteen minutes. There was an abundance of flowers and ornamentals, including a variety of orchids, on display in the front window. I had a good feeling that this was the place.

My plan was simple. I would charm the proprietor, talk up the quality of the orchid on the woman's lapel, and then finesse the name and address of the woman in the wheelchair. I walked in and heard the tinkle of the bell jostled by the door as it opened and closed. I was about ready to start my assault of charm and persuasion when the proprietor walked in from the back. We both did a bit of a double take as we saw the other. It was the mother.

"Didn't we meet in church yesterday?"

"Yes, we did. I was so taken by the orchid your friend was wearing that I had to search for one myself. Did she buy it here?"

"No, she didn't buy it here. She grew it here. We own this place."

There was obvious pride in her voice.

"Well, you can be proud of your business here. It's lovely. By the way, my name's Joseph Vance."

"It's a pleasure to meet you, Mr. Vance. I'm Vivian Calabrese. Are you new to New Cambridge?"

"Please, call me Joe. I'm just passing through. I'll just be staying a short while in your beautiful town, I'm afraid. I'm staying at The Wayfarer."

"Oh, it's a lovely inn and Mrs. Tate is such a pleasant woman. What do you do for a living?"

"I have the most stereotypical of nomadic occupations. I sell encyclopedias."

"Well, given the fact that you correctly identified the *Cattleya*, you obviously review the product you sell."

"I have a fair amount of time to myself and I love to read. How long have you had this florist?"

"My husband and I opened it twenty-five years ago when Mary just started high school. Now it's just Mary and me. Lou passed away seven years ago now."

"I'm sorry to hear that. I'm sure he was a fine man. The two of you have done a wonderful job. This is a great florist."

"It's where Mary is the happiest, tending to the flowers and plants. She loses herself in them, sometimes too much. I'd like to see her get out among people more. I won't be around forever and when I'm gone, she'll be alone."

She was quiet for a moment. I said nothing because I sensed she was going to say more and for me to speak would be an intrusion. As expected, she continued on.

"A prestigious university had already accepted her. She planned on becoming a veterinarian and had a brilliant life ahead of her. Then, in an instant, her life changed forever."

"What happened?"

"We had only recently bought our first car, a Model A Ford. Lou was very forward thinking and insisted that each of us learn to drive it. Mary was actually the best driver of the three of us. She borrowed the car to head to a party one of her friends was holding. The roads were icy, but we thought she could handle the drive. She couldn't. The car careened out of control and went off the road and down an embankment. She wasn't located for nearly two hours. When they finally found her, she was nearly dead. She received multiple injuries, both internal and external. She required six hours of surgery, but the damage to her spinal cord was too extensive. She's confined to a wheelchair for the rest of her life.

"After her accident, she was in the hospital for six months followed by years of painful therapy. Unfortunately, the therapy could only help her somewhat physically. No amount of therapy could help her regain emotionally or mentally. I know I only just met you and this is a lot of personal stuff to be telling you but yesterday when you complimented her orchid, it was the first hint of a smile I'd seen on her face in weeks."

With that, she leaned over and grabbed a pot with six brilliant purple and white orchids that she handed to me.

"These are for you. Thank you."

"I really didn't do anything, but I'd like to see if there is something I could do. How about if I take the two of you to dinner? I noticed a restaurant near my B&B."

A wistful look came over her face.

"That would be McAllister's. It's an excellent restaurant, but I haven't been out to eat in years. The only thing I'm able to get Mary out of the house for is church. Perhaps you could come over for dinner one evening."

"That sounds perfect. I'd bring a bouquet of flowers, but that would be a little ridiculous since I'd have to buy them here, so I'll get a nice bottle of wine."

She laughed. "How about Wednesday, six-thirty? We live at Seven High Street. It's about a three-minute walk from the inn."

When I arrived at the appointed time, I was cordially welcomed, but it was obvious the two women had had a row. I guessed that Mary did not approve of her mother inviting me for dinner. I was invading her space without her consent. I knew I had my work cut out for me after Mary gave me a greeting, but then settled into a sullen despair as we sat in the living room for hors d'oeuvres and drinks before dinner. Years later, I went to see a performance of *The Glass Menagerie*. As I was watching the play, I thought back to this evening and the role I was playing as the Gentleman Caller.

Vivian was trying so hard to bring her daughter out of her shell. Perhaps she was trying too hard. I imagined I was only the latest attempt. I determined I would make it her best and final one.

We chatted about this and that, but the conversation was primarily between Vivian and me. Mary spoke only when directly asked a question and then her responses were only one or two words. Most times, when I help a person, I take time to get to know them. It can take a week, a month, or sometimes more to evaluate a person and his or her situation. I have to ensure that the person is sincere. I have to make my best guess that changing this one decision will change that person's life for the better. I have to make sure that the change sought is not for monetary gain, or at least not solely for that purpose. I had absolute power in my hands. I got to decide who deserved to go back and improve their lives and who did not.

In most instances, I would cultivate a relationship over time to gather my observations and make my determinations as to worthiness. In Mary's case, I wouldn't have this luxury. I'd have to act that very day. Otherwise, she would live with her current fate the rest of her life.

I would start with small talk, but I couldn't let it stay small for too long. The trick was to look for an opening in the conversation to move in. If it were just Mary and me, I'm not sure I'd be able to do it. At some point, the person has to say out loud what particular decision they want to change. Otherwise, I can't help him or her. However, Mary was so mute that she very well might not have been in the room. Luckily, Vivian was there.

Vivian could talk enough for the three of us, especially when she talked about her husband, Lou. He had passed away seven years earlier, but the way she spoke of him it was as if he was in the room with us right then and there. He'd had a heart condition for a number of years until it simply gave out.

Vivian told story after story involving Lou. Some involved him alone. Others were about the two of them and still others revolved around the three of them. Vivian got more animated as she recollected the man she loved for many years but, with each tale, Mary got more withdrawn and despondent. Her darkened mood was most evident when the tales involved her.

I sensed I had to act very quickly. Mary would excuse herself and go to bed early. I'd never see her again.

"It's lovely to hear stories of a happy home and family. Unfortunately, that isn't my situation. I'm afraid I don't have warm relationships with my parents. We used to be very close, but then I said something terrible and I haven't spoken with them since."

I was lying. At that point in time, I had a wonderful relationship with my parents. It wouldn't be until four years later that we became estranged. Right then, however, I thought I'd go back to the basics and use the original story of Francis Wentworth and his Correction for Richard Marsh to press my case.

"That's very sad. There's no hope for reconciliation?"

"No. I've tried many times, but they won't forgive me. I only wish I could go back in time and not say the thing I said. I can't though, can I?"

Neither woman could respond.

"Yes, I'd love to take back what I said. I guess each of us has one thing or another in our lives we'd like to take back, don't we? An ill-advised decision we made that, looking back, we wish we never made. How about you? You have one of these such decisions?"

Vivian nervously considered the question. She looked over at her daughter.

"I would have forbidden you going to that party that night. I should have tackled you. I should have blocked the door. I gave in to you and I shouldn't have. That's the one decision I wish I could have back."

Vivian put her head in her hands and began to sob. I was part way there, but not all the way. I needed Mary to say it, not her mother.

I expected Mary to soften at the sight of her mother crying but the exact opposite happened. She stiffened and seethed as her mother spoke, but still she said nothing. I was losing hope. Then she let her mother have it.

"How dare you feel sorry for yourself! I'm the one in a wheelchair for the rest of my life."

"I, I didn't mean."

"You didn't mean! You didn't mean! If I've so ruined your life, please leave. I don't even know why we're doing this, trying to put on airs we're normal for a man we just met. Maybe you should leave."

I stood my ground and wasn't going anywhere. I stared at her intently.

"What do you want from me? What do you want me to say? Okay, my life sucks and it's all my fault! I wish I never left the house that night to go to that damn party! There, are you happy?"

"Yes," I responded. I smiled, leaned over and put my hand on her shoulder. She glared at me for taking such liberties. I closed my eyes as all went dark. When I next opened them, I was in my room at the inn. It was getting late, so I left my room and walked downstairs. Mrs. Tate was in the living room.

"How are you this evening, Mrs. Tate?"

"I'm doing well, Mr. Vance. Thank you for asking."

I was going to ask her about Mary and Vivian, but then I thought better of it. I remembered talking with her about them a few days earlier but I had learned long ago that, after a Correction, I could not be certain of which reality I now lived in. A Correction can have ripple effects. It is always better to keep my cards close to the vest until I know for certain.

The next morning, I walked the mile to Calabrese Florist and Greenhouse. The sign was similar, but somewhat different from when I saw it a few days ago.

I walked in, tinkling the bell as I entered. A man was behind the counter. I recognized him immediately from the photographs. It was Lou Calabrese, the beloved father who in the previous reality had passed away years earlier. I thought back to what Vivian had told me. Her husband had a weak heart that ultimately gave out after years of strain. His daughter's accident had been perhaps the biggest strain in his life. The Correction, the saving of his precious daughter from a horrific accident, removed the stress on his heart and, as a result, here he was, alive.

"Good morning, can I help you?" he asked.

"I'm just passing through for a few days. I'm staying at the Wayfarer and I always love to have some fresh flowers in my room when I travel. Mrs. Tate, the inn's owner, said this is the place to come."

"How is Wendy? I haven't seen her in ages."

"She's doing quite well. She's a perfect host. I'm stuffed from the magnificent breakfast she laid out for me this morning."

"What kind of flowers are you interested in?"

"Orchids. The *Cattleya* variety. I saw a nice one in the window that would be perfect."

"I'll fetch it for you."

As he was walking to the window display, I decided to play a hunch.

"I selected the Wayfarer because they accept pets. I love to travel with my Airedale. I noticed this morning, however, that he was rather listless and I was wondering if you knew of a veterinarian in town."

His face beamed.

"You don't have to go very far. It just so happens that a couple of fine veterinarians are next door. In the interest of full disclosure, they happen to be my daughter and son-in-law."

"You sound justifiably proud."

"I am."

I paid for my orchid and then headed out. I looked to my left and there was a sign hanging on the front of the house next door. It read: Mansfield Veterinary Clinic. I walked over and on the door were the names Dr. Mary Mansfield, DVM and Dr. Michael Mansfield, DMV. I walked in.

There was one woman holding a Siamese cat on her lap in the waiting area. Vivian was seated behind the receptionist's desk. She looked up when I entered.

"Good morning." She noticed the orchid I was carrying. "I see you've been to our shop next door. I hope my husband was nice to you."

"Oh, yes, extremely. I was in a church recently and a woman was wearing one of these on her lapel. I was so taken with it I had to get one of my own for my stay at the Wayfarer Inn."

"It's funny, my daughter often likes to wear one on her lapel."

Just as she said this, the door behind her that led to the offices and examining areas opened. A middle-aged woman restraining an exuberant golden retriever puppy emerged. The puppy was curious about everything, but most notably the Siamese cat. The cat stiffened but did not otherwise react. Following closely behind was Mary, wearing a white doctor's coat and sporting a smile of utter joy and contentment. She was obviously happy with her life, doing what she wanted to do. She said a few things to the woman about the care of her dog and then signaled for the other woman to bring the cat in. It was then she noticed me.

"Do I know you? You look very familiar."

"I get that a lot. I have one of those faces, it seems."

"Nice orchid you have there. *Cattleya labiate*, if I'm not mistaken."

"You are quite correct. I bought it next door."

"I thought as much. I helped cultivate them back in high school before turning my attention to furrier life forms. What brings you here?"

"I have a listless Airedale back at the Wayfarer and your father said this would be the place to bring him."

"Of course, bring him in. My mother can set you up. It's been a pleasure chatting with you, Mr.?"

"Vance, Joseph Vance."

"Well, I better get to my next patient. Siamese cats can get quite temperamental if you ignore them for too long."

"It's been a pleasure, a distinct pleasure."

She walked back through the door. I turned to Vivian. "I'll get back to you with a time that's good. Thank you. You've got a nice family, Mrs. Calabrese."

"Why thank you, Mr. Vance. Thank you very much."

I went back to the inn. I packed my bags, settled my bill with Mrs. Tate, and left town.

There was a different story I wanted to tell you but, I'm ninety-nine and scattered. Mary Calabrese was one of my best success stories, so I love to tell it. I'm tired now, so you must wait until tomorrow for me to tell you more. I'm off to bed.

9

I'm a bit rested, so let me tell you the story I was originally going to tell you before I irretrievably digressed. I was describing the process we go through to determine if a person is worthy of a Correction. Mary was an example where the worthiness was so blatantly obvious that it would have been a sin for me not to help her. Let me now relate the story of Carl Ostrow.

The name Carl Ostrow might sound familiar to many of you. A few years back, he was the National League home run champ his first two years in the majors. He could do it all: hit, hit with power, run, field and throw. Old time ballplayers said he had the sweetest, most natural swing since Joe Jackson. He had his Hall of Fame ticket all but punched, but then, during spring training of his third year, he blew out his left knee. After that, he hung around professional baseball but he was only a vestige of the player he had been. The official word was that he rushed his rehabilitation and came back too quickly. Most people in the know, however, attributed his professional decline to his fondness for vodka and cocaine.

He'd been retired for five years when I ran into him. It was in a bar in the Carroll Gardens section of Brooklyn. He was regaling the other patrons with his exploits on the field. In return, they paid for all his drinks. I arrived at eight-thirty. By eleven-thirty the crowd had thinned out and he was sitting by himself. Occasionally he'd chat with the bartender, but otherwise he sat alone with his thoughts and a drink in his hand. I went over and took the seat beside him.

"Good evening, Mr. Ostrow. My name is Joseph Vance. This is my first time in this bar. You seem to be a regular."

"Yep, we go way back. Good place. What's your name again?"

"Vance, Joseph Vance. Call me Joe."

"Alright, Joe. Nice to meet you. You buyin'?"

"Sure." I ordered us another round. We chatted about anything under the sun, but inevitably the conversation made its way back to his playing days and exploits on the ball field. This was probably what he thought people wanted to hear most about him. This banter resulted in the maximum number of drinks being bought. I was okay with this at this stage in our relationship. We could get into meatier issues at a later date.

We were still there at one-thirty when the bartender announced last call. Ostrow and I were the only ones left. Whereas I had nursed three beers over that time, Ostrow downed one vodka martini after another. The result was that he could barely find the door.

"You want that I get you a cab, Carl?" the bartender asked the former ballplayer.

Ostrow was about to nod his assent when I spoke up.

"I'll get him home. I parked my car on the next block."

The bartender went back to the business of cleaning up. Ostrow squinted at me.

"Do I know you?" he asked in a slurred voice.

"My name is Joseph Vance."

"It's nice to meet you, Mr. Vance," he slurred. "Thank you for offering me a ride home. Much appreciated."

I walked—or, more precisely, carried—him to my car. He flopped into the passenger seat and dug out a laminated card with his address on it, which he handed to me. I guessed he was often in this state, and this was the easiest way for him to tell the cabbie where to take him.

Once he settled into the seat, he soon fell into a deep slumber. His brownstone was about a mile away, which took me only a few minutes to drive. I parked in front and opened the passenger side door. He flopped over onto the sidewalk. Getting him into his place would not be easy, but I was young and strapping, so I managed. I fished through his pockets and found his house key and let us in. I wasn't about to try to get him up the narrow stairs, so I led him into the living room and deposited him on the sofa.

It was after two in the morning. My apartment was in Manhattan and I wouldn't get back for at least another hour. Exhausted, I spent the night at Carl's place. After settling into an armchair, I promptly fell into a deep sleep.

Despite the rather uncomfortable sleeping accommodations, I slept straight through to the morning. When I opened my eyes, the first thing I saw was all six-three of Carl Ostrow standing over me brandishing a Louisville Slugger bat.

"Who are you? What are you doing in my house?"

He brought the bat into striking position. I cowered.

"We met last night, at the bar. My name's Joseph Vance. We talked for hours. The bar closed down, but you were in no shape to get yourself home. I drove you here. It was too late for me to head home, so I flopped down here."

He lowered the bat somewhat but was still wary of me as he considered what I told him. Gradually, a dim recollection of the previous evening seeped into his consciousness and he relaxed.

"Thanks for getting me home. Sometimes, I don't know when to stop myself."

"How about we go out and get some breakfast? I saw there's a diner just around the corner."

"Yeah, that would be good."

We ate our breakfasts in relative silence. Unlike the previous night, he was not "on" this morning. At one point he looked across the table at me. He stared at me for a full minute before I said something.

"What?" I asked.

"I was just trying to figure out your deal. What do you want?"

"Why should I want anything?"

"My experience tells me that everybody wants something. Everybody's looking for an angle, trying to get their claws into me. I had a little fame and made some money. People want to be near me to see if they can absorb some of my fame and all of my money."

"Who says I'm not one of those people? Maybe I'm hanging around to rob you blind."

"Maybe you are, but I don't think so. You're different." Carl's body relaxed as he sat back in his chair.

"Am I?"

"Yeah, but I can't quite put my finger on it."

"Well, you keep working on it. I'll be right over here eating my breakfast. Let me know what you decide." I returned to eating my omelet.

He laughed. "I'll do that."

After that, we could talk more freely about a variety of subjects, not just his on-the-field exploits. He seemed to appreciate the opportunity to talk with someone in this way. For all his fame, he was a very lonely person.

After we finished breakfast, I told him I had somewhere to be. He seemed disappointed. I asked him if he'd like to get together for breakfast again the following week. He brightened up and said he'd like that. Every Saturday morning over the course of three months, we'd get together for breakfast at the diner.

Usually, Carl would show up with a hangover from his barhopping the previous night. He asked me if I wanted to join him at the bars, but I told him I wasn't interested. If nothing else, I couldn't keep up with him but I needed my focus to be on the real him, the private him. He was fine with my answer, but he thought it worth a shot.

It wasn't until our fourth breakfast that he opened up and talked earnestly about his life. During the week, he worked in his uncle's produce market in the Park Slope section of Brooklyn. I went to see him there once. It was a bustling, successful market that people came to from all over the city. He masterfully worked the crowd, just like he did at the bar, but without the alcohol.

During one of our breakfasts, he told me about the 'one that got away'. Her name was Susan Albright. They started dating in eighth grade. By junior year in high school, they were talking about marriage and a life together. It was also during that year he started to blossom as a ballplayer. He was getting stronger and faster. He could do it all, and he was attracting attention from major league scouts. The more attention he received from them, the less he gave to Susan. Despite being ignored, she remained the dutiful girlfriend, until she got word that he was being less than faithful.

He signed a contract the day he graduated high school, and he played the rest of the year with the minor league club out in the Midwest. The following year, the Cardinals invited him to spring training and he found himself starting left fielder for opening day. His golden ticket was stamped. He was on his way to stardom.

He paused, deep in his thoughts, after telling me this all this.

"Boy, that was some ride, but it all came way too young. I could have used someone looking out for me. My Dad had passed away when I was eleven and my Mom was busy raising my younger brother and sister. Once I left town, I was totally on my own. Susie would have been perfect. She was always the sensible one and would have looked out for me. But I dumped her."

"What happened to her?"

"She went off to college, where she met a guy. I think they've got a couple of kids, living a good life."

He seemed to be truly sorry that he didn't stay with this woman. He'd kept tabs on her over the years, so it was obvious he still had feelings for her. The way he talked about her, she sounded grounded. Perhaps she would have kept him off the booze and he'd be happier now. However, even if he were to reveal to me that he wished he hadn't deserted her, I couldn't help him. Although staying together and getting married would have been the best for him—and maybe her—it was an ironclad rule that once children are involved, we can't send someone down a path that could negate their lives. If I had helped Carl and Susan to come back together, the children she had with another man never would have happened. I asserted a lot of power in my work, but that's a line I couldn't cross. But I still hoped I could help Carl to give him a better life.

Hoping to plant a seed, I tried my proven tactic of bringing up the mythical schism I had with my parents. Perhaps he would offer a similar story of something for which he would give anything to go back and change. He wasn't biting. The best I could get out of him was that he wouldn't have taken that pitch the umpire called for a strike in the last game of his second season. If he had only swung at it, he said, he might have connected. If he connected, the Cardinals might have rallied to win and would have been in the World Series.

He also reasoned that if he made that hit, he wouldn't have been so desperate to prove himself during the next spring training. As a result, he probably would not have blown out his knee and his career would have been extended.

I tried to get him away from talking about baseball. Seeing him operate at the produce stand, he obviously had it in him, but my efforts were to no avail. I had to sigh. This was the best I was going to get, but it was not enough for me to proceed. Even if he had gotten that magic hit and launched his team into the World Series, I can't imagine that his life would have been all that different. If nothing else, there was a strong possibility that the enhanced adulation would have corrupted him even more severely than he currently was. One problem with The Correction was that I had no idea what the new life path would be. We like to highlight the success stories like Mary Calabrese, but there is a strong possibility that things can still turn sour after the change.

I suppose there wouldn't have been any great harm in letting Carl go back and swing at that pitch. Maybe the fresh path his life would take might have been better, but I didn't think so. It's a rare gift we offer, we can't squander it.

I gave it one last shot. I asked him if he ever thought about what his life would be like if he had never pursued baseball as a career. He was a fairly intelligent guy and probably would have done well if he went to college to get an education. He looked at me like I had two heads. Baseball was intrinsic to his very being. He couldn't imagine himself without it.

I conceded defeat. I lied to him. I told him my father was sick and was asking for me. I had to go back home to him in the Midwest. He was truly sorry to see me leave. I was sorry, too, but there was little I could do. I promised to keep in touch, but you know how it is.

Three months later I was in Cleveland and I read a short piece on him in paper. It was actually his obituary, but because he had achieved some celebrity, he got a notice in the sports pages a thousand miles away. He was driving his car on a winding road north of New York City and drove into a bridge abutment. The article didn't mention whether alcohol was involved, but I knew it was.

Such a waste.

10

Over the centuries we've had to stop ourselves from doing a Correction for a different reason. Our job has always been to help individual people reclaim their lives. It has never been to change history. Sometimes our Corrections can't help but inadvertently change history, even if they're done for someone we deem to be historically insignificant. One can never predict the impact an individual may have on the world, especially if given a second chance.

Jacob Reynolds (my great-great-great-great-grandfather) came within a hair of altering history. Whether the Correction he almost made would have led to an improvement in the world is subject to debate, but it has never been our place to insert ourselves into the affairs of the nation, or the world.

Jacob was a tea merchant living in New York City with his wife, Sarah, and their two sons, Efrem and Samuel. By 1804, Jacob's business was flourishing once again after languishing for over a decade during the Revolutionary War. Because he maintained good relations with both the British and Americans throughout the conflict, his business grew to its prewar vitality after the hostilities concluded and The United States began its foray into the world as an independent nation.

New York had become the center of the country and the center of the New World. It was an exciting place to be and Jacob embraced it with both hands. Every Wednesday, he loved to go for lunch at Fraunces Tavern, the historic tavern in the Wall Street neighborhood in Manhattan. If New York was the center of the world, Fraunces was the center of New York. Much of the history of this young nation had taken place here.

The Sons of Liberty, a secret society dedicated to independence, met here before the Revolution. General George Washington bid farewell to his officers at Fraunces after British troops evacuated New York in November 1783.

In an event close to Jacob's heart, after the British Parliament enacted the Tea Act, American patriots forced a British naval captain who tried to bring tea into New York to give a public apology at the Tavern. Then, like in Boston, the Americans, dressed as American Indians, dumped the ship's cargo into New York Harbor. Years later, Jacob claimed he took part in this dumping, but this was never confirmed.

Sometimes he dined alone, sometimes with friends, and other times he would take clients for one of Fraunces' bountiful lunches. On this day in July 1804, the place was inexplicably packed. Jacob was ready to turn around when a stool opened up at the bar and he grabbed it.

He was trying to get the barkeeper's attention to order his lunch when a well-dressed man hurried into the tavern and sat in the remaining seat. He looked distraught. Jacob thought he recognized the man, but he couldn't place him or remember the name.

"Are you okay, friend?" he asked.

The man said nothing in response as he stared off into space. When he spoke, it was to yell for the barkeeper to bring him a drink. By this point, he was shaking. The barkeeper arrived, and he ordered a whiskey, which he downed in one gulp. He then turned to Jacob.

"I'm sorry. You inquired about me and I ignored you. I'm afraid I've had quite a terrible morning. I may need to flee the State, but I needed a drink in a familiar place to collect my thoughts."

"What happened that makes it necessary for you to flee?"

"I shot a man in a duel. It was over in New Jersey. I gravely wounded him. I doubt if he'll last the night. I should have just shot over his head, like he did to me. The point would have been made, with no one getting killed. I'm such a damn fool. A damn fool."

"A duel? Can't say I've ever known anyone who's fought in a duel."

"I'd known him for many years, and the accumulation of insults and slights and other offenses finally became too much to ignore. I had to settle this once and for all on a field of honor. The problem is, there was little in the way of honor involved."

The man once again went quiet. He seemed a lot calmer than when he arrived at the tavern. When he walked in, he seemed at the end of his rope. He had talked himself down, but there was still an undercurrent of unease in his manner.

Jacob thought this would be a perfect opportunity for a Correction. He could not think of a downside. It would involve no kids. He would save a man's life. This man would not profit from the Correction, but the man could erase this terrible memory from his mind. He would be at ease. All Jacob had to do was to get him to say that he wished he never dueled or that, if he had, he shot wide like he said his opponent had. It would be an easy Correction with no foreseeable repercussions. Still, he had to do his due diligence before performing his ritual.

They talked some more about the duel. It was a fascinating account. Jacob found it astonishing that the victim's son had died in a duel on the same spot three years earlier. There was much intrigue. It occurred to Jacob that he had never introduced himself, nor had he learned the gentleman's name. Neither had he learned the name of the man's dueling opponent.

It did not concern him that he did not have this information. He did not deem it especially relevant to his decision. Jacob was on the verge of getting the man to state his wish that he had never had this duel. After this, he would put his hand on the man's shoulder to consummate The Correction. Then he stopped as the tavern erupted with commotion when three men rushed in.

"You hear about what happened across the river? Alexander Hamilton was shot! Yeah, he was in a duel with Aaron Burr in Weehawken. Word has it he won't survive. They brought him back to New York to die!"

Jacob looked at the man sitting beside him. He did recognize him. It was Vice President Aaron Burr. Jacob had seen him in Fraunces once before, rubbing elbows with the elite of New York. Now he was here, having just come in from shooting Hamilton.

The entire bar was buzzing about the duel. It would not be long before someone recognized Burr. They would surround him wanting to know what happened. He thanked Jacob for the conversation, put a couple coins on the bar and hurried out.

Given this new information, Jacob was uncertain whether he actually would have gone through with this Correction. It was not the family's style to perform Corrections that altered history. This would have been one of those gray areas.

It's not as if his action would have sparked a war. In fact, Alexander Hamilton was such a national hero that he wouldn't see any downside in saving his life.

Still, however, it was always better to keep Corrections low-key where they have minimal impact. There was too much in the way of unintended and deleterious consequences that one could never anticipate, even when dealing with people who have had a minimal effect on history. When dealing with someone on the scale of Alexander Hamilton, the possibility of dominos falling along the line for years to come is much more possible. It was better to sit back and not do anything in cases like this. That's exactly what Jacob Reynolds did.

11

We have no way of knowing what the impact of the Corrections we make will be. Let me try to explain. We "authorize" the Correction and the people go immediately back to the decision or action they wish to alter. As a result, Mary stays home instead of heading out to that party. But then they live a life from that point forward. We have no control over what they do over the months and years that follow the Correction. There's plenty of opportunity for them to make new ill-conceived decisions. We stay in the present, however, and only see the people after they've lived that life.

We proceed based on an educated guess and then hope for the best. It is an educated guess guided by eight hundred years of Correction experience passed down from generation to generation, but it still is a guess. Another example will illustrate.

My great-great-great-grandfather, Efrem Reynolds, was in Charleston, South Carolina in May 1856. He lived in New York and was down south on business. He wasn't an especially religious man, but he "got the call" to attend the First Episcopal Church one Sunday. In short, he was being guided to go to that church to help somebody.

I often wished our voice—or whatever it was that guided us—was more specific. It would be much easier if we were told a name or shown a face of the person we were to help. Instead, we were told to be at a place (usually a bar or a church) and the person we were to help would become clear. I can't tell you the number of hours I wasted after I've arrived at a place, surveyed the crowd and then latched onto the wrong person. It's not until I talk extensively to this person it becomes obvious he or she was not who I was sent there to help.

Efrem approached the church and noticed a dozen carriages in front of the church. With each carriage was an African driver waiting for their respective masters to finish the service. Their owners had obviously ordered the drivers not to interact with each other, probably so that their banter would not interfere with the church service. As a result, all the drivers either sat on their carriages or stood silently beside them. Efrem wondered for a second whether he had been sent to help one of them, but he decided not. The message definitely was for him to go inside the church. He walked in.

Before sitting in a seat in the pews, he surveyed the crowd. He finally settled on a stocky, bearded man, approximately thirty-five years old. He sat toward the front with a woman Efrem assumed to be his wife. She was very far into her pregnancy. The young man looked down at his lap as they sat there, waiting for the service to begin. When the music started up for the first hymn, he rose with the rest of the congregation, but Efrem noted that the man was not fully participating. There was obviously something deeply distressing him. Efrem would concentrate his efforts on him.

The service wound its way through the scriptures, the Apostles Creed, another hymn, a rousing sermon and the offering. Before the closing hymn and finally the benediction, the minister asked if there were any announcements or concerns from members of the congregation. One parishioner got up to ask for prayers for his mother, who had taken ill recently. Another got up to remind people of a church supper that would take place the following Saturday. The preacher was about to move on when the wife prodded the young man to stand up. Reluctantly, he complied.

He stood there for a few moments, not saying a word. Then he spoke.

"I took a life last night. It was my slave, Andrew. The Bible says, 'Thou shall not kill.' but that's exactly what I did. I seek forgiveness."

There were many murmurs throughout the congregation, but they were murmurs of support. The pastor spoke up.

"It speaks volumes about your character that you speak of the need for forgiveness, but you need none. How you seek to handle your property is your business, my brother. Unfortunately, sometimes we have to put our beasts down. It's for their own good, as well as ours. Rest assured that, in the eyes of the Lord, you have committed no sin."

The gentleman sat back down in his pew. Despite the words of the preacher and approvals of his fellow parishioners, he did not look mollified. He wore an expression of deep guilt. It was a guilt that he would carry the rest of his life. He was the person Efrem was there to help.

Efrem remained in his seat after the service ended and closely studied the gentleman and his wife, who had both stayed seated while the rest of the congregation filed out. When they got up to leave, so did Efrem. The gentleman's and Efrem's eyes met as they got closer.

"Good morning. My name is Efrem Reynolds. I was very moved by your, let's call it, confession."

"Thank you, Mr. Reynolds. I'm Wesley Adams and this is my wife, Emma. I've known Andrew since we were boys. We grew up together on our plantation. It bothers me deeply that I shot him. He was disrespectful to my wife, who as you can see is with child. I could not let it stand. He tried apologizing, and he probably did not mean it the way it came out. But my temper got the best of me. I should have accepted his apology. I would still have to punish him—perhaps a public whipping or some such punishment—but I should not have shot him dead. I sure wish I did not pull that trigger. And on top of that, I now have to find myself another skilled carpenter."

Usually, we like to do more research on our subjects to ensure that the subject is worthy and also that there aren't any foreseeable side effects. Efrem would have liked to do his homework, but this seemed like such an obvious case for a Correction it was impossible to resist proceeding then and there. By applying the Correction, a man would be alive. What possible downside could there be?

Efrem put his hand on Wesley Adams' shoulder. Within seconds, Efrem stood alone in the sanctuary. The minister walked in.

"Hello, can I help you?" the preacher asked.

"No, I'm just passing through and I like to stop in at a church to pray before I move on."

"Well, take your time."

"Thank you. Oh, do you know where I can find Wesley Adams?"

"You just missed him. He was here for this morning's service. I suspect you can find him back at his plantation, the Adams Manor. It's about a mile to the west of the city."

"Thank you."

Once the minister disappeared, Efrem departed the church, certain he had done the right thing, a good thing. As most of us have traditionally done, we waited around to see the effects of our handiwork. It's partially an issue of pride as we view the positive impact that we had on improving someone's life. It's also to make sure that we had a positive impact but, if we didn't, to evaluate what we did wrong to not do the same thing again.

Efrem returned to the inn where he was staying. He figured that there was not much he could do on a Sunday. He'd look into things first thing on Monday.

When he woke the next morning, he went down to the parlor for his breakfast. There were local newspapers on the table. He picked one up to read while he ate. He skimmed a few stories but then he stopped dead in his tracks when he reached page five. The bottom half of the page was an advertisement for a slave auction to be held the next day, Tuesday, at two in the afternoon.

He wasn't shocked or appalled to see this announcement. Although he grew up in the North and had an abhorrence of slavery, he'd been in the South often enough to know that it was a reality down in these parts. These auctions happened all the time.

What dismayed him was a certain section of the advertisement. This appeared to be a local auction where plantations in the area sold off or traded some of their slaves. Each plantation listed the slaves they were selling as either individual or family. Beside each person was a brief description of any special skill the slave possessed.

One listing caught his eye. The plantation was Adams Manor. There were three individual men and three families the plantation was looking to sell off. Under one of the families, three people were listed: a man, a woman, and a child. The man's name was Andrew. He was 27 years of age and described as a carpenter. Under him was Eliza. She was also 27 years old and was a domestic with kitchen experience. The child was Hannah. She was six and described simply as healthy.

Efrem had felt satisfaction that he had allowed Adams the opportunity to go back and not kill Andrew. However, in his haste he had misread Adams. The way Adams spoke of Andrew, he made it sound like the two men had a bond. Even though they existed in a master-slave relationship, Efrem misinterpreted that they had a type of friendship. This was not true. Adams may not have killed Andrew, but he didn't consider him a friend. Andrew was property, and skilled property at that. Adams could buy or sell any of them on a whim or when it was economically advantageous or necessary.

What was most disturbing was that the advertisement made it clear that the master could sell the family as a unit or he could sell each individual member separately. It was not clear how the auctioneer determined the final disposition of the family, but Efrem imagined that the goal was the maximum return of profit. If selling family members individually resulted in a larger total price than selling them as a group, then the family would be split.

Normally, after we make our Correction, we become disinterested observers. We take our notes and learn our lessons so we will not repeat the same mistakes in future Corrections. Having already meddled with time and history, we should back off so we don't mess up any further. Efrem, to his everlasting credit, could not just sit back. He was going to take matters into his own hands.

He always travelled with a fair amount of money in his valise. He rarely ever needed the cash, but it was just the way he was. Here, he would likely spend every cent he had, and he would be happy to do it. He just hoped he had enough.

The next day, he arrived at the auction yard a half hour before the auction was to begin. There already was a crowd of about fifty people. He tried to gauge how many of these people were to be serious bidders. Specifically, how many people would he be bidding against for Andrew? He didn't know in what order the auction would proceed. The advertisement listed the Adams Manor slaves toward the end. While he did not relish the idea of witnessing human being after human being paraded and inspected on the auction block, he hoped they operated in the order outlined in the paper. He had never been to an auction, let alone a slave auction. Any delay before Andrew and his family were led to the block would give him an opportunity to observe and learn before he entered the bidding.

He had another reason for wanting Andrew's auction to be later in the process. On the list were two other slaves with carpentry skills. If they went before Andrew, there would be a better chance of there being less competition for his services. As a result, the asking price would be less. Efrem had a substantial amount of cash, but he had no idea how much a slave costs, let alone three of them. He was afraid of being outbid. In addition, he reckoned that the men he was bidding against would be local. If they did not have ready cash on their persons, they could make a quick run to a bank. All of Efrem's money was in a bank in New York City. Although the telegraph system had been in operation for well over a dozen years, Efrem had no idea if lines ran between Charleston and New York. Even if they did, he had no idea what process he could use to access his funds. He would have to work with the money he had on hand.

He positioned himself in a spot where he could see most of the surrounding participants. He could also be in a position to offer his bids with a minimum of ease. About ten minutes before the auction was to begin six men entered the area and stood beside the block. Among these men was Wesley Adams. Efrem surmised that they were the representatives or owners of the plantations. They were here to monitor the proceedings and ensure their maximum profits, but not to take part.

Efrem felt a wave of animosity as soon as he saw Adams. He brushed it aside. He did not want his judgment clouded as he moved ahead.

Soon after, the auctioneer entered. He made a few introductory remarks and then got down to business as his assistants ushered the first slaves up to the block. In all cases, they wore chains and shackles on their ankles and wrists. The petrified and mournful looks on their faces were likewise universal.

The bidding began as the auctioneer acknowledged each bid in rapid-fire bursts that defied description. The bidding for the first few slaves started at fifty dollars and each ultimately sold for about two hundred dollars. If this remained the level of bidding, he definitely would have enough since he had around $1,500 in his pocket. The first few were farmhands, however, and he would have to wait another round to see how much more skilled slaves went for.

Next, the auctioneer offered up a carpenter. Efrem became especially alert. The bidding started off slightly higher at one hundred dollars but there was limited interest as only two men offered bids. When the bid got to two hundred ninety dollars, one of the bidders conceded. This gave Efrem a good feeling.

Next up was a family consisting of a man, a woman and a girl. Efrem figured the girl to be three or four years old. She tried to hide behind her mother's skirt, but one of the auctioneer's assistants forcefully grabbed her by the arm and pulled her out so that she'd be in full view of potential bidders. The father instinctively took a step to protect his daughter, but then thought better of it. Instead, he held out his hand. She took it to stand beside him. The assistant was going to grab her once again, but the auctioneer waved him off so he stood down.

The bidding for the family was a more complicated affair as it was a mix of bids for the entire family as a unit, but occasionally someone would throw out a bid for one of the individual family members. Somehow, the auctioneer kept it all straight in his head so that he determined that the cumulative bids for the individuals exceeded the last bid for the family as a unit.

The assistant went back on the block and forcibly extricated the daughter from the father and returned her to the mother. He then led the father away to a new master while the mother and daughter were given to another. The wife wailed in anguish as they took her husband away. The assistant produced a whip, which he loudly cracked. He glared at the wife, daring her to continue crying, giving the distinct impression that, if she did, the next crack of the whip would be on her back. Understandably, the wailing stopped. The girl began to cry, but the mother soothed her and kept her tears to a minimum.

Another six slaves were put up on the block and each was quickly sold before Andrew, his wife and daughter appeared. Andrew was a large, imposing man, especially next to his diminutive wife. He was also a lot darker than she was. All had the typical petrified look on their faces.

The man who bid for the previous slave with carpentry skills opened the bidding but he only wanted Andrew, not the other family members. He offered fifty dollars. Efrem countered with sixty dollars for the family unit. The man countered with seventy for Andrew. Efrem threw out eighty. Then another man threw out forty dollars for the wife, Eliza. Efrem did the math and bid one hundred twenty for the family.

Out of the blue, a man who had not yet participated in the auction offered fifty dollars for the girl, Hannah. Efrem countered with one hundred eighty for the family. The bid for Andrew was increased to one hundred dollars. Efrem shouted out two hundred twenty. There was yet another bid for the girl and Efrem upped his bid to three hundred. At this point, both the men who were bidding for the females shook their heads. The man who wanted Andrew realized he would have to bid for the entire family and offered two hundred fifty. Efrem countered with three hundred and the other man conceded. The gavel came down and Efrem was now a slave-owner.

He went to the block and collected the three slaves. They resignedly came down to him. He walked them over to a clerk sitting at a desk off to the side. The clerk had been recording the results of the auction and issuing the bills of sale and certifications of ownership. Efrem paid the stipulated three hundred dollars, signed some documents, and received his paperwork.

The assistant pulled out a key and unlocked the locks on the shackles for the three slaves. The chains and shackles belonged to the auctioneer. It would be up to the new masters to put their own shackles on their new purchases. Efrem, of course, did not own any shackles and would not use them if he had. He nodded to Andrew and together the four people walked out of the square. Before they got very far, Wesley Adams intercepted them.

"Goodbye, Andrew," he stated to the slave, but he did not offer to shake his hand. His eyes were glistening with tears. Andrew did not respond. Rather, he continued to look down at the ground. Adams then directed his attention to Efrem.

"Treat him well," was all he said as he turned and walked away. Efrem shook his head. Adams obviously cared for this man, but the pressures of the society they lived in were too much for Adams to bear. Andrew was simply property to him. Efrem led them away.

Efrem had hitched his carriage a couple blocks away from the auction block. He led the three slaves the two blocks in complete silence. His carriage was more of a coach with two bench seats and a retractable roof that could be brought up in the case of inclement weather.

When they arrived at the rig, Efrem spoke up.

"Andrew, why don't you and your wife sit in the back and I'll drive the coach with your daughter up front."

Andrew looked perplexed.

"Massuh, you sure 'bout dat? You ain't from 'round here, ere ya?"

"I'm from New York."

"Dat's way up nort, in'it?"

"Yes it is. Why?"

"Folks down dese parts may look funny if dey see y'all drivin' and us in de back."

"I see. You're probably right. You drive and I'll sit beside you. Eliza, you and your daughter sit in the back. What's her name?"

"Hannah," she meekly responded.

Efrem knelt down in front of the girl. He tried looking her in the eyes but she stared at the ground and said nothing.

"Hello, Hannah. My name's Efrem. It's nice to meet you. You don't have to be scared. You will be safe from now on. I promise. Let me help you into the carriage."

He held out his hand. She hesitated, but then reached out and took it. He then helped her climb into the back of the carriage. Then he held out his hand to Eliza who also hesitated but eventually took it and climbed up and sat beside Hannah. Efrem then turned to Andrew, who had been watching him skeptically.

"Shall we be on our way, Andrew?"

Both men climbed into their seats. Andrew gave the reins a shake and the horses started forward. They rode through the streets of Charleston. Efrem told Andrew when to turn. Finally, Andrew had to ask a question.

"Massuh, where we goin'?"

"North," was Efrem's simple reply.

"You got plantation up nort?"

"We're just going to keep heading north until we get to my home."

Andrew considered this for a few moments, but he thought better of saying anything more. They rode on in silence, but once they left the city limits Efrem asked Andrew to stop the carriage. He turned to face them all.

"Andrew, Eliza, Hannah, I owe you an explanation of what's happening here, but I can't tell you just yet. You don't know me and have no reason on earth to trust me, but that is what I want you to do. Trust me."

Eliza spoke up. "I do. I trust you."

Andrew looked wary but said nothing. He prodded the horses, and they resumed the trip north. As they proceeded along, they encountered a few other buggies and people, but none paid them any mind. It wasn't until they approached the border between South and North Carolina that Efrem became alarmed as three armed men on horseback approached them. He reached under the seat and pulled out two sets of chains. These were chains he would use in case the rig got stuck in mud or if he had to haul something. He handed one set to Andrew and then one set to Eliza.

"Quick, put these chains over your wrists. Don't let these men see you putting them on."

The men drew their horses up next to the carriage with one man, who Efrem assumed to be the leader, in the front and the two others behind him. He could see each of the men looking over him and his three passengers.

"Good afternoon, gentlemen. Glorious day, isn't it?"

"Hello," the man responded. "I'm James Appleton, Sheriff for Marlboro County. And you are?"

"My name is Efrem Reynolds."

"They belong to you?" he asked, pointing at the three slaves.

"Yes, I just purchased them."

"You did, did you? You don't sound like you're from around these parts. In fact, you don't sound like you're from the south at all."

"You're very astute, Sheriff Appleton. I'm from New York. That doesn't mean I can't own slaves, does it?"

"No, it doesn't. It's just highly unusual."

"Well, I bought them to help my cousin. She owns a farm in Fairfax County, Virginia. Her husband died a couple months ago and needs help. I was down in Charleston on business and I saw a notice in the paper about an auction, so I thought I'd pick up a slave or two to help her out. Turns out I could get her an entire family for a very reasonable cost."

"You're not against slavery?"

"I'm not for it or against it. Right now, it'll help my cousin keep her farm, so I'm for it."

"You have paperwork proving they're yours?"

"I do indeed." Efrem pulled the bill of sale and proof of ownership out of his coat pocket and handed them over to the sheriff. Right after he had bought the family at the auction, Efrem contemplated taking them over to the government office to file for the slaves' manumission when he bought them, but then he thought better of it. Now he was glad he didn't. Freeing slaves, even legally doing so, would not go over well with these types of men.

Appleton looked the papers over, and then casually asked a question. "What business are you in that brings you down to South Carolina?"

Efrem knew that the sheriff was trying to trip him up, but he was prepared.

"I'm a tobacco broker. I negotiate and arrange shipments of tobacco from various southern ports to New York. Men in the North love your cigars. I have paperwork if you'd like to see it."

"No, that's okay."

"At the very least, let me give you and your men some cigars."

"Now that I won't refuse."

Efrem reached back into his bag and grabbed a handful of cigars, which he handed to the sheriff.

"Well, thank you kindly," Appleton said as he handed the papers back to Efrem. "We've had some Yankees come down from the north and steal our slaves over the past year. I caught one just last week. Just like you, he was riding along in broad daylight, but he had stolen property. He tried hiding them under some blankets in the back of his buckboard. He's in my jail right now and we've returned the slaves their rightful owner. Your papers seem to be all in order, however. You can be on your way."

"Thank you, sir. You all have a good day."

The three men rode off as Efrem told Andrew to proceed north. A few miles later, just after they had crossed the border into North Carolina, Andrew looked over at Efrem. He then pulled the carriage over to the side.

"You all right, Massuh?"

Efrem looked stricken. He had turned ashen and was shaking. A peaceable man, the confrontation with the sheriff and his men concerned him. What would he have done if the situation had gotten violent? They still had North Carolina, Virginia, and maybe even Maryland to go through before he could get to what he could consider more friendly territory. Yes, the paperwork had gotten him through this scrape, but will it be sufficient the next time?

He figured he had packed enough provisions to last them a week, but this trip in a slow, full carriage would take at least twice that long. He did not know how to forage off the land. Perhaps Andrew or Eliza knew how, but he doubted it. He was nervous about how he would handle buying food. He was nervous about leaving the three of them alone, vulnerable to anybody, while he went in to the store to make purchases. Would leaving them in the carriage right outside the store be safe? Would bringing them in with him draw too much attention? Should he send Eliza into a store, figuring she would be the least threatening to a shopkeeper? All these things were playing on his mind until he finally answered.

"Yes, Andrew, I'm fine. Let's keep moving."

"We going to Virginia?"

Efrem was reticent about telling them the truth about where they were heading. He always liked to be truthful with other people and contemplated telling Andrew and Eliza their ultimate destination, but after his encounter with the sheriff, he thought it better to keep them in the dark. He could imagine a scenario where someone would turn to his companions to ask them where they were heading and Hannah innocently blurting out that they were going to New York.

"Yes, we're heading to Virginia."

Still, Andrew and Eliza, and to a lesser extent Hannah, had to sense that Efrem treated them far differently compared to anyone from their former lives. They saw a difference from the first day when Efrem helped Eliza and Hannah up into the carriage. Since that time, he had shared meals with them, provided for their health and welfare, shared the covering over the carriage when it rained and other things that they had never experienced before. They appreciated the treatment, but they were wary that it could change for the worse in a matter of seconds. A wrong word, a misinterpreted look or just the master's whim were enough to sour the master on a slave and immediately result in harsh treatment. Past experience told them that Efrem would at some point start treating them harshly. The question was when.

The carriage plodded along up through North Carolina into Virginia. When nighttime came, they pulled off the main road and the four of them slept in the carriage. The time came when they were running out of food and they needed to locate a small town with a general store. Efrem had Andrew pull up in front of the store and the three remained there while he went in to make the purchases. He placed the order. He thought it necessary to maintain the master-slave appearance, so he asked if the shopkeeper minded if he could have his "boy" come in to help carry the goods out to the carriage. "Of course, that would be fine," was the cheery reply. Andrew came in and hauled out the bags of food. They were just about out when Efrem noticed a jar of stick candy. He reached in and pulled out a peppermint one. "I'm a sucker for these. Have been ever since I was a kid. How much?" "On the house. Enjoy."

"Well, thank you kindly. Have a good day." Efrem stuck the candy in his pocket.

They loaded up the provisions and went on their way. About a mile out of town, Efrem reached into his pocket and extracted the candy. He turned around and handed it back to Hannah.

"You ever have candy before?"

Hannah shyly shook her head no.

"Go ahead, try it." Efrem pantomimed licking the stick. Hannah looked at her mother, who nodded to her, so she complied and put the stick to her mouth. Immediately a look of delight and wonderment spread across her face as she licked it again and again. A tear came to Eliza's eye as she watched her daughter's enjoyment. She later told Efrem that it was at that moment, through this minor act of kindness, that she knew they were going to be all right, that it wasn't going to all fall apart at any moment. Efrem was going to watch out for them.

They continued on. Andrew, who was a man of few words anyway, seemed even more withdrawn and deep in thought. He saw the same thing as his wife, but he couldn't let himself believe that things would work out. He had to keep his guard up at all times. After a few minutes, Efrem spoke to him.

"Andrew, may I ask you a question?"

Even this was a novel experience for Andrew. He was used to having orders barked at him. Because he was a skilled carpenter, his masters would occasionally asked him a question relating to carpentry, but never could he remember anyone requesting his permission to ask him a question.

"Yes," he responded.

"Do you know why Mr. Adams put you and your family up for sale?"

"He say I insult Mrs. Adams. I no do dat, suh."

"I believe you, Andrew. What did you say to her?"

"She had new hat. I say she look nice. That all. I promise."

"I believe you."

"I know Massah Wesley since we was young 'uns. He always nice and friendly-like until he marry Mrs. Adams. She no like me but I try to be nice. After I say she look nice, Massah Wesley all angry. He say he should kill me right dere, but he don't. He say I hasta go. I beg but he say they's an auction in couple days and he gonna sell me. Day of auction, he say he sell 'liza and Hannah, too. Maybe we stay together but he no promise. Thank ya kindly for lett'n me stay with dem, Massah Efrem."

Efrem cringed any time they called him Massah, but he still thought it better to maintain the master-slave illusion for the few remaining days of their journey.

"No family should be torn apart, Andrew."

They continued their trek up past Richmond into northern Virginia. As they were approaching Washington, D.C., Andrew asked, "We in Virginia, ain't we?"

"Yes, Andrew, we've been in Virginia for quite a bit now. We'll be out of it as soon as we cross the Potomac River and enter Washington, D.C."

"Ain't you leavin' us in Virginia like you tole dat man last week?"

"No, Andrew. I lied to that man. I was afraid of what he would do if I told him the truth about where we are going."

"Where is dat?"

"I'm taking you home to New York with me. Once we get there, I'm setting you free, you and Eliza and Hannah. I have some friends there who can help you get a place to live and find a job. I want to see Hannah get an education, and you and Eliza, too, if you want."

"Why?"

"Why what?"

"Why you do this?"

"It's the right thing to do. I couldn't save you from being killed only to then let you be sold away."

"I don't get it."

"I believe this is what Wesley Adams wants for you. He seemed to have an affection for you, but he lives in a society where it's difficult for him to act correctly. He's too weak to fight it. Don't ask me how I know this, I just do. Andrew, I couldn't bear it if they tore your family apart. I've been away from my wife and child for a month now, and I miss them terribly. I can't imagine the pain I would endure if I were to never ever see either of them again."

Andrew seemed to accept this explanation and went about his driving. It was getting dark, so Efrem suggested pulling over for the night. They didn't pull off to a side road like they had been doing, but Efrem was feeling confident. The four of them had come so far and were getting so close to safety. He thought they'd be safe for one night. They had some dinner and then settled down in their spots to sleep.

A few hours later, Efrem awakened when he heard rustling near the carriage. He leaned down to pull the pistol from under the bench, but he couldn't find it, no matter how much he groped for it. He lifted his head just in time to see the butt of a rifle being rammed in his direction. He moved his head, but not enough to totally evade the blow. It glanced off the back of his head. It was enough of a thump to stun and disorient him. Going in and out of consciousness, he reached out to help Eliza and Hannah, but he was so dazed the assailant easily pushed him aside.

The assaulter reached in the back of the carriage and grabbed both Eliza and Hannah. "I'm gonna have some fun tonight and then Ma will finally have herself a nigger girl to help around the kitchen." As he pulled at both the mother and daughter, they screamed for Andrew. Efrem tried to focus his blurred vision on where Andrew should be, but he wasn't there. The assailant had pulled Hannah out and threw her to the ground. He was dragging Eliza out of the carriage by her hair.

Suddenly there was a flash from about ten yards away, followed by a loud report from a gun. Eliza found the hand grasping her hair loosening. There was a thud as the man dropped to the ground. Andrew sprinted to the carriage. He scooped up Hannah and placed her gently in the seat beside her mother. He went back to the inert body of the attacker. He grabbed the rifle off the ground and placed it in the carriage. Andrew slid his hands under the arms of the dead attacker and dragged the body into the woods. Hiding the body behind a fallen log, he threw some leaves and mulch over it. He then jumped into his seat and urged the horse forward.

Efrem was still groggy and tried to mouth some words, but nothing coherent came out. Andrew said, "You just rest, Massuh Efrem, you be fine." Andrew proceeded on for about ten miles up to near where the ferry shuttled people and carriages back and forth across the Potomac River. He dared not approach anybody with Efrem in his semi-conscious state, so he pulled over off the road so they could rest.

A few hours later, as daylight dawned, Efrem woke with a start and a terrific headache. He tried to remember the events of a few hours ago, but nothing came to him. He looked over at Andrew and then back at Eliza and Hannah. Realizing everyone was safe, he relaxed back in his seat.

"Where are we?" he asked.

"Ferry to cross the riva just up dere," Andrew responded.

"Did something happen last night?"

"Man attack you and Eliza and Hannah wid dat gun. I shoot 'im."

Efrem looked down on the floor and saw the rifle.

"I see."

"I put body in woods. Dey not find him for a bit."

"I see. Did you use my gun?"

"Yassir, I in trouble? I kill a white man."

"You're not in any trouble. You protected your family. I think we got away, and if anyone tracks us down, I'll swear that I shot the man. It's my gun, after all. Oh, and thank you for saving my life. Let's cover up that rifle and we'll cross the river."

Efrem was wondering if he'd have to produce paperwork to prove that the slaves belonged to him, but the ferryman didn't care. Efrem paid the toll and

Andrew drove the carriage onto the ferry. Twenty minutes later, they were in Washington, D.C. While Washington, D.C. was a southern city which had a fair number of slaves, Efrem felt a wave of relief wash over him. They were out of the South, technically at least. Life would not be easy for his charges, but at least they would have their freedom. They would be free for the remainder of their lives.

Andrew and his family were familiar with city life, having spent much time in Charleston over the years. However, Charleston was a slow-paced, sleepy southern city, especially compared to where they were going to live, New York City. Thus far on their trip, for safety Efrem had been careful to skirt any big towns and cities. They went around Durham and Greensboro, North Carolina and Richmond, Virginia. However, he knew that eventually they would arrive in New York and Efrem was afraid the size and activity of that city would overwhelm them. To get them progressively more comfortable in northern cities, he decided to go through urban areas starting with the District of Columbia and then Baltimore, Wilmington, Trenton, and Newark. These were small cities but they were bigger and more bustling than Charleston. This would reduce the shock when they finally arrived in New York City.

Efrem was relieved when they rolled into New York and the looks on his friends' faces were that of wonderment, not fright. The size and constant activity of New York awed them, but the city didn't overwhelm and crush them.

Efrem had friends who could help. They were surprised when he showed up at their doorsteps with a Black family, but the surprise immediately gave way to action. One of his friends, Albert Hastings, was a prominent member of the Resettlement League, an organization devoted to working closely with the underground railroad to assist runaway slaves. Hastings secured a small apartment in a building occupied primarily by colored folk. Then he arranged a job for Andrew with a house builder who employed a mix of colored and non-colored men. Eliza took a part-time housekeeping job with Hastings' wife.

After going home to his wife, Abigail, and his daughter, Sally, Efrem's first order of business was to free the three slaves. Hastings connected Efrem with an attorney who had experience with the process of manumission, the legal freeing of slaves. The first thing he had to do was to fill out the forms for each of the three soon-to-be ex-slaves, which the attorney would file with both the State of New York and the State of South Carolina.

The forms asked for the names of the slave to be freed. The bill of sale only listed the first names—Andrew, Eliza and Hannah—the name of the person who owned them—Efrem Reynolds—and their previous owner—Wesley Adams. Generally, many slaves adopted the last name of the master they belonged to, but since the bill of sale was silent on their last name, Efrem was in a bit of a quandary what to put down on the manumission form. He approached Andrew.

"Morning, suh!" Andrew exclaimed when he saw Efrem approach him.

"Hello, Andrew, everyone treating you all right?"

"Yeah suh, Massuh Efrem. Every day be like Christmas."

"That's good to hear. I'm working on the paperwork to set you, Eliza and Hannah free and I have a question for you. The form asks for your full names. I've only known each of you by your first names. The bill of sale that I have only has your first names and lists you as the property of Wesley Adams. Should I put Adams down as your last name?"

"Dat's what they call us down south. You say we can be called sometin different?"

"I don't see why not. This is a new start for you. I don't see any reason why you can't be called whatever you want to be called."

"Den I want to be called Andrew Reynolds, if dat okay."

Tears filled Efrem's eyes.

"You okay, Massuh Efrem."

Efrem recomposed himself.

"Yes, I'm quite all right. I'm excellent, as a matter of fact. One thing you'll have to do is to stop calling me Master. From now on, you're a free man. You'll have no master; not me, not anybody. It's a pleasure to meet you, Mr. Reynolds."

Efrem kept close contact with the entire family, but his primary focus over the ensuing years was Hannah. Over the course of their trip north, he had found her to be an intelligent and inquisitive child. He wanted to nurture that intelligence. He enrolled her in school. Hannah was easily admitted to a free school for colored children operated by The Resettlement League. Her work was hard, but she thrived on it. Before long, Hannah was mastering everything the school could throw at her. To ensure that she was learning, Efrem would come to her apartment and tutor her two to three times per week. He also taught Andrew and Eliza to read and write.

When the war began in 1861, Efrem volunteered for the service. He received a commission as a lieutenant in the 59th New York Volunteer Infantry Regiment. Just before he was about to leave to join his unit, Andrew came to him.

"Good luck, suh. Ya'll come back t'us."

"I will, Andrew. I will."

Efrem went to shake Andrew's hand, but instead, Andrew came forward and gave him a huge hug, which Efrem returned. "Come back, suh." Andrew repeated.

Efrem was away a little more than a year. He served honorably, but he was seriously wounded in the right leg at the Battle of Antietam. Surgeons amputated his leg just above the knee. He fought an infection and a fever for over a month, but he was finally well enough to be shipped home. When he got off the train, not only were his wife and daughter there to greet him, but so were Andrew, Eliza and Hannah. Unbeknownst to Efrem, Abigail had assumed the role of watching over the three and had become friends with them. Sally and Hannah, who were about the same age, appeared to have hit it off very well.

A few days after Efrem came home, Andrew paid him a visit to ask his advice. He had heard that a regiment of Black soldiers was forming up in Massachusetts, and he wanted Efrem's advice about whether he should join up. He wanted to, but he didn't want to leave Eliza and Hannah without a provider.

Efrem was proud of his friend for wanting to enlist to fight a war that would help to free his fellow African slaves. He almost told him to do it, that he and Abigail and Sally would look after his family, but then he stopped himself. His mind went back to the battle in which he lost his leg. His unit went into the battle near the Dunker Church with just under four hundred soldiers. Within a matter of less than two hours, seventy-one men were killed and one hundred fifty three were wounded. He still had nightmares about the men who died to the right and left of him. It was hell on earth. He figured that, as a slave, Andrew had experienced enough hell.

Efrem had already gone further than any Corrector had ever gone before. The most a Corrector would do after the Correction was to check on the result of his work. He or she would be a casual observer and then move on. By helping Andrew and his family escape, Efrem knew he was interfering far beyond the extent he should be, and by doing so, he could fundamentally alter history, but his humanity would not let him act otherwise.

Efrem steered him into staying with his family. If Andrew had persisted, Efrem would have, of course, supported him. Andrew, however, so trusted his savior and mentor, he didn't pursue the subject any further. He would stay in New York with his family. It turned out to be a wise decision in July 1863 when the New York race riots broke out. On July 13, a white longshoreman with a large club confronted Eliza as she walked home. She ran two blocks to her apartment where Andrew was waiting for her. The man was close behind when she closed the door behind her. He beat on the door when Andrew ran for his rifle. It was the same rifle he had taken off the attacker many years ago.

He yelled for the man to go away. When the attacker refused and continued to beat through the door, Andrew fired. The door splintered and the banging stopped. Andrew opened the door to find the man writing in pain, holding a wound to his gut as he lay on the ground. Andrew gathered up Eliza and Hannah, and the three of them ran out of the apartment building and onto the street. They did not stop until they got to Efrem, who took them in.

After Andrew explained what happened, Efrem hid the trio in the basement of his house. In the meantime, Abigail went back to the scene of the shooting. As she approached the building, she noticed a trail of blood that led up to the front door and then into the building and up the stairs to the third floor apartment. A pool of blood lay in front of the door. She surmised the man had dragged himself away. She entered the apartment and noticed that Eliza kept a bucket of water with a mop in it in a corner of the kitchen. She grabbed the bucket and mop to swab down the pool of blood and the trail leading away from it.

She re-entered the apartment to gather up as many clothes and supplies that she could carry. She also grabbed the rifle, figuring it would not do Andrew any good if the rifle was found by police at his home. Even though he was acting in self-defense, she knew that the white man, not the black man, would get the benefit of the doubt. As it turned out, the assailant was only able to get a few blocks away before he bled out and died, unable to tell anybody who shot him.

Once the rioting died down, Andrew and his family moved to Brooklyn along with many other African-Americans. Efrem resumed his tutoring of Hannah and wondered if there was a way for her to continue her study in a university. Both she and Sally, who had long been her inseparable friend, expressed interest in wanting to pursue careers. Hannah wanted to be a doctor, a lofty dream for a woman of that era. It was a nearly impossible dream for a Black woman, but she would not let anybody or anything deter her. The war was now over and the buoyant feeling of victory in the north contributed to her feeling that she could do anything she wanted.

Efrem spoke with his friend, Albert Hastings, about the possibility of Hannah and Sally advancing on to university. Hastings was not optimistic, especially regarding Hannah. Universities were increasingly opening their doors to women throughout the country, but admitting an African-American woman was a true rarity. However, he said he would ask friends in the academic world if they knew of any possibilities.

Two days later, Hastings called on Efrem. "Well, Efrem, we really learn something every day. More universities are admitting women, even Black women, than I realized. I had dinner with a friend who lives in Washington, DC, but is visiting here in New York. He is a close friend of Otis Howard. Howard is a decorated war hero and is now head of the Freedmen's Bureau. He is looking to establish a university in Washington that will be open to everyone, male, female, black, white. I told my friend about both Hannah and Sally and how exceptional they both are. He said he would speak with Howard upon his return to DC. He didn't see any reason the girls couldn't be in the inaugural class. He said he'd telegram as soon as he got word."

Efrem was both elated at the news and saddened that Sally and Hannah would be so far away. He was glad that they would have each other as they went through school. It's tough for anybody to be away from home for the first time, but being with one's best friend would ease the pain.

He was especially concerned about Sally. She had only recently learned that she had inherited his gift, that she could help people with a Correction. He told her the true story about the Correction that saved Andrew's life and his subsequent purchasing of him, Eliza and Hannah to get them out of slavery. She learned about other Corrections he had done over the years. None of them were as momentous as the one involving Andrew, but they all seemed to help the person as their lives moved forward from the erased mistake.

At first, Sally did not believe her father. She wondered if the trauma of war had done something to his mind. However, as he described his "condition" she gradually realized he was telling the truth. She could remember how she felt when he did a Correction. She could sense it. As the firstborn, she could see both realities when her father made a Correction. These days, most people would call what she felt an extreme 'déjà vu'. Her mother and anyone else she knew could only see the revised reality.

Efrem knew that, once he explained Corrections to her, Sally would do her best to use her newly learned power appropriately. Still, he was concerned. Family lore told of all the good done through Corrections, but he also knew about the occasional times things went awry, resulting in unintended consequences. The story of the original Corrector, Francis Wentworth, whose rushed Correction resulted in the negation of a child had been repeated as the ultimate cautionary tale over the centuries.

Often, when something went wrong, it happened because the person doing the Correction was inexperienced and did not think through the ramifications. The tradition had been to tell the firstborns of their gift when they entered their teens. That way, they would be at home and under the tutelage of the parent when they made their initial Corrections. However, Efrem was away at war or convalescing from his wounds when traditionally he would have trained Sally. Now, when he finally taught her, she was leaving home.

He trusted his daughter, and he trusted that he and Abigail had done a fine job in raising her. Her heart and instincts would always tell her to do the right thing, but it is only human nature to try a new gift out as soon as possible. It's exciting and heady to have such power. Who wouldn't want to play with a new toy?

Efrem, Abigail, Andrew and Eliza shed many tears at the train station when they went to see Sally and Hannah off for Washington. There was a bit of an argument about whether Hannah would be allowed to ride in the main coach section. Sally said she didn't mind riding with Hannah in the colored car, but they were advised that the car was filled. The conductor told them they would have to catch the next train, but Efrem would not hear of it. He made such a fuss that the conductor went to get his supervisor.

The supervisor arrived, obviously ready to back his conductor and bar the girls from boarding, but then he saw Efrem.

"Where d'you lose your leg?"

"Antietam."

"I was there. 12th Massachusetts Infantry. I was wounded in the cornfield. Lost many buddies that day."

"I was in the 59th New York Infantry. Dunkers Church. We both saw the hell of it that day, didn't we?"

"Yeah, sure did."

He looked over at Sally and Hannah. "So, what do we have here?"

"That's Sally, my daughter and Hannah, who is like a daughter to me. They're going down to Washington to become doctors."

"That's quite impressive. Welcome aboard, ladies."

The conductor was about to protest, but all it took was one look to make him back down. The group finished their goodbyes, and the train sped away.

12

Sally and Hannah both became doctors. They each met men in Washington who they married and raised families. Hannah and Bill Smith's first child was a boy, named Efrem. Sally and Mark Vance's first child was also a boy. She had also wanted to name her son Efrem, but Hannah beaten her to the punch. She thought it might be strange to have both boys share what was increasingly becoming a unique name. She opted to call him John. John Vance was my grandfather.

Hannah's husband landed a job in New York, so they moved back there where she established her practice. Over the next forty years, she spent much of her time administering to the immigrant poor of the Lower East Side. Sally remained in Washington. She likewise practiced much of her medicine in the poorer sections of Washington. Hannah and Sally would get together a couple times a year to catch up. They both found it somewhat ironic that each was practicing medicine primarily in areas populated by those of the other's race. Neither said they ever felt any unease. They were both welcomed and loved by their patients and by the communities.

Sally found that working with the poor provided her with perfect opportunities to practice her gift for people she felt really deserved Corrections. She was so trusted that her patients freely talked about themselves. They would confide in her and reveal their innermost secrets and fears. It was easy to get them to tell of one decision they wished they hadn't made or an action they hadn't taken in their lives. She would them touch their shoulder and The Correction would happen.

Sally was fastidious about keeping records of The Corrections she performed. In all, she performed nearly 300 Corrections. She always made sure there weren't any children whose existence may be in jeopardy. Her records showed not only the name, address, and other basic information about the person but also the decision/action corrected and, to the extent she could find out, the end result of The Correction.

I have her notebooks, and they make for fascinating reading. Many of the patients for whom she did Corrections remained in the neighborhood and remained her patients. Others ended up following different paths, and she never heard from them again. For those who stayed, she noticed a change in their demeanor and attitudes. She helped lift a heavy weight from their very souls. Her talks with them were a lot freer and did not have the sense of foreboding they previously had.

She continued to practice medicine until the day she died in 1917 at the age of 70. Her last Correction was three days before her death. My father told me he believed this Correction led to her death.

She had celebrated her seventieth birthday a week before. John, who was now an attorney and lived in Philadelphia with his wife and son, came to Washington to celebrate with her. Sally's husband, Mark, had passed away five years earlier, so Sally lived alone. John had been trying to get his mother to retire and move to Philadelphia. He did not like the idea of her wandering the streets alone at her age. She waved him off, saying medicine was her life. She was going to continue helping her people until she could no longer stand. He conceded it was a lost cause.

She also told him she was going to continue making Corrections. As the firstborn, he had taken on the mantle, but he knew he would never be as productive as his mother. As the firstborn, he could sense when his mother had done a Correction. One time he was in the middle of cross-examining a witness in a murder trial when the sensation came over him. He had to stop himself and smile. The judge asked him, "Mr. Vance, are you done with this witness?" John shook his head and responded, "No, your honor," and then he continued.

Sally could not uproot herself, nor could she desert her patients, but she did have to admit that she was terribly lonely. She and Mark had been married for over forty years. He was her constant companion and confidante. While he was aware of her gift, she was never sure if he believed her. He never felt the difference and only saw the world through untrained eyes. Probably, he saw his wife as eccentric and maybe a bit off, but he loved her so that he overlooked this oddity in her.

One day, Mark told her about a regret he had, something he would change in his life if he could. It had to do with his younger brother, Adam, who had taken to alcohol and gotten increasingly dependent on it as his life went on. Mark was always a lot more popular than Adam. One day, Adam shyly asked his brother if he could stay home and play with him. Mark brushed him off and ran off to play ball with his buddies. Adam never asked him again. He increasingly folded back into himself. As he got older, he used alcohol to help him through his days. When Adam was thirty-five, he committed suicide.

Mark always wondered what would have happened if he had been more solicitous of his brother and said he'd stay home to play with him. Perhaps his brother would still be alive.

Sally was almost ready to grant her husband's wish and let him go back to that point, but then she stopped herself. She did it for selfish reasons. She explained that she had no control over what happened in Mark's life from the point of The Correction forward. Perhaps getting closer to Adam could set Mark's life on a path where he and Sally never met. She couldn't take that chance. Neither could she take the chance that John or their two other children would never have been born.

Also, doing The Correction wouldn't prove anything, at least not to him. The revised action he took—playing with his brother—would be his revised memory. He would remember nothing about running off to play with his friends. Sally also had her doubts whether Mark playing Adam would have saved Adam. He obviously had deep-seated problems that probably would have come out regardless of how his brother treated him. She truly believed that her husband was carrying a burden on his shoulders that was not his to bear.

Sally explained all this to Mark and used examples of the patients she never saw again once she performed their Corrections. At first, he was miffed that she would not offer to help him and his brother, but he soon came around and their relationship did not suffer. Sally was never sure whether her explanation made sense to him or whether he was just playing her, knowing that she could not do what she said she could do. Sally could have been furious with Mark if the latter were true, but in the long run, it didn't matter to her. They never mentioned it again.

Mark had been gone for five years, and Sally sorely missed him. She missed his wit and repartee. She missed having someone her own age and experiences to talk with. Whenever she attended a few social gatherings, she found many of the people to be shallow and uninteresting. Hannah came to see her several times a year, but as each had gotten older, various age-related maladies made these reunions less frequent.

One evening Sally was walking home from clinic. The year was 1917. It was a beautiful fall day, so she sat for a few minutes in a small park along the way. The park was bustling with people, mostly parents watching their children play. Sally was enjoying the activity when a dapper, gray-haired man approached her. "Do you mind if I share your bench?" he asked.

"Please do."

"I love this little park, especially this time of year," he stated. "I grew up right over there. No matter how far I've gone in this world, I always seem to gravitate back to this spot."

"You travel a lot?"

"I used to. I'm retired now. I was with the State Department for 30 years. I was posted to the Far East and in Egypt for extended periods, but more recently I was stationed in Europe."

"That sounds fascinating."

"Like anything, it was a job, but yes, it was fascinating. I met so many people and saw so many things. I also like to think I did some good along the way."

"I'm sure you did. I would have loved to have gone to Europe someday. I grew up in New York but have lived most of my life here in Washington. My job has always required I stay here. I guess travel to distant shores will have to remain a dream."

"Who knows? Dreams often come true. What was your job?"

"I'm a doctor. I haven't yet retired. Who knows if I ever will? Ever since my husband passed away five years ago, my son's been trying to get me to move to Philadelphia to live near him. I just can't leave my patients. I run a clinic in Southeast."

"You're the one who's led a fascinating life. When I was young, my mother wanted to be a doctor. I sorely disappointed her when I chose this career path. She got over it, however, when I arranged for her to meet President Roosevelt. My name's Terrence McNally, by the way."

"It's a pleasure, Terrance. I'm Sally Vance."

They chatted and lost track of time until Terrence happened to notice that darkness had fallen.

"I'd better be heading out."

"I imagine your wife will start wondering where you are," Sally breezily stated, hoping her intentions weren't to blatantly obvious.

"Nope, no wife. My Alice passed away a decade ago."

"Any kids?"

"No, we weren't too lucky on that score. Can I walk you home? I'd feel like a failure as a gentleman if I let a fine lady as yourself in the dark."

"That would be nice, if it's not out of your way."

"Not in the least."

They walked and talked the fifteen minutes to her home. He shook her hand in a gallant manner and said good night as he took his leave. Sally was disappointed he did not mention wanting to see her again, but it did not dismay her. She was never a woman to sit back and let things happen. If he wouldn't pursue her, she would pursue him.

When he said his name, something clicked in her mind. She recognized it but did not remember where she heard or saw it. Her guess was that she read it in the newspaper, so the following day she went to the library in her community. She asked if they kept back copies of the Washington Post, the newspaper she had read every morning with her coffee since the 1870s. The librarian advised her that the library had back copies going back at least twenty years. She must have seen his name in the last four years, so that is what she asked for. The librarian said that would be possible. They kept up to five years on-site. Any more than that could be brought in from the warehouse. They walked her to the room in which the newspapers were housed. She dove in.

She didn't remember seeing his name in recent memory. It had to have been at least three years earlier. So, she started with the oldest papers in the pile first. Four hours and eight hundred newspapers later, she finally found what she was looking for. She took copious notes on the front-page article in the June 29, 1914 edition. She copied it word for word. She returned the newspapers to their places, thanked the librarian, and went back home.

When she got there, one of her assistants from the clinic was waiting for her. He was frantic but looked relieved when she walked up the drive. It occurred to her that she never sent word to the clinic that she was going to be out. She was embarrassed because she attributed her oversight to a schoolgirl crush.

"Ms. Vance," the man stated, "we was all worried about you. It ain't like you ta not come in ta work like dis."

"I'm sorry, Malcolm. Something came up and I simply forgot to send word that I wouldn't be in today. Please send my apologies to everyone for causing them to worry."

"I will, Ms. Vance. So long as you's awright."

"I am, and I'll be sure to be there tomorrow. Okay?"

"Dat's good, Ms. Vance. See ya tomorra."

As Malcolm walked away, Sally couldn't help but smile. A part of her was pleased that they missed her as much as they did. She always took herself somewhat for granted, but it was gratifying that her absence was so keenly felt. The real reason she was smiling was the reason for her absence. It occurred to her that she had been acting like a moonstruck and lovesick schoolgirl. She hadn't felt that way in an awfully long time and, while it would mortified her if anyone knew, she was tickled pink to have that feeling again.

She hadn't eaten all day so she made herself a sandwich, after which she went back to the park. She sat on the same bench and waited. Again, she watched the kids play, but she was too anxious to truly enjoy the scene. After an hour, she got up to leave. She was disappointed, and she was also embarrassed that she had succumbed to a schoolgirl crush the way she did. "Oh well," she sighed, "it was fun to dream. Now back to the real world."

She slowly exited the park and headed home. She turned the corner and nearly bumped into him. Her heart rate sped up immediately.

"I just came from your home. You weren't there."

She laughed. "I hope not since I've been here for a little while."

"Waiting for somebody?"

"Just passing the time."

"Maybe you'd like to pass time with me for dinner. There's a quaint Italian restaurant called La Gondola not far from here. I don't know if you're familiar with it. I've eaten there many times. Would you care to join me?"

"I would."

The two picked up where they left off the day before. They found even more things in common, including their fathers. When Sally told him about Efrem saving Andrew and his family from slavery and then serving in the Union Army, fighting at Antietam, Terrence recounted that his father's story was very similar. He was a noted abolitionist in the New York area who likewise volunteered for the army when the war began. His father was an accomplished equestrian, so he ended up in Phil Sheridan's calvary. He served a full three years in the calvary, ultimately rising to the rank of colonel. They wondered whether the two men knew each other, given that they traveled in similar circles. Neither was around to ask, though.

Sally's relationship with Hannah and her family impressed Terrence. He said he looked forward to meeting her very soon. Sally took this as an excellent sign that Terrence was planning on a long-term relationship. She was planning on that.

13

John Vance stood up to begin his cross-examination of the defense's witness in the Amos Smith murder trial. Amos Smith, the son of the Mayor of Philadelphia, had been charged with the premeditated murder of his wife, Hortense. Smith claimed her death was accidental. He had been cleaning his firearm, and it accidentally discharged, killing her instantly. However, there were so many inconsistencies in Smith's statements that the police and the prosecutors thought otherwise. John had lined up witness after witness who testified about a history of abusing his wife and threatening violence.

The mayor had attempted to exert influence to get the prosecution to back off of his son. This made the District Attorney even more determined to pursue conviction. He told John to go in with both guns blazing and John relished the opportunity.

The witness put forward to provide a defense for Amos Smith was so weak and had so many holes that John was practically salivating at the chance to get at this guy. He had to refocus himself, however. He pulled a letter from his mailbox just before he left for the courthouse. His mother was telling him that she and Terrence McNally were going to wed. John was in shock.

John met Terrence two months earlier. The former diplomat seemed nice enough. He was an accomplished man. He was pleasant company and was obviously quite in love with Sally. His problem was that his mother had only known this man for about six months. That was hardly time enough to decide to marry someone.

He knew his reaction was not logical. His reservations flowed from his emotions. John's father, Mark, had been dead nearly six years, but a large part of him still thought of his mother and father as a couple. They should forever be a couple and he resented an interloper, no matter how great a man he may be, inserting himself into his mother's life. She had gotten increasingly lonely since his father passed on, but he still resented anyone who could actually reduce or eliminate that loneliness. Time and again he had offered for Sally to come live with him in Philadelphia, but she constantly refused. He thought she was being unreasonable.

One thing he had noticed was that his mother's rate of Corrections had significantly slowed down since she met Terrence. He did not think that was a bad thing. He always had a concern that she might have been too prolific, that she didn't do enough research before performing her Corrections. Something was bound to go wrong. The one thing that saved her was that she primarily performed Corrections for the downtrodden and non-powerful, people who lived on the fringe. Before, changing these people's lives would help them but would have little impact outside of their limited worlds. He was very selective in his Corrections and he was teaching his son to be the same. He was glad that his mother, as she entered her golden years, was perhaps coming to the same conclusion.

This was the frame of mind he was in when he arrived at the courthouse. He temporarily put his mother out of his mind and focused on this case. Once this trial was over, he would travel to Washington to talk with his mother. He actually was softening the more he thought about it. His mother deserved happiness and at her age she couldn't wait around for an extended courtship. A slight smile creased his lips as the judge entered the chambers and everyone rose. John regained his focus and went to work.

After a day of jury selection, John presented the State's case. Three days later, the prosecution rested, and the defense was presenting its case. The defense attorney walked his first witness through a series of questions. John got up to start his cross-examination. He paused a few seconds to let the witness sweat a bit. He was two words into his first question when everyone in the room disappeared. His head started to spin, but that stopped in a few moments. Still, he was disoriented.

He found himself sitting in a conference room with seven other attorneys. His boss, Deputy District Attorney Arthur Avery had finished his plans for the

Harkins murder case and was now droning on about who to call as witnesses in the Stryker fraud trial. "John, what do you think?" By this time, John had insinuated himself into this different reality. "I agree with the list of witnesses but I'd reverse the order of the accountant and Stryker's sister. The accountant can lay out the numbers to get the jury used to the facts and then we can get into the emotional account of how Stryker left his sister and their parents destitute. Ultimately, we need the jury to make their judgment on facts. If we hit them with the emotion first, they may not pay attention when the boring stuff is being presented to them."

John was surprised that everybody agreed with his assessment since his mind was not totally there. A part of it was subsumed by the Amos Smith case and his mother's impending marriage, even though he was realizing that those events no longer were relevant or real.

He was gradually becoming aware of what had happened, but he did not want to face the truth. Avery had adjourned the meeting and the various lawyers had left. Avery was gathering up his papers and noticed John still seated, staring off into space.

"You okay, John? You don't look well."

"I'm okay. Art, do we have a pending case against Amos Smith?"

"Amos Smith? The mayor's son?"

"Yeah, him."

"You're kidding, right?"

"No, why?"

Avery pulled a folded newspaper out of his briefcase, opened it up and handed it over to John. There, on the front page was the headline "Mayor's Son Killed in France". He read on.

Amos L. Smith, son of Philadelphia Mayor Thomas B. Smith, was mortally wounded yesterday at a battle at Château-Thierry, France, about sixty miles northeast of Paris. He succumbed to his wounds and died in a Paris hospital hours later. Lieutenant Smith was part of the American Expeditionary Forces or AEF under the command of General John J. Pershing. The AEF joined British and French forces to halt an offensive by the German Army. The aim of the offensive is to capture Paris and ultimately compel the Allied forces to sue for peace to end this conflict that has dragged on for nearly four years and resulted in the death of millions of soldiers and civilians.

John looked over the rest of the front page headlines and saw that they were all related to a conflagration in Europe known as The Great War. In a daze, he handed the paper back to Avery. "Thanks, Art." was his monotone statement.

"You remember we were building a case against Smith for murdering his wife, don't you? Before we could nail it down, he enlisted and was shipped off to France. We figured we'd pick a trial back up after he got back. The Germans saved the taxpayers a whole lot of money, didn't they?"

"Sometimes these various cases get jumbled in my mind. I knew we were working on something but I hadn't heard about it lately."

"I'll catch you later."

"Yeah, I'll see ya, Art."

John's mind raced between both realities, one of a tenuous peace, but peace nonetheless, and one of devastating conflict. His mother had shown him the November 1914 newspaper article crediting Terrence's efforts in brokering a long-term agreement between Germany, Austria-Hungary, Britain, France and other countries. The agreement had cooled tensions between the countries and headed off hostilities that seemed imminent. Despite occasional flare-ups, this peace was enduring and had lasted to the present day in 1918.

By this time, John was fully aware of 'The Great War' and its record of carnage and death. This had become the world's current reality.

He ran from the courthouse. His first stop was the Western Union Office, where sent a very simple message. *Mother have you done a Correction? Stop Be there ASAP. Stop John.* Then, dreading the worst and not thinking he could take time to return to the office, he dashed off a second telegram to Arthur Avery. *Art Mother is ill Stop Had to run to DC Stop Will not be in court for Harkin case tomorrow Stop John* He ran eight blocks to the Broad Street Train Station. A train for Washington, DC was departing in forty-five minutes. He bought a ticket and boarded the train when it pulled into the station.

He had never been so apprehensive in his life as he was on the train ride south. On the one hand, a part of his being was now fully aware of The Great War, as if he had been reading the headlines every day about the war for the past four years. On the other, it was as if he'd been in a four-year sleep and awakened to a much more brutal world than the one he was in when he first closed his eyes. Could his mother somehow be responsible? If so, how? What horror was she now going through?

Once he got into Union Station, he jumped on a streetcar he knew went close to his mother's house. He ran the two blocks to the house and banged on the door. Getting no response, he tried the door, but it was locked. He reached into the flowerpot where she always kept an extra key. He let himself in.

"Mom! Mom!" he shouted as he rushed around the house. He bounded up the steps and hurried into her bedroom. That was where he found her, lying on the floor beside her bed. He knelt down beside her. Her body was cold. There was no pulse. She was gone. He sat down on the floor beside her.

"Mom…what happened? What happened? What happened?"

He sat beside her for over a half hour, but then he slowly got up. He had to contact authorities to let them know of his mother's death but first he wanted to search for some answers to basic questions. What happened here? How could a Correction set the stage for this devastation to occur? What was his mother trying to accomplish?

His mother kept meticulous reports on all of her Corrections. She had converted her guest room into a library where she kept all her records. That's where John was going to start. Luckily, she arranged her record-keeping chronologically, so it did not take long to find the most recent. He started at the end and worked backward. As he suspected, he found a Correction pertaining to Terrence McNally.

Last week, Terrence asked me to marry him. I enthusiastically agreed. We'd only known each other for a very short time, but we knew it was right. He had been alone for a long time. So had I. It would be good for each of us to have someone to be with. But we were both looking for more than just a companion. We loved each other. I know that John will need some convincing, but he'll come around once he comes to know Terrence. I've been so excited I feel like a schoolgirl.

As we'd gotten to know each other, I sensed there was something troubling him deeply. I didn't want to pry, but if we were to commit to spending the rest of our lives together, I thought I had a right to know. It wasn't until we were talking about places we should go after our wedding that I finally said enough. He had to tell me what was wrong.

I'd traveled nowhere other than an occasional trip to the Delaware shore and trips to New York to visit Hannah whereas he'd been all over the world, both in his official capacity and as a tourist. I told him I was at his mercy what the best spots in the world were. I said I'd always wanted to see the big tourist attractions: Paris, London, Rome, but I also said I'd love to see some out of the way countries and cities with reputations for beauty, but are not as well-known. I threw out Thailand and Japan as possibilities, but then I mentioned Sarajevo in Eastern Europe. I'd heard it was a beautiful city. I've always liked the name.

It was also the scene of Terrence's most significant diplomatic victory, and I thought it would give him a chance to show off to me. Instead, upon hearing the name of this, his expression changed to one of profound sorrow. He tried to recover and put on a good face, but the point had been made. I had to find out what it was about this place that had such an impact on him. It took a while, but he finally admitted what it was. He said it was easier for him to write it out than to say it to me, so here it is in his own words.

We had just finished the negotiations, and we were exhausted. Germany had proven especially belligerent and demanding. It was almost as if they were looking for any excuse to go to war. They wanted us to throw up our hands and walk away from the table. However, we were very patient and looked for areas of compromise. Finally, late in the day on June 27, 1914, all the parties reached an agreement. There would be no war. The French thought we gave up too much to the Germans, but they gave in and agreed to the terms. No one had yet signed the documents, but that was strictly a formality. We scheduled a formal signing ceremony for two days hence, on June 29.

We were ebullient and thought we'd earned ourselves a celebration. Our entire delegation went out for drinks and dinner at the finest restaurant in Sarajevo. I have never been a big drinker, and I had a bit too much, I'm afraid. We left the restaurant at around one in the morning and I drove a group of us back to our hotel, about a mile away.

Because of the drink combined with exhaustion, I was not at my best driving. We were all talking and still having a good time when a man stepped into the road. I could not help but hit him. I pulled the car over to check on the man, but James Farrell, my second-in-command, insisted that we move on. We all knew the car had killed man instantly; there was nothing we could do for him.

I was beside myself with grief and wanted to stop, but James's arguments were persuasive. His key point was that the peace agreement was still very tenuous. Whether it was logical or not, news of a diplomat driving a vehicle after drinking a fair amount of alcohol and then killing a local resident of a country seen as an ally of Germany could be enough to get Germany to back out. We drove on.

Over the next few days, I insisted that James follow up and get whatever information he could on the victim. He objected at first, saying that any contact we made would only draw attention to ourselves. I insisted and ordered him to do whatever it takes to find out about the man. Rather than working through the police, which would undoubtedly have set off alarms, he contacted a journalist friend who had contacts with local newspapers.

His name was Gavrilo Princip. He was only nineteen-years-old. The son of peasant· farmers, he had traveled to the city of Sarajevo to get an education and better himself. I took that away from him.

The papers were all signed and the period of peace began, but, for me, my period of turmoil also began. I got the name and address of his parents who live in the small hamlet of Obljaj, Croatia. I anonymously send them one thousand dollars each anniversary of his death. It doesn't assuage my conscience nor does it bring their son back but hopefully it makes their lives a little easier.

John did not need to read on further. He knew the story. Gavrilo Princip assassinated Archduke Franz Ferdinand of Austria and the Archduke's wife, Sofia, Duchess of Hohenberg. The assassination of the Archduke served as the spark that lit the kindling of what would soon be known as The Great War. By running down Princip, Terrence inadvertently kept The Great War from happening.

John was pretty sure he knew the rest of the story, but he finished reading his mother's account anyway.

Four years later, Terrence was still being torn apart by this one action. He had taken a life. It was an accident, but he felt responsible. It was killing him. Many people feel lucky when they get away with something. Terrence only felt intense guilt. He felt someone should hold him accountable for his actions. He once said he was going back to confess and take whatever happened, but the State Department forbid it. They still feared of a spark that could ignite into war. Germany still itched for war. The American government would not be the one who gave them an excuse.

Terrence would just have to live with this for the rest of his life. That is unless someone who had a special power intervened. I considered this very carefully. One thing that would keep me from allowing Terrence a Correction was purely selfish. We allow the person a chance to go back a reverse a decision—in this case Terrence would choose not to drive because he was drunk—but we never know how or even if that person's path changes from that point forward. There was a possibility that Terrence could head off in a different direction and we would never meet. This was a possibility I was willing to take. I love him and cannot stand to see him suffering so. I also did not envision his life would change very much through this Correction. His career and life would be the same whether or not this peasant boy lived or die.

After I read his account, I talked with him about it. A fair number of tears were shed, but finally I got to hear the words I needed to hear, "I wish I never drove my automobile that night." I put my hand on his shoulder and he was gone.

I had never had such a feeling after one of my Corrections as I did now. I could not stand the intensity or the pain I was feeling. It was not until an hour later that it all hit me. I knew I was responsible for keeping Gavrilo Princip alive. I knew I was personally responsible for allowing the Great War to start.

Sally's account ended there. John went back to her bedroom and saw her lying there. She had taken her actions so personally that it caused a massive heart attack. He looked down with love on his mother. She had spent her life devoted to helping others. Her heart could not accept the fact that she was in any way responsible for the death of millions of people.

14

After attending to his mother's funeral and estate, John Vance was about to return to Philadelphia, but he decided there was one thing he needed to do first. He went down to the street and hailed a taxicab. He gave the driver the address, 501 O Street in Georgetown.

The taxi let him off at this address. It was an elegant brownstone typical of the area. He went up the steps and rang the doorbell. A short while later, Terrence McNally answered the door.

"Hello, Mr. McNally. My name is John Vance. You don't know me, but I'd like to ask you a question."

"It's never the questions that worry me; it's usually the answers. So, ask away."

"Do you believe the war would have happened anyway if you fully executed the peace treaty you were negotiating in June 1914 in Sarajevo?"

McNally had a look of astonishment on his face. "How do you know about those negotiations? They were top secret."

"I just know that they occurred. You even had a verbal agreement by all parties. The Germans threw up objection after objection as they attempted to derail the talks, but eventually you reached a tentative compromise. France thought that too much was being given to Germany, but they reluctantly accepted the terms. The next day, Gavrilo Princip assassinated the Archduke of Austria and all your work went out the window. The rest as they say, is history."

"And your question is again?"

"If Princip hadn't killed Franz Ferdinand and all the attendees returned to the table to sign the agreement, we would have had peace instead of war. My question to you is, in your learned opinion, would that peace have held?"

"We've never met? You sure look familiar."

"I get that a lot. I have one of those types of faces, I guess."

"Why don't you come in so we can chat properly."

John and Terrence entered the brownstone and sat down at the kitchen table.

"How do you know about our commission?"

"Let's just say a friend of a friend told me."

Terrence didn't respond but was deep in thought. John imagined he was going through the small list of people involved in these talks to figure out who had talked. John was tempted to tell him that Terrence himself was the one who spoke up. When he said things about the conference to his mother, the existence and success of this peace initiative was widely known and widely publicized.

"Why have they kept the efforts of the commission—not to mention its very existence—so secret? You would think we would want the world to know that we sought peace," John remarked.

"I thought so, too, but we were ordered not to say anything until at least the war was over. They never gave a reason for the blackout. Most of us thought maybe the Administration did not want anything that could be projected as a failure. They even threatened us with prosecution under the National Secrets Act if we talked of this commission. I'm therefore surprised anyone would have said anything to you."

"However, I know about it. I need your assessment as to whether the peace would have lasted. Would there still have been war?"

How Terrence answered would be critical. There were several iron-clad rules that his family had adhered to over the generations. Most of these rules were put in place for humanitarian reasons. There would be no Corrections if they involved children. The Correction shouldn't be done if the change was exclusive for monetary gain.

It was also decided many centuries ago that no one would perform a Correction if the change would knowingly alter history. Corrections, it was very early thought, were to help a single person, not to change the world. If nothing else, this was too great a responsibility for one person to bear. Sally Vance knew this so personally that it took her life. But, depending on Terrence's response,

John would violate this precept. If Terrence believed that there would have been a lasting peace, he would have tricked Terrence into going back and undoing his mother's Correction. Princip would have been run over, again, and millions of lives would be spared and his mother would be alive.

John knew he was venturing into uncharted territory here. He had no idea whether the new Correction would result in the same result of killing Gavrilo Princip days before he carried out the assassination. Even if it did, there would be no way of knowing whether this time an associate of Princip would carry on for his fallen comrade and assassinate Franz Ferdinand. Despite all these uncertainties, John was willing to proceed, depending on the answer he got.

After considerable thought, Terrence gave his reply. "I believe the Germans want war. There's something in that country's makeup that demands it exert its dominance over others. The German people have a vision of themselves as a superior race who have an obligation to subjugate other countries and peoples. So, in answer to your question, I don't believe the peace would have held. The Germans would have found some pretext to demand war or would have manufactured some affront to their national pride that they must answer. The English and French, who are seeing a diminution of their worldwide influence, would see a need to respond. The Americans would respond exactly like we did. We'd hang back until we can see that our involvement would have the greatest impact and would catapult us forward as world players. Yes, inevitably a world war would have broken out. All we were doing was trying to delay the inevitable."

"Thank you for that honest response."

"Why is it important for you to know?"

"You wouldn't believe me if I told you. I thank you for your time."

Before Terrence could press him further, John got up, shook his hand and headed for the door. Terrence showed him out but asked nothing further.

If Terrence had answered that he believed the commission headed off war for a long time, if not permanently, John would have had a dilemma on his hands. He would have to ignore everything he had learned about influencing history to coax Terrence to wish he had driven that night. He would also have to ignore what he believed his mother would have wanted. If he went through with this Correction, he could just hear his mother's admonitions against what he had just done. She would be the one person other than himself who would know the full story. She would be alive, but she would know not only the history she had changed but of John's work as well. The thing is, her change was inadvertent; his would be on purpose.

Terrence's admission that, despite his best efforts, war was inevitable, made John's life easier. It relieved his mind that his mother bore responsibility for a horrific war. Perhaps she can rest in greater peace with this knowledge. He also knew that he could continue to perform Corrections and that he could pass on the tradition to his son, James, who was now coming of age to take on the responsibility. John added on one more rule. He must never do a Correction for anybody of any prominence. While it wasn't Terrence's position that resulted in his running over Princip, his prominence put him in a situation to do so.

15

I've related to you about some of my Corrections, but I've told you precious little about myself. Let me rectify this situation. I was born in 1919, a year after The Great War—the war inadvertently "caused" by my great grandmother Sally. My parents were James and Mary (Oliva) Vance. I did most of my growing up in New Jersey, across the river from Philadelphia.

My childhood was uneventful and somewhat sheltered. I was the first-born of three children, two girls and one boy. My dad worked at the Philadelphia Naval Shipyard and my mother was an elementary school teacher. My lawyer grandfather wanted my father to follow in his footsteps, but Dad was good with his hands and lazy in studying his books. That's not a good prescription for creating a future attorney. Dad spent forty years at the shipyards, building ships through two world wars. He was especially proud of his work on the battleship USS New Jersey.

My mother was my teacher in second grade. If I went into the school year expecting an easy time of it because Mom was teaching, I was sorely disappointed. She was tough. I wouldn't have been surprised if she was tougher on me than on the other students, but I was in second grade at the time, so what did I know.

Around the house, I often got the feeling that my parents were watching me closely. I didn't know it at the time, but I now believe they were looking for signs that I had the gift. They were watching me to see whether I reacted whenever Dad did a Correction. The thing is, I didn't sense or feel anything. Nothing. They were resigning themselves to the fact that the string had stopped. There was to be no carrying on of the mantle by the first-born of the family.

Then, when I was nearly nineteen, I felt my first sensation. My father lied and told me that there had been instances of "late bloomers" previously in the family. He was my Dad, I believed everything he said. I had no reason not to.

After that, he gave me a crash course in Corrections. He told me all the lore that my forebearers handed down over the centuries. He showed me the secret volumes of all that they had written down. Just the catalogue of Corrections maintained by my Great Grandmother Sally comprised several thick books. I couldn't get enough. It filled me with the spirit of helping people.

Dad made me start small so I could get a feeling of the power I had. My first Correction involved helping a neighbor who had backed over and crushed his five-year-old child's scooter. I met my neighbor, Mr. Creegan, in front of his house and got him to wish that he had looked for the scooter before he backed the car out of his garage. I put my hand on his shoulder and he disappeared. I looked around and there was Teddy playing on his scooter on the sidewalk. I felt like I could conquer the world. I ran in and told my Dad what I had done. He was brimming with pride.

Since I was nineteen when I performed my first Correction, this one Correction was the extent of my apprenticeship. My Dad said I was ready. "You were born ready," he said.

Dad wanted me to get an education. He sometimes regretted he didn't follow in his father's footsteps and become an attorney or some similar profession. Perhaps his son could be an attorney. I was willing to give it a try, so in 1939 I enrolled at Rutgers University. I consider myself to be of above average intelligence, so school should have been easy for me. However, I've learned that I possess a below average attention span. As a result, I dropped out of school after little more than a year.

Dad did not want me just sitting around. In late 1940, he got me a job at the shipyard, but I only stayed on this job for a little more than a year. This time, it wasn't because of any personal failings that caused me to submit my resignation on December 9, 1941. I left to serve my country.

My parents had mixed feelings about me enlisting in the army. My mother claimed I was too young. She said I worked in a shipyard, an essential industry. I would therefore not be eligible for the draft. She was only worried about me, like any mother would be. I told her I could not hide out for the duration of the war. I had to do my part.

My father worried that I would be killed, but he was concerned not only for my well-being. I could die before I married and produced an heir to perform Corrections. The string had gone on for over seven hundred years. He didn't want it to stop on his watch.

Ever since I was a young boy, my father held out Great-Great Grandfather Efrem as the ideal of what a man should be. He risked his life helping Andrew, Eliza and Hannah escape slavery. Then when the Civil War erupted to help other escape a similar fate, Efrem would not say that he had already done his part. No, he enlisted in the Union Army. He lost a leg, but that was a sacrifice he would gladly make if it meant freedom for all Americans. I explained to my parents that I could do no differently. Otherwise, all those stories they told me were only stories, not life lessons.

They really did not have a suitable response to my argument nor could they do anything to stop me. I'd already enlisted and would report to Fort Devens in Massachusetts in three weeks. There wasn't anything anyone could do about it.

I went through basic training and was assigned to the Army's II Corps infantry unit. I guess I showed something because I earned corporal stripes just before we shipped out to England in June 1942. Boy, were we green. We displayed our inexperience early the next year.

In November 1942 we sailed to Oran, Algeria in North Africa. Rommel's Afrika Korps was at its peak of strength at that point in time, but we were cocky Americans, ready for anything. In February 1943 we proved that we weren't ready as we thought we were and the Germans routed us at the Kassarine Pass in Tunisia. The Nazis crippled our inadequately armored tanks one by one, and then their offensive began. Armored vehicles supported the German infantry. We were in full retreat. They were annihilating us. We fought the best we could, but we were outgunned, outmaneuvered and out-whatever you want to say by the seasoned Germans.

I was only grazed slightly in the arm during the battle but two of my closest buddies, Frankie Costello from New Jersey and Al Leonard from Ohio, were blown apart by tank fire. In both cases, I quickly snatched their dog tags off their necks so that we had a record of their death and we could notify their families.

One little footnote, after I got my "wound" treated at the medical field station, it got recorded as a wound. The next thing I knew, our squad's lieutenant tracked me down and handed me a Purple Heart. I asked him what it was for. He said it was a wound. I told him a bullet just nicked me. I didn't deserve a medal. He said it wasn't worth the paperwork to try to refuse it or send it back. I stuffed it in my knapsack and forgot about it.

It had gotten to a point where we either couldn't or wouldn't retreat any further. We had finally achieved some high ground and hooked up with some British troops to blunt the German advance. We dug in and were returning fire. The soldier beside me—I never knew his name—took a bullet in his upper chest. He immediately clenched his right hand over his wound while his left hand reached out and gripped onto the right sleeve of my shirt. His grip was like a vise as he pulled me close. It was obvious to both of us his death was quickly approaching.

"Tell my wife I'm sorry I cheated on her. Tell her I love her. I love only her. Tell her."

He was shouting at me to be heard over the deafening explosions around us, but his voice was quavering. The intensity of his grip increased as he writhed in pain. He only had less than a minute left. He knew it; I knew it.

"Promise me you'll tell her." He was a lot calmer. He knew death was approaching.

I didn't know this man's name or where he was from. I didn't I know who his wife was nor did I need to know.

"Who did you cheat with?" I asked him.

He looked into my eyes. "Amy. Amy Salter."

"Repeat after me: I wish I never slept with Amy Salter."

He mustered one last bit of energy. "I wish I never slept with Amy Salter." Then he closed his eyes. I put my hand on his shoulder and he disappeared. I was in time. If he had died before I tried the Correction, he wouldn't have vanished. He went back in time and chose not to cheat on his wife.

I had no idea where he was now. The ripple in his personal history altered his path. Perhaps he had originally enlisted because he cheated on his wife and she told him they were through. Now, however, there would have been any need for him to enlist. Or maybe he was drafted. Maybe he was here in Tunisia. Maybe he was in the next foxhole. Maybe he'd been killed already. I had no way of knowing and no way of checking on him. This Correction had no impact on the German shells raining down on us right now, so I wasn't going to go looking for this guy. I hope he made it, but if he didn't, at least his wife would have an unsullied memory of him. I picked my rifle back up and started firing again.

I survived the battle, obviously, and then I survived the invasion of Sicily and then the D-Day invasion of Normandy. I guess I had some power looking over me.

After the war, I was speaking with a fellow veteran who fought in the Battle of the Bulge under Patton. One night he went to sleep in the woods, certain he was going to die the next morning. He said it seemed like such a distinct prophecy that he was shaking with fear. His fear was so pervasive that he didn't think he'd be able to sleep, but his body was so exhausted sleep eventually overtook him.

As he slept, he had a dream. In his dream, his elderly grandfather who had died fifteen years earlier came to him. The old man calmly told him he was going to survive, that no harm would come to him in the upcoming battle. He said he woke up the next morning brimming with confidence. He had to calm himself down to make sure he just did his job and not do anything rash. He survived the battle without a scratch.

I didn't have any dreams but I often wonder if I didn't have someone looking over me. Perhaps Grandpa Michael, who first appeared to Francis Wentworth in the thirteenth century, was watching over me. Perhaps he had been protecting our family, generation after generation, guiding us as we went along. Who knows?

16

After the war, I came back to New Jersey, unclear what to do with the rest of my life. My father still worked at the shipyard, but shipbuilding was winding down. He had some pull and probably could have gotten me a job, but it wasn't what I wanted to do.

Our little town offered me little opportunity, and I didn't really like Philadelphia so I moved into New York City. I loved the city but could only find the odd job, so it wasn't long before I went back to New Jersey. I missed the bustle of New York and the quaintness of small town life got old very quickly. It got especially old because I lived close to my parents. My father never missed an opportunity to pressure me to get married and have a child. He even had a wife picked out for me.

I'd known Victoria Snell since we were kids. Our families were close. She was smart and funny. She seemed like a perfect match for me. I liked her a lot. She professed to love me. I didn't think I loved her, though. I'd probably end up marrying her, but I figured I'd put it off as long as I could.

I had to think of a job that allowed me to travel, so I took a position selling encyclopedias. This job gave me a chance to learn, but not only about the new places I visited. Every night before I went to bed, I'd read another entry in the encyclopedia. I was a lazy student when I was in school, but now that I was on my own, I couldn't learn enough. I absorbed every page of the encyclopedia and then hungrily turned to the next page to learn more.

I was on the road ten months out of the year, mostly by design. I could rationalize that I was building a nest egg, but in truth I was putting off the inevitable as long as I could. I had to stop avoiding my responsibilities. I conceded I had to get home so I could propose to Victoria and start a family. Then, on one of my sale forays, I met Olivia.

The year was 1946. I was in Charleston, South Carolina. I went there to sell encyclopedias, of course, but I also went to pay a tribute to my Great-Great-Grandfather Efrem. Like most of my family, he kept a scrupulous record of his life. He said where he lived, which church he attended, where he heard Wesley Adams' regrets about shooting Andrew and many other locations in the city that were important to his life. I was planning on making this tour, but I had to take care of some business first. I wanted to sell at least two sets of encyclopedias before I could settle down for some vacation time.

I chose an upscale neighborhood to start my door-to-door canvas. Often, I go first to a more middle class area of a city. The people are nicer. I get fewer doors slammed in my face. This time, however, I went to where the money was.

After getting my sixth Southern genteel refusal, I was about ready to head over to a more modest neighborhood, but I tried one more house. It was an immense white two-story mansion with four impressive pillars lining the front porch. I knocked on the door. The wood was so substantial that I wondered if anyone could hear my feeble knocking, but within a few seconds the portal opened. Facing me was a mass of shoulder-length raven hair surrounding an alabaster face. The woman appeared to be about my age.

"Can I help you?"

I have a usual opening line that I've found effective, but I was so flummoxed by this beauty that I blurted whatever popped into my mind.

"Would you like encyclopedias?"

She laughed. "Who doesn't like encyclopedias?"

I recovered somewhat. "Oh, you'd be surprised. The residents of six houses in this neighborhood have rejected me already."

"Maybe it's that opening line of yours."

"Perhaps it is. Maybe I should close the door and start over again. If every time I opened a door I was greeted with such a lovely face, I wouldn't care if I never sold another set of encyclopedias in my life."

"Okay, now you're hitting your stride. What's a wombat?"

I don't know why, but I was not blind-sided by this question. "It's a marsupial native to Australia."

"Who fought in the Crimean War and when was it?"

"The Crimean War was fought between 1853 and 1856. Russia lost to an alliance made up of the Ottoman Empire, England, Sardinia and France."

"Who was Zoroaster?"

"He was an ancient Iranian prophet who lived in the 6th or 7th century BC. He established Zoroastrianism, the world's oldest continuously practiced religion that, in a nutshell, predicts the ultimate conquest of evil."

I was not sure why she was asking all these questions, but I was enjoying it. I found it rousing.

"Who was Peter Minuit?"

"He was the third governor of New Netherland, which later became New York. Historians widely credit him with purchasing the island of Manhattan."

She paused.

"Did I pass?"

"If I were to buy a car, I'd make sure that the guy selling me the car knew it inside and out. Why wouldn't I ask the same of someone selling me a set of encyclopedias?"

"Fair enough. Does that mean you're think of buying a set?"

"Not necessarily. I'm thinking that, since you seem to have as much knowledge as the encyclopedia, it might be cheaper to marry you instead."

"Is that a proposal?"

"Not necessarily, it's a little difficult marrying somebody whose name I don't know or who doesn't know my name."

"I'm Joseph Vance."

"I'm Olivia Wyatt."

"Now that our introductions are out of the way, was that a proposal?"

"Not necessarily, I don't think I could imagine marrying someone who's never even taken me out to dinner."

"Would you join me for dinner this evening? Since I'm new to this city, I will leave it to you to pick the restaurant."

"I never would have guessed you weren't a native."

"I do have a bit of a northern accent, don't I?"

"I personally find it charming. I get off work at six. Pick me up then?"

"You're working?"

"Why, yes. I'm the nanny for the Robinson's two children. You didn't think I owned all this, did you?"

"So, I don't suppose you'll be purchasing a set of encyclopedias, will you?"

"No, but the Robinsons will, once I tell them how wonderful they are."

"But you haven't seen them yet."

"If they gave you all that knowledge, they must be wonderful. Do you have a card?"

I produced one and gave it to her.

"Mrs. Robinson is due home from the hairdresser in an hour. Don't worry, I'll sell her on the need for all this knowledge for the kids. My sales pitch will be much better than yours. See you at six then?"

I went back to my hotel to collect myself, clean up, and get ready for my date. I probably should have hit at least two more homes that day to drum up sales. One more sale would warrant a trip to this city. But I was too flustered and distracted to do any more work that day. Her forwardness and sardonic humor really got to me. I was still pinching myself at my good luck.

I had dated a few girls in my life, but no one other than Victoria on a steady basis. Olivia caught me totally off-guard and kept me off-balance. I spoke with her for ten minutes, but she was the most intriguing person I'd ever met in my life.

When I went to this neighborhood earlier, I had taken a cab and then walked around. This time, I drove my rental car and arrived back at the mansion at precisely six. She walked out, not in a dress or any attire that I would imagine her wearing to a nice restaurant. She wore casual tan slacks and a loose-fitting white shirt. Her hair was pulled back in a ponytail. She took one look at me in my suit and tsked repeatedly.

"This will not do. This will not do at all. You'll be totally out of place."

"Where are we going?"

"Eloise's, best restaurant in Charleston if not the Carolinas. But it's very casual. I guess I neglected to mention that, didn't I? We should go back to your hotel and you can change. Let's be quick, though. That place fills up quickly."

We swung back to the hotel. She waited in the car while I ran up and changed. Less than ten minutes later, I was back down to the car.

"That's much better. Let's go."

She guided me as I weaved through the city as I headed east towards the port area. The neighborhoods became increasingly less affluent as we drove along. She had me take one more turn and then told me to turn into a parking lot next to what appeared to be a huge unpainted shack. The parking lot was packed, and I didn't think we'd get a spot, but she pointed to one right up next to the building a spot that had a crudely lettered 'Reserved' sign in front of it. The parking space was directly in front of the main door, over which there was a red neon sign that told the world that they were at Eloise's.

Even before we got out of the car, we could hear the music of a jazz combo. Once we stepped out, the song was more distinct.

"Ah, Duke Ellington, *Take the A Train*."

Olivia looked impressed. "That is quite a set of encyclopedias, isn't it?"

"I've acquired some bits of knowledge over the years outside of the encyclopedia. My Dad is a jazz fanatic. I'm going to know Duke Ellington, Count Basie, Louis Armstrong and all the greats."

We walked in and the place was packed. The band, consisting of a female lead singer with a husky sultry voice, a trumpet player, a clarinetist, a bass player and a drummer, was in one corner. I surveyed the crowd who, except for one table of six, two other customers, the drummer and now Olivia and me, were all Black. Olivia was spying on my reaction as we walked in. I think she was gauging my reaction to walking into a room full of Black people. I was so into the band I hardly noticed who was there. I think that's what she wanted to see because, when I looked down on her, I saw her smiling up at me. I smiled at her in return.

As soon as we walked in a few feet, a big black woman wearing a form-fitting red cocktail dress and extremely high heels rushed over. Her hair was piled up in a bun on top of her head. She picked Olivia up off the floor, gave her a bear hug and spun her around. Olivia squealed like a five-year-old.

"You been away too long, Livy."

"Auntie, I was here just last week."

"Like I said, too long. Who have we here?"

"This is Joseph Vance. He just sold me a set of encyclopedias. Well, he sold one to the Robinsons, anyway. Joe, this is Eloise Walker. She owns this place."

We shook hands. Eloise was eyeing me warily, but I passed at least initial muster as she welcomed me. She then took Olivia by the arm and led her over to a corner table. They chatted as they walked along.

"We had a tough time reserving your table tonight. A couple rough hooligans tried to claim it, but your Uncle Oscar set 'em straight. He said, 'Our Livy's comin' tonight so's you better move them asses off those chairs if ya knows what's good fer ya.' "

"C'mon Auntie, Uncle Oscar wouldn't scare a fly. You're the one who told them to move their asses, right?"

She broke into a full-throated laugh. "Little lady-like me? I could never use such language. You two sit right down and I'll start bringin' out some food to ya."

Eloise left. I turned to Olivia. "It's hard to hear over the band, but did you call her Auntie?"

"She's my aunt. Actually, she's more like a mother to me. My parents died of the influenza when I was two. Aunt Eloise and Uncle Oscar took me in and raised me. Before your mind runs all over the place, my dad was white and my mom was black. They couldn't get married, but somehow they figured out a way to have me. When they died, my father's family wouldn't have anything to do with me. My aunt and uncle took me in, no questions asked. They raised me as their own. Their world became my world. But then, because of my skin color, I've since had to straddle both worlds, never belonging in either."

"That's fascinating."

"You really think so, don't you?" It was an observation, not a question. "This is always the place I bring my first dates. I don't go out on a lot of second dates."

"I can't imagine any man not wanting to see you a second time or a third or fourth or fifth time."

"You're either very sweet or a very smooth talker. Given how you stumbled over your sales pitch, I'm leaning towards sweet. There's something sweetly naïve about you. Not many guys I date are at ease when they walk in here. I've had some who instinctively put their hands on their wallets. Why are you different?"

"It all started in Charleston."

"I thought you'd never been to Charleston."

"Never have. This is my first time down here. My connection goes back three generations. My great-great-grandfather Efrem Reynolds was down here on business in the 1850s. While he was here, he became aware of the plight of an African slave who was being auctioned off along with his wife and young girl. He bought the three of them and then drove them north to New York. Along the way they encountered a sheriff who questioned where he was taking the slaves and a road bandit they had to kill. In New York, Efrem set them free and set them up with jobs and a place to live. His story is part of our family lore. I thought I owed it to him to return and visit the places he wrote about."

"Why did he do such a thing?"

"Efrem was in the tobacco trade. He did some business with the owner of the slaves and got to know the slave named Andrew. He couldn't abide Andrew's family being split up. It just wasn't right."

"And you said my story was fascinating."

I was tempted to tell her that Efrem first heard of Andrew through a Correction that saved the slave's life. I didn't think that to be the type of thing you mention on a first date. I really did want a second date.

Olivia excused herself. I assumed she just had to go to the bathroom but when she came back with Aunt Eloise and an older gentleman who introduced himself as Oscar.

"Joe, tell my aunt and uncle the story you just told me."

I did as she instructed. When Olivia brought them over, her aunt had the same wary look on her face as when I first walked in. As I told her the story I could see her visibly soften. By the end, there was a discernable tear in her eye.

"Auntie, Joe is looking to pay tribute to his great-great-grandfather by finding places he and Andrew and—what did you say the wife and daughter's names were?"

"Eliza and Hannah."

"Yes, Eliza and Hannah, do you think Ms. Lily can help him?"

"It's worth talking to her. Why don't you come by tomorrow evening for dinner and we'll ask her?"

Eloise and Oscar got up to leave. They had a place to run, after all. But before they left, Eloise gave me a big hug, nearly as big as the one she gave Olivia when we walked in. Once they left, I turned to Olivia. "Who's Ms. Lily?"

"Our neighbor. Nobody knows how old she is, but she's got to be well over ninety. I wouldn't be surprised if she's over a hundred. Her body's failing her a bit lately, but she's still sharp as a tack. A real feisty lady! She didn't really accept me, a white girl, living right next door. She grew up a slave, after all and then lived through the era of the Klan and Jim Crow. They lynched one of her husbands. It was natural she'd not warm up to any white people. I wore her down, though, and we're very close now. She may be very cold to you, but if she sees you mean something to me, she'll warm up to you."

"So, I mean something to you, do I?"

She blushed for a second, but then recovered quickly.

"You mean at least as much to me as a set of encyclopedias."

"That's a start, anyway. I do have one question that's been puzzling me since I first met you, but I'm trying to figure out a way to say that won't offend you."

"Go ahead and ask. I promise I won't take offense."

I was still nervous. The evening was going so well. I didn't want to derail it, but I had to ask.

"How do you know so much? It seems anything I raise as a topic, you're conversant on it. I have a couple of friends who are attorneys and they say one of the cardinal rules of lawyering is never to ask a question of a suspect you don't already know the answer to. When I was trying to sell you the encyclopedia, you fired out a series of questions on a variety of topics to test me. You obviously knew the answers when you asked. How?"

"Aunt Eloise and Uncle Oscar believed in education. They knew how to read and write and do a little figuring, but they're both the smartest people I've ever known or ever will know. They wanted me to do better and get a proper education. The schools in our part of town were either nonexistent or very poor. Until his eyes started to fail him, Uncle Oscar was Mr. Robinson's chauffeur for many years. Uncle Oscar mentioned their dilemma with educating me and the next thing we knew, Mr. Robinson funded a school in our neighborhood. He promised me a place there. As I got older, he got me into progressively nicer schools. He finally got me admitted to Allen University to become a teacher. I had just graduated and was about to take a position as a teacher when his son and daughter-in-law were in a terrible accident. Mr. and Mrs. Robinson became guardians of their grandkids. I never reported for my teaching job. Instead, I went to the Robinsons and told them I would be the nanny to their grandkids. They're both in their upper sixties and keeping up with an eight-year-old and a six-year-old was way too taxing. That's what I've been doing for the last five years and that's where you met me today."

"I repeat my previous assessment of you: fascinating."

We talked throughout the night. Eloise kept bringing dish after dish until I was absolutely stuffed. Finally, the place was closing down, and it was time to head out. I headed back to my hotel. Olivia stayed with her aunt and uncle for the night.

The next morning when I woke, I wondered whether the previous evening had been a wonderful dream. Much of my life and the Corrections I perform very often feel like dreams. It's difficult to separate reality from make believe. I went to a few houses to try and sell some encyclopedias, but my heart wasn't in it so I gave up. My mind was too focused on Olivia to think about anything else. I went back to my hotel room and pretended to read a book.

At six I arrived at the Robinson mansion to pick up Olivia. When she stepped out the door and gave me the sweetest smile I could imagine someone giving another person, I knew it wasn't a dream. She clinched it when she got in the car and gave me a kiss on the cheek. Off we went to meet Ms. Lily.

We pulled up in front of Ms. Lily's home that she shared with her daughter. Her daughter, Mabel, was officially her caretaker, but Ms. Lily was such a cherished institution that she was everybody's mother or aunt. The entire neighborhood took part in watching after her. When we arrived, it was a warm spring evening, so Ms. Lily and her daughter were sitting out on the porch. Mabel introduced herself and then said she was going to go inside to bring out some refreshments and we should make ourselves at home.

As Olivia predicted, Ms. Lily was suspicious of this white stranger who showed up on her porch but after Olivia reached over and took my hand, the old lady smiled. Olivia told me to repeat my story. By now, on the third telling, I was getting quite practiced with it. I could even throw in a few details that had slipped my mind, things like the name of the church where Efrem had first met Wesley Adams.

Ms. Lily heard me through and then sat silent for a moment as she collected her memories of a time and a life so long ago. Then she spoke. I am not even going to pretend that I could understand even a third of the words from her toothless South Carolina drawl. Luckily, Olivia understood every word and translated for me. Following is my recollection of her translation.

"I was born on a plantation in Georgia but, before I learned to talk, my mama and me was sold to Magnolia Philips Plantation near Charleston. I spent my younger days picking cotton beside my mama until she was sold away. Then I picked cotton alone. I did not know anything about any other plantations than Magnolia Philips. I was never allowed to go into town like other slaves, so I never would have met Andrew, Eliza or the young girl Hannah.

"When the war started, things didn't change too much for us slaves. The only difference was that we did not see as many young white men around as we used to, but that didn't make things any better. In fact, things steadily got worse. The men left behind were the ones who weren't good enough to go to war, so they felt they had to be meaner than before to get the same amount of cotton.

"Our food was never good, but as the war went on, it got scarcer and worse. Eventually, some slaves left the plantation. There was no one to chase them down. It was mostly the men who ran. The women had no place to go. I stayed.

"Then at one point these men in blue uniforms carrying guns arrived at the plantation. By this time, the overseers had all skedaddled. There were hardly any men, black or white, left. This fella in a blue suit walked up to me and says, "You're free." I answered, "What does that mean?" "He said I could go anywhere I want. I didn't belong to anybody anymore and could leave the plantation if I wanted. "Where can I go?" "I don't know," he replied. "Is there food there?" "I don't know," he answered once again. I was going to ask him more questions, but I think the answers would have been the same, so I thanked him kindly. He went on his way. He seemed very pleased with himself for helping to free us. I guess he was doing right, but I did not feel any different than the day before when I guess I wasn't free.

"I finally ventured into the city. The armies had slaughtered all the livestock and poultry. They picked the vegetable gardens clean. The city couldn't be any worse. I had nothing keeping me on the plantation. I had no family there.

"Conditions in Charleston weren't any better, but I could survive. I found a room in the colored part of town and was found a few odd jobs here and there. I got by.

"About five years after the war ended, I ran into Nate. I knew him at Magnolia Philips Plantation before he ran off. He had taken a shine to me back then, but I didn't like him too much. He was a braggart with a big mouth. But now that I saw him again, I was hungry for a man. We moved in together. He asked me to marry him, but I didn't see the need for it. We were together for ten years and had two sons. Then one day he didn't come home from work.

"I thought his big mouth would get him in trouble one day, and I was right. He said the wrong thing to the wrong white man. They found his body hanging from an oak tree in the middle of the forest two days later. I knew it was worthless trying to get justice. In fact, I knew I could end up like Nate.

"Some friends took care of me and the kids for a year until I got back on my feet and could take care of myself. It was then that I met Andre. He was the nicest man I ever met. He'd been a slave down in Georgia his entire life, but after the war he drifted north. After Nate, I didn't want or need a man, but Andre was different. He made me laugh. I hadn't laughed in, I don't know how long. I didn't want any more kids, but we had two anyway, a boy and a girl. Andre loved those kids, but he didn't love my kids from Nate any less.

"We had very little, but we never starved. Andre was our rock. He even made sure we all went to church every Sunday. It was not something I was used to doing, but if Andre thought we should do it, I thought we should do it.

"One day Andre asked me to marry him. Unlike with Nate, I agreed. It felt right. A preacher married us in the local AME Church. It was a grand affair. I never felt prouder."

Ms. Lily paused to take a sip of water. I was enjoying the story of her life, but I had already resigned myself to the fact that she knew nothing about my family. I'd have to be satisfied with the record I had of events. Over the coming few days I'd look for the places Efrem had written about, hoping to recreate his story. It was as if Ms. Lily could read my mind because she then started a new thread of her discussion.

"It was in the 1880s when my daughter, Ethel, got real sick. I tried everything I could think of, but she kept getting worse. I was about to give up when somebody told me about a doctor who had set up a free clinic about ten blocks away. I wrapped Ethel in a blanket and carried her the ten blocks. When I got to the small storefront clinic, there was a long line of people waiting to see the doctor. I despaired of ever getting in when I saw a teenaged boy who had just finished talking to a man a couple of people ahead in line. He had a pad on which he wrote something down.

Next he came to me. He was such a good-looking young man. He smiled and introduced himself. His name was Efrem Smith."

As soon as she said the name 'Efrem' my ears perked up and I sat up straight.

"He told me his mother was the doctor and his job was to talk to the people in line to find out what ailed them. He was to decide whether somebody was so sick they should come to the head of the line. I uncovered Ethel's head. He looked at her, opened her mouth to look inside and then put his hand on her head. She was burning up. He gently grabbed me by the arm and asked me to come with him.

"He walked me by the line of people into the storefront. Some people grumbled as we passed them, but most could see how sick my daughter was so they didn't make a fuss. The young man walked in ahead of us and went up to the doctor, a slender black woman who was tending to a man with a large slash in his arm. Efrem whispered in her ear and she looked over at me. She gave instructions to her son on how to treat the man's wound and then walked over to me.

"She didn't introduce herself as she took Ethel away from me and laid her down on a cot. She worked on bringing her fever down with cold compresses while she ground up some medicines she forced Ethel to take. Efrem attended to the other people as they came in the clinic while the doctor worked on my daughter.

"Eventually, the boy closed the door and told the remaining people that they'd have to come back first thing in the morning. The doctor told me to make myself comfortable because Ethel was going to be there all night. She would not let us leave until the fever broke. The doctor went back to attend to my daughter.

"An hour later, the doctor came over and sat down beside me. 'Your daughter is resting now. She'll be okay, but she must stay calm for the next couple of days. She has scarlet fever. It's a good thing you brought her here. Scarlet fever can result in death if not treated, but we got it in time. Oh, I realized I didn't introduce myself. I'm Doctor Hannah Smith. You met my son, Efrem. He's going to be a doctor, too.'

" 'Thank you, doctor,' I responded. I asked her where she was from. You could tell she wasn't from around these parts. She said she came down from New York but was born in Charleston. She said she came down to help out for a couple of weeks and maybe set up a clinic. I asked her why she was doing this. She said a man named Efrem saved her many years ago. Efrem had bought her and her family at an auction and then drove them north to set them free. She wanted to help her people here who weren't as lucky as she was.

"Until she became too old to make the trip, Dr. Hannah and Efrem came back south every year for a couple of weeks to help us. Then Dr. Efrem came on his own for a number of years. He raised money to hire additional doctors and nurses so that the clinic was year-round."

Ms. Lily talked for another half hour, but I wasn't listening that closely. I had the best confirmation I could ever have about the effect of a Correction. If Efrem's Correction had only saved Andrew's life, it would have been enough but it did so much more. Hannah would have continued to be a slave. She never would have become a doctor. Her son, Efrem, perhaps never would have been born. He never would become a doctor.

I looked into the clinic that Eliza had started and found that it was still running. I went to visit it. It was called the Hannah Smith Clinic. There was a plaque honoring her in the lobby. The plaque mentioned my great-great-grandfather Efrem. It was a modern facility now with a number of doctors and nurses.

Not only would have Ms. Lily's daughter probably died if it weren't for Efrem's Correction, but he helped hundreds upon hundreds of people over the years. It was a legacy I was proud of and hoped I could live up to.

We left Ms. Lily's with such a buoyant enthusiasm it was difficult keeping our feet on the ground. What made me truly happy was that Olivia, a beautiful woman I'd known for only a few short days, was as delighted as I was. She was elated that my family had someone like this in it. I didn't want to destroy the mood, but I thought it important that I find out why.

"Olivia, can I ask you a question?"

"Certainly."

"Why?"

"Why what?"

"Why all this? Why am so lucky to have you by my side? Why don't you want to just go on dates where we can learn about each other, go dancing, have dinner?"

"Your accent."

"My accent?"

"I told you about the local guys who run away as soon as they learn I'm the product of a mixed marriage. I'm so tired of going on first dates and nothing else. And it wasn't only white guys who cut and run. Plenty of black guys did as well. I guess I could have just "passed" as white and settled for some man who would treat me well so long as I never acknowledged my heritage. You heard how Ms. Lily did such a thing with Nate. He was handy and gave her some security, but she settled. I don't want to do that. When I opened the door and you spoke, I said to myself this guy is different. I was also taken how stumbling you were. I had a sense that you were a great salesman, but when you saw me, you couldn't put two coherent words together. It was sweet. But then when you started talking about things that matter to you, I saw the real you and I liked what I saw. That's why I'm here with you. And I hope to keep being with you."

I pulled her close and kissed her. She kissed me back. I was into something good. I thought back to the story about my ancestor, George Allenwood, and his voyage to America. He met the woman of his dreams, waitressing in a pub three days before he sailed. He convinced her to leave everything she knew and sail with him. On the trip over, they married. I was convinced I was in a similar situation with Olivia.

"Livy, I hope you don't mind me taking the liberty of calling you that. It just felt right."

"It feels right to me, too."

"Livy, I know we only just met each other, but when something feels right, you know it. I know that was part of your joking banter when you talked about marrying me."

"Who said I was joking?"

"Will you marry me?"

"I will. I'd marry you this second, but it's not legal down here. We'll have to go somewhere where it is legal. I've always wanted to live in New York."

Olivia came back to New Jersey with me. Mom and Dad were greatly surprised when I showed up with this woman. I shocked them when I told them we were going to marry.

17

I want to come back to something I said earlier about not having the gift for Corrections until I reached the age of nineteen. Throughout my youth, my father prepared me for the eventuality. I think I mentioned that our parents don't encourage us to do Corrections until we are mature enough to handle the responsibility. And even with this maturity, mistakes or ill-advised Corrections still happen.

Despite this trepidation, parents are eager to work with their offspring, testing them on their abilities at the earliest age possible. My father was no different. I was no different with my son. My father told me all the stories. I was a sponge. Like I was later in life when I read the encyclopedia, I absorbed everything he told me. Naturally, my boyhood hero was Efrem but I fell in love with Emily and all the rest in between.

When I was fifteen, my father thought I was ready and wanted to test my abilities. I tried, but there was nothing. I tried numerous times, but nothing happened. I was frustrated for myself, but I also felt like I let my father down. He claimed I didn't disappoint him, but how could I not have? This was a family tradition that went back over seven hundred years. I was the one who was breaking the string.

Over the course of the next four years, my father and I repeatedly attempted Corrections. Each time, we failed. Then, one snowy morning just after I turned nineteen, I woke up feeling different. The world was much clearer. It was like I was extremely near-sighted my entire life and everything was blurry but now I was given my first pair of glasses and everything came into focus. The thing that was even stranger was that I now remembered doing Corrections from my early teens.

I sensed this had to be everything my father and I had been talking about for years finally coming to fruition, but I was very concerned. I wanted to run to my Dad to tell him, but he was out of town. He'd left the day before to go on a trip "for business". He'd never taken a business trip before so it surprised both my mother and me, but we thought little of it.

When Dad arrived home the next day, I could barely wait to tell him what I thought happened. Dad was delighted, but he was not as surprised as I thought he would be. Mom asked him how the business trip went and Dad stumbled through a response, but he said it went fine. They achieved everything they wanted to. Mom didn't look overly convinced, but she let it drop.

I told Dad that I now distinctly remembered performing Corrections for at least five years now. He said that my mind was playing tricks on me. His simple explanation for the delay in my abilities coming out was that I was a late-bloomer. The mind was just kicking in and there was bound to be confusion. He said there had been examples of this happening in the family in the past, but he couldn't offer any names or specifics. I thought it somewhat suspicious, given how obsessed my ancestors had been with recording every aspect of their lives. I would have thought that something like concern about a first-born not carrying on the family tradition would have been major news. Still, I accepted my father's word for it.

I made up for lost time in carrying out Corrections. I really made up for it when I was in the military. There were many, many screwed up soldiers who regretted actions they had taken in their lives. I helped them all. I suppose I was like my Great-Grandmother Sally in the frequency of Corrections I performed. I was luckier than her in that my Corrections did not result in a world war or anything as calamitous as that. I focused on the nobodies who populate the world. Changes in their circumstances had little of an impact outside of their respective orbits.

I got a call from my mother. She was calling to tell me she was divorcing my father. She found out he had cheated on her. I was under the impression that the cheating was recent with my mind going back to his "business trip". It wasn't. The cheating had happened nearly three decades earlier, two years before I was born. He was only coming clean about it now.

To make matters even more confusing, my mother said she wasn't divorcing him because of the cheating itself. She was leaving him because of how he handled it. She called Dad a murderer. She said that, since the murder directly affected me, I had a right to know the story.

The year was 1917, two years before I was born. My father was exempt from the newly instituted draft because he worked at the Philadelphia Naval Shipyard, an essential wartime industry. Construction of new ships at the shipyard continued at a pretty healthy pace that would only increase as American involvement in World War I gained steam. As a result, the shipyard was steadily hiring new employees. One of the new employees was a young, pretty Puerto Rican woman named Lydia Sanchez. They hired her on as a secretary in the main office.

Being a Latina woman, especially an attractive one, made her a target of abuse by several of the more uncouth louts who worked the docks. The abuse she took was brutal and sexually tinged. She complained to her superiors, but they did nothing. In fact, they put the blame partially on her.

One day, James (since I hadn't yet been born, I feel a little strange calling him Dad) had finished his shift and was walking through the yard, heading for the exit when he heard a muffled scream. He ran toward the sound. Turning a corner, he saw a man standing over Lydia who was on the ground, cowering in fear. The man obviously had assault on his mind. Without saying a word, James ran at him full speed. The man turned, but it was too late. James lowered his shoulder and rammed it into his chest, driving him back ten feet into a brick wall. The back of his head slammed into the hard surface and he lost consciousness as he crumpled into a heap.

James turned to Lydia and held out his hand.

"Can I help you up, miss?"

She was still shaking and didn't react at first. He kept his hand extended.

"It's okay. You're safe now. No one's going to harm you."

She took his hand and stood up. She looked up to him and then burst out in tears as she leaned into him and cried into his chest. He put his arm around her and gently patted her back.

"There, there. Let's go get a drink to calm you down."

They went to a local bar and had a couple drinks. They chatted about themselves and their lives. When Lydia seemed calm, James said he would walk her home. He did not want her walking the streets of Philadelphia by herself as dusk approached. When they reached her apartment building, she took his hand and invited him up. He wavered for a second, but then followed her in.

His bosses would occasionally ask James to work a second shift, so when he didn't come home that night until the wee hours of the morning, Mom thought nothing of it. Mom and Dad didn't have a telephone at the time. There was no way for him to get in touch. The next morning, Mom asked him how work was. He said it was very busy. Technically, he didn't lie to her. He just didn't tell her the entire truth.

In the morning, he went to work and then during his lunch break he went to the main office to check on Lydia. She was not there. He asked about her. One of the other secretaries said she didn't show up. Neither did she call in. After his shift, he went by her apartment. Nobody was there. As he was leaving, he passed a neighbor in the hallway who told him that she saw Lydia leaving earlier in the day with a suitcase in hand.

James checked with the office a few days later and they said she probably wouldn't be coming back. He didn't want any further relationship with her. He was concerned about her health and well-being. He went on with his life as the devoted husband, chalking this one dalliance as a onetime stray, never to happen again.

It wasn't until 1937, when I was around seventeen and was showing no sign of being gifted that he once again thought of Lydia. He had lied to me when he had said there were cases in the family over the centuries of first-borns who were late bloomers. Ever since the earliest days, parents could see that their eldest child exhibited a specialness practically from birth. Dad knew that and therefore sensed there must be another cause to my slowness.

His suspicions were confirmed two years later when a young man around my age showed up unannounced at our house and asked to speak with my father. Dad wasn't home at the time and he said he'd come back. I asked him who he was and whether he had any message for my father. He said nothing and exited.

Later, when Dad returned, I told him about the visit. He seemed somewhat perplexed, but then a flash of realization crossed his face. Dad told me he needed to talk with the young man, alone. When and if he came back, I was to get my father immediately. Under no circumstances was I to let Mom speak to him. His instructions were quite specific and were not negotiable. He told me to repeat what he had just advised me.

The boy came back an hour later and Dad was ready for him. He answered the door with his coat in hand as he and the young man went out for a walk together. Dad returned alone, two hours later. He went into his room without saying a word, closing the door behind him. I had no explanation who the young man was or what he wanted with Dad, but soon things returned to normal. We went about our lives and forgot about the incident.

Years later, Mom called to tell me she was divorcing my father. She told me about the young man who had visited that day. I didn't have the heart to tell her I knew the man she was talking about, that Dad had ordered me never to tell her about him. Then she told me some things I didn't know. He was my step-brother. The man's name was Luis Sanchez. Lydia Sanchez was his mother. James Vance, my father, was his father. He had come that day to tell my father of his existence and to tell him that Lydia had recently passed away. He did not want anything of my father. Luis just wanted to meet his father before he joined the army. He said his mother spoke lovingly of my, or rather his, father and how he helped her at a tough time in her life. She also appreciated that Dad gave her a son.

She had never asked Dad for help or even advised him of Luis's existence because she knew it would ruin our family. Luis just wanted to say thanks before he shipped out.

My inability to perform Corrections became crystal clear. I wasn't Dad's first-born; Luis was. But then, after Dad confessed to Mom, he explained how, at nineteen, I became the first-born.

I do have to digress a bit here for a moment and discuss the role of spouses. Going all the way back to Francis Wentworth, his wife Martha truly believed in his ability to perform Corrections, but other spouses have been more skeptical over the centuries. They couldn't see the various realities that the Corrections brought about. There was no way to prove to them that there had been a change.

I told Olivia about my abilities soon after we were married, but I was never sure whether she believed me. She believed that I believed it, and that was enough for her. Perhaps if we had more time together, I could have convinced her.

My mother was a full scale believer. Some people who would otherwise be considered 'outsiders' had some insights into our powers. My mother was one of those believers. Maybe if she didn't believe, she wouldn't have filed for divorce.

In 1938, Dad had performed a Self-Correction. He had gone back and not slept with Lydia Sanchez. They had never conceived Luis. By default, I became the first-born. It wasn't until 1946 that he told Mom about his cheating and then his "annulment" through Self-Correction.

She could forgive the infidelity, especially one that happened such a long time ago. What she could not forgive was that Dad had erased a human life. Luis ceased to exist. There was no record of him. There was no memory of him. Even Lydia would never have any recollection of the boy she had brought into this world, a young man who was her world. As a mother, that was a line that Mom could not cross.

Self-Corrections were frowned upon. There was too much temptation to use a Correction to amass a fortune. All one had to do was to track stocks, the lottery, the racehorses, or some similar endeavor, determine a winner and then go back with a wish to play the winning numbers. Corrections should be for a higher purpose, not to improve your personal condition. At least that was what the party line had always been. It will never be known how often Self-Corrections actually happened.

While a part of me agreed with my mother, he was still my Dad. I would not cast him aside for someone I'd only met for thirty seconds. I felt sorry that Luis was no more, but it didn't really affect me, so I wasn't that sorry.

In addition, Mom told me that, when Dad made his confession, he said he did the Self-Correction for me. I was the rightful heir. He agreed that what he did to Luis was a tragic sin that he would live with for the rest of his life, but if he had to do it again, he would without question. To him, it was also a sin what he had done to me over the years. He had made me feel like a failure. Despite his constant assurances that there was nothing wrong with me, his continually testing me and then seeing that I came up short told me differently. Now I could continue the family tradition, and I was ready for that responsibility.

18

My parents never went through with their divorce. Their separation lasted a little less than a week. My mother moved out, stayed with her sister for five days, and then went back to my father. He welcomed her back with open arms.

Mom regretted moving out almost as soon as she did it. My aunt called me after the second day to ask me if there was anything that could be done to bring Mom and Dad back together. She said Mom was moping around and absolutely miserable. It was obvious she still loved her husband and could not imagine the rest of her life without him, but she just couldn't go back. My aunt, who was a delightful woman but could be a bit of a busybody, couldn't get an explanation from my mother what unforgivable act my father did so she was plying me for some insight. My aunt naturally assumed he cheated. I, of course, could not tell her the real reason for the split. If nothing else, she could never believe it if I told her.

It took five days for Mom to come up with a way for her to come back to Dad. She could never bring herself to forgive him for wiping away a life, but she sorely wanted to go back to him. She called me to bounce her plan off of me.

"Joey, how are you?"

"I'm okay, Mom. The real question is how are you doing."

"I'm miserable. I miss your Dad so much. He made a mistake, and he knows it, but the mistake he made he did for what he thought was the right reason. He did it for you. I'm afraid I'm driving your Aunt Shirley mad, poor woman. But you know I can't tell her the real reason I left."

"What are you going to do, Mom?"

"That's why I called you. You're the only one who can understand, the only one I can talk to about this."

"Yes, I am."

I couldn't hurry her. She'd get to the point and tell me what she was proposing to do in her own good time. If I rushed her, she might back off. I really wanted my parents to be back together—I thought they should be back together—so I had to be patient.

"Joey, you know about these things better than I do. Can your father do more than one Correction on himself?"

"I don't think I follow you."

"Your father admitted that he did what he called a Self-Correction where he went back and never slept with that woman, Lydia. The guilt of what he did—erasing a life—forced him to confess to me. We've both been miserable ever since. I want to be with him and he wants to be with me, but we can't, given what I know. What I'm asking is, can he go back and not confess to me? I wouldn't be the wiser, would I?"

"No, you wouldn't remember any of this."

"Ignorance can be bliss, can't it?"

"I suppose it can be."

That is what my mother did. She went to my father and asked him to do another Self-Correction. He readily agreed. The next time I saw them, they were back to where they were prior to their "divorce". My father had a melancholy look on his face, however. It was obvious he did not like deceiving my mother, but it was better than being away from her. He had the satisfaction of knowing that he confessed to her. It was her choice not to accept this confession.

As for my mother, there seemed to be bliss in her ignorance. She went on with her day as if nothing had happened, probably because in her mind, nothing had happened. There was one moment when she looked at me with what I saw as a glint in her eye. It was as if she were thanking me for helping her make the right decision. It could have been my imagination, though.

19

Eloise was disappointed when we told her the news that we would be moving out of Charleston, but it didn't surprise her. "I always knew you'd leave this sleepy city someday. You have too much to offer the world to be cooped up here forever. Thing is, I'll never be ready for you to leave. You better invite us to the wedding and have a room for me and Oscar when we come up to visit!"

Then she turned to me. "And you better take good care of her. I won't be around to keep an eye on you to keep you honest, but I'll track you down if you don't." Then she reached out a took my hand. "I'm only kidding. I know you'll take care of her. Every time I see the two of you, I see the look on your face. The love you have for this woman is so obvious. You can't help but take care of her."

I mentioned how resistant my parents were to Olivia. They thought I had my future all planned out with Victoria, and then I arrived with this other woman. I attributed their reaction to being blindsided like they were. I probably should have called them before we left Charleston to give them a chance to get used to the idea. I didn't see the need because I thought they'd be so won over the first time they met Olivia, just the way I was. I miscalculated, but I figured they'd come around.

They came around. Over the next few months, they got to know Olivia and saw in her what I had. Both Olivia and I wanted to move into New York as soon as we could to start our lives together there. However, we had hunted down an apartment in New York but it wouldn't be available for a couple months so we made the best of Jersey. We would get married there.

We planned to wed two months after we arrived. Olivia worked closely with Mom in arranging the details of the wedding. Mom was thrilled that Olivia included her in the arrangements. It was to be a relatively small affair with close family and friends at my parent's small church near our home in New Jersey.

The day of our wedding arrived. We had hoped that Eloise and Oscar would arrive a day or two early, but business at the restaurant was such that they could not get away. They would arrive on the day of the wedding. Olivia had told Mom about her parents dying during the influenza pandemic and that her aunt and uncle raised her. However, she didn't include one detail when she talked about them. She rarely mentioned their race when she talked to people, not out of shame, but because in her mind that shouldn't matter. They were family. Period. She didn't like the way people often made preconceived judgments about Black people before even meeting them.

The morning of the wedding, I drove up to Trenton with Dad to pick them up. We went down to the platform to greet them. The train pulled in, and they were the first to get off. Eloise yelled my name in her booming voice and ran to give me one of her big hugs while Oscar struggled with the suitcase. Meanwhile, Dad stood there shellshocked. He recovered enough to be gracious when I introduced them, but he was relatively silent on the trip home. Nobody really noticed since Eloise was enough to fill up the car with nonstop chatter.

Eloise and Oscar settled into their hotel room to rest up and prepare for the wedding. Dad and I drove back to his house. Dad was still silent for a bit, but then he spoke up.

"Why didn't you tell us?"

"Tell you what?"

"You know what. You forgot to mention the little fact that Olivia was colored."

"Aren't we all colored? She looks about the same color as you, Dad. In fact, in certain lighting, her color is whiter than yours."

"You know damn well what I mean. You can't marry that woman!"

"I can't?"

"Our line has been pure for over seven hundred years. I'll not have you sully our family with her!"

"Sully? What about all the talk about Grandpa Efrem over the years and what he did?"

"He didn't introduce them into the family. He didn't dilute the first-born."

I was about to counter but then I thought better of it.

"Dad, in honor of Francis's first Correction, I think we should stop this conversation before one of us crosses the line and says something the other can never forgive, although you've flirted with that line already. I love Olivia and I'm going to marry her. I want you at out wedding, but if you're convinced this is a mistake, you're free to not attend. Here we are at your house. I have to get home to change. Maybe I'll see you later, maybe not."

Dad got out the car and walked up to his front door. I looked at him for a few seconds before driving on. It was like I was seeing my father for the first time ever, and I did not like what I saw. I had to calm myself down. I would not ruin Olivia's day.

My father did attend and he was congenial. The day was not ruined. I was distracted, but all I had to do was to gaze upon Olivia's lovely face and all my anxieties immediately melted away. Before I knew it, we were husband and wife and I couldn't be happier.

20

It was July 1948, a month after our son, Nathan, was born. We were living in a walk-up apartment in the Chelsea section of Manhattan. Before we married, I asked Olivia where she wanted to live. I would live wherever she wanted. I expected her to say she wanted to stay in Charleston. It would have been natural for her to remain with the familiar, with her roots. I was surprised when she announced that she'd love to live in New York. She said she'd love the size and activity. She said she needed a change.

A year later, I walked by the nursery and looked in. Olivia was rocking our son back and forth as she nursed him. It was such a wondrous scene, I couldn't help but stop and gaze on them for a minute.

Olivia was looking down on Nathan with such love. She's a beautiful woman on her worst of days; here, in this setting, she was downright beatific. To complete the tableau, she was humming a song that I couldn't quite make out, but it was lilting and sweet. I've never felt luckier in my entire life. I couldn't understand why I was so lucky, but I would not fight it.

After a short time, she noticed me standing there. She shared the smile she was giving Nathan with me. I didn't think it possible, but that smile made me feel even more blessed. I walked in and stood behind her as I put my hands on her shoulders. She nestled her head into my chest.

I wanted as much time as I could get with Olivia and Nathan, so I quit my job selling encyclopedias. That job required me to be on the road, away from home, for long periods of time. I took a job at a nearby Oldsmobile dealership. I quipped with Olivia that I would be in trouble if somebody quizzed me on the automobiles as much as she did on my encyclopedias. Fortunately, nobody probed me beyond my rudimentary level of knowledge on the automobiles I sold.

Selling cars to a wide range of people gave me numerous opportunities for Corrections. Folks had a way of telling me too much information when they were buying a car. Perhaps it was because an automobile was a substantial investment, many people would feel the need to get me on their side. Perhaps they thought I'd give them a better deal if they buddied up to me. Maybe they were right, but I had limited authority to cut prices.

I was in this job for four years. There was one Correction that sticks in my mind from that period. It happened in September 1949. Willie Urbanian came in to buy a car. We recognized each other immediately. I didn't know him well, but I saw him around the neighborhood when we were kids. I went to high school with his brother, Al. Willie was eight years younger than Al, so he was the pesky little kid who hung around his big brother that the rest of us didn't really want around but we tolerated him.

Willie idolized his older brother. When the war started and Al enlisted in the Army, Willie wanted to follow him. Unfortunately, he was only fourteen. He wouldn't be eligible to enlist for another four years.

He was biding his time in high school, waiting for the moment that he could enlist, when his mother came to the school to tell him that Al had been killed at the Battle of Saipan in the South Pacific in June 1944. I had heard that, upon hearing this news, Willie ran out of the school, tears in his eyes. Nobody heard from him for three days. Finally, he came back home.

He graduated high school, but he did nothing after that to advance his life. After a year of this, his father kicked him out of the house, telling him to pull himself together and get a job. Since he had no job prospects, he enlisted in the army. The war was over, but there were plenty of peacekeeping duties around the world. He figured that along the way he could pick up some skills that he could put to use in private life. Unfortunately, that didn't work out so well.

After he got his discharge papers, he had a hard time holding a job. In between drifting, he made some friends who probably weren't the best for him. As a result, he walked into the dealership two days after he walked out of prison where he had served an eight-month stint for burglary. He seemed deeply chastened and embarrassed about his prison sentence. Still, he didn't know what he wanted to do with the rest of his life.

He came to the dealership, ostensibly to look for a car, but I think he'd gotten word that I worked there. He remembered my friendship with Al and he needed someone from that time to talk to. I was busy with another client, so I asked him if he could join me for lunch. At noon, I met him at a tiny French restaurant, Chez Napoleon, a couple blocks from our dealership.

"Thanks for meeting with me, Joe. I'm really not in the market for a car."

"I kind of figured that out, Willie. It's good seeing you again."

"Me, too. I needed somebody to talk to. My parents love me, but I've let them down so many times. My friends have either moved away or don't want anything to do with me. I remember how you were with Al. I don't know if you heard, but I just got out of prison."

"I had heard. I'm glad you're out."

"It was tough in there. I don't want to go back. I just don't know. I'll admit it, I'm very weak. I've been so angry since the Japs killed Al in the Pacific. I just don't know what to do."

"I can see if we need any help around the dealer. We always seem to need help in the shop."

"I appreciate that, but I don't want to put you in trouble. I'm such a screw-up."

"If you could do anything you wanted to do, what would that be, Willie?"

"You know, I enlisted in the Army because I didn't know what to do with myself. Even though being in the Army got Al killed, I kind of owed it to him to carry on. Anyway, I was pretty good at being a soldier. I even got promoted to corporal. I don't know why I came back home when my tour was up. I guess I was doing well and I could now come back, find myself a wife and settle down with a family. That obviously didn't work out the way I thought it would. You enlisted, didn't you?"

"Yes, I fought in Europe."

"I wish I was born earlier. I would have liked to have fought for something. I went to Germany for a year, but it was more police work than soldier. It was pretty boring. I spent much of my time protecting our supplies from starving people. I guess that got to me, so I got out."

"Even with that, are you saying you would have preferred to have stayed in army?"

"Yeah, I guess that's it."

"Say it."

"Say what?"

"Say that you wished you didn't leave the Army, that you had re-enlisted."

"Okay, I wish I re-enlisted in the Army."

I put my hand on his shoulder and he was gone. I found myself alone in the restaurant when the waiter came over to take my order. I had zoned out for a minute, so he had to ask me for my order a couple of times.

"I'll have the steak au poivre, please."

Six months later, I contacted Willie's parents to find out how he was doing. They were very excited. They had just gotten a letter telling them he had been promoted to sergeant. He was really thriving and was talking about making the army a career. Before we hung up I gave them my address and asked them to have him contact me when he got a chance. He wrote me a couple letters. They were all upbeat.

Then, a year and a half later, I received a letter from his parents. They apologized for not calling me with the news, but they couldn't stand talking about it. Instead, they sent me a clip from the local newspaper. It read:

Yesterday, Cherry Hill native Sergeant William S. Urbanian was killed in combat near the village of Chonan, Korea. Sergeant Urbanian had rescued three of his fellow soldiers who were under fire by enemy forces. Enemy gunfire mortally wounded him as he returned to extricate the remainder of his squad. Sergeant Urbanian is survived by...

I didn't need to read anything more. I was saddened that Willie died way too young and that I held some responsibility for his death. That feeling was counterbalanced by my pride in helping him find his purpose in life. Instead of being aimless, he was a leader. He had achieved the rank of Sergeant. He died rescuing his men. This was far different from the shell of a man I talked to in the restaurant. Without his Correction, I could only imagine that his future would have been tenuous at best. He probably would have ended up back in prison, or worse.

21

It was September 1953. I was riding high as the top Oldsmobile salesman in the New York metropolitan area. Olivia was expecting our second child. Nathan had just started first grade. He was already a star student. We were very proud of him.

Now that our family was growing, we were looking for a larger home. I was leaning towards getting a house in Queens or The Bronx, but Olivia loved Manhattan and she wanted a larger apartment there. I couldn't believe that a woman who was born and raised in a small city with a much slower pace of life could thrive in Manhattan. I've known many people who'd gotten totally overwhelmed at even the thought of New York City. That gave one more thing to make me marvel at how special Olivia was.

We had a string of visitors for a few weeks. First, Eloise and Oscar came north and spent a long weekend with us. We hadn't seen them in over a year and it was wonderful getting together with them. For our wedding, they only made it as far as New Jersey, so this was their first trip to New York. They obviously were in the group that found New York overwhelming, but that feeling was overcome when they saw Olivia and Nathan. They were thrilled that Olivia was expecting, and they spent much of the weekend spoiling Nathan.

Two weeks later, the Robinsons came to visit us for a long weekend. They arrived on Thursday afternoon. We had a wonderful evening together. Unlike Eloise and Oscar, they were comfortable in New York. On Friday, I had to work and Olivia was really feeling her pregnancy so we couldn't be with them to show them around the city. My parents volunteered to come into the city and be their tour guides. By this time, Dad and I had mended fences and we were on good terms again.

We had last seen the Robinsons a few years earlier when they flew into New York to catch a ship for a cruise to Europe. My parents were in town and we all got together for lunch before the Robinsons sailed off. Dad and Mr. Robinson hit it off immediately. So, when I told Mom and Dad that the Robinsons were coming in for a visit, they jumped at the chance to spend the day with them. We would all get together for dinner that evening after I got off from work.

I woke up early and prepared breakfast for Nathan and me. Olivia wanted to sleep in so I kissed her goodbye and then walked Nathan to school. He was so excited about an art project he was working on. I asked him when I'd be able to see it. "Not until it's done, Daddy," he seriously responded. "Fair enough," I responded, suppressing a smile at my son's solemn response. I walked him up to the school front door and opened it for him to walk in. I knew enough not to walk in any further. No little boy wants people to see him as a little boy. I hovered there as I watched him trot down the hallway, hang his jacket on his assigned peg on the wall, and then determinedly run to his classroom. I had to wipe away a tear of pride and joy before walking away.

I proceeded on to the dealership, still on my family high. I had a couple appointments with prospective clients who needed a car, but were still on the fence about whether that car should be an Oldsmobile or another brand. I rehearsed my patented sales pitch in my mind so I'd be ready to seal these deals.

I was looking over my notes when I had a strange feeling, a tingling. My initial thought was: "Oh, Dad's doing a Correction." This one was different, though. The tingling feeling immediately shifted to dizziness. The dizziness lasted only a second as everything went black. I could feel myself slumping to the floor. There was nothing I could do about it.

When I woke up, I was sitting on a bed. I looked around. Nothing was familiar. I was in a hotel room. Over in the corner was my suitcase and the case in which I used to carry my sample encyclopedias. My new reality was slowly seeping into my brain. Reality terrified me. I went to the phone on the desk and punched in the number to get an outside line. Hearing the dial tone, I dialed '0' and, after a few rings, an operator came on the line. "How can I help you today?" a cheery feminine voice intoned.

"I'd like to place a collect call to New York, 212 Monument 7-2997."

"Your name, please."

"Joseph Vance."

The operator connected the call. The line rang a couple times. With each ring, I was saying to myself, 'Olivia, please pick up. Please pick up.'

My heart sank when a woman picked up, but it wasn't Olivia.

"Hello."

"I have a collect call from Joseph Vance. Will you accept the charges?"

"I'm sorry, but I don't know a Joseph Vance. Perhaps you have the wrong number."

"This is 212 Monument 7-2997, correct?"

"Yes, that's my number, but I don't know anybody by that name. I'm sorry."

She hung up, and the operator was about to disconnect when I asked her to try one more number. "Can you try New Jersey, 609 Volunteer 2-0615. Also collect."

"Yes, sir."

A few seconds later, I heard another female voice. This time it was familiar and she accepted the call.

"Hi Mom."

"Hi Joey, how's Pittsburgh?"

I'd only realized a few seconds earlier that I was in Pittsburgh.

"It's fine, Mom. Is Dad there?"

"No, he went out for a while. You know that since he retired he can't stay in one place very long. We're both so thrilled you finally proposed to Victoria. You're not getting any younger, you know. I had lunch with her mother last week to talk about the wedding plans. We're both so excited."

I'd only a few minutes earlier remembered Victoria Snell, my fiancée. We'd been dating for four years and I finally broke down and asked her to marry me. Dad had especially been pressing me to marry her so we could start producing an heir. He needed a child to carry on the seven-hundred-year tradition of performing Corrections. I had dragged my feet for too long.

I needed to talk to Dad to find out what happened to Olivia and Nathan. He must have done a Correction that backfired. Somehow he created a situation in which Olivia and I did not meet. We did not marry or have children together. Because of this action, I was thrust back into this other reality with Victoria and encyclopedias. My big problem was that, as a person gifted with the ability to perform Corrections, I couldn't be blissfully ignorant of my other reality, the reality that had the love of my life.

In my current reality, I wasn't against marrying Victoria, but I obviously wasn't in any great rush. I gave up my job selling encyclopedias so I could be near Olivia. I had no such motivation to get a new job to be near Victoria. I kept my old job that sent me around the country.

Now that both realities collided, I knew I could not in good conscience marry Victoria. I wanted and needed to be with Olivia. She was my wife, my only wife.

I had to talk to Dad to figure out what happened and how to fix this situation. Just like he did with Lydia Sanchez, he could go back and reverse what had happened. He had made it clear he didn't like me marrying Olivia, but he'd want my happiness, wouldn't he?

Mom prattled on for a little longer, and I let her. It wouldn't do to talk things over with her. While she was a spouse who understood Corrections and accepted that they were real, this situation would be impossible for anyone to grapple with. Dad was the only one who would know that what I said was the truth.

I told my mother I had some work to do and would call back at seven. She said she'd make sure Dad was home.

"Hi Dad. What Correction did you do today?"

"I haven't done one in a couple weeks. Why?"

"You had to have done one. That's the only explanation."

"The only explanation for what? Tell me what's happened! You're scaring me, Joseph."

"This morning, I lived in New York. I kissed Olivia goodbye, dropped Nathan off at school and then went to my job at the Askin's Oldsmobile Dealership. While I was there, I passed out and when I woke up, I was in a hotel room in Pittsburgh. I was still selling encyclopedias. I called my number and a stranger answered. I have no idea where Olivia is. I've heard the stories about children who get caught up in Corrections. I'm scared to death that Nathan— my son—is no more. I need to find out what happened. The only conclusion I can make is a Correction gone bad."

"I swear to you I haven't done a Correction in two weeks. I believe everything you say, but I have no idea who Olivia or Nathan are. As far as I know, you live alone two blocks from us. You've been selling encyclopedias, not cars, for over a decade. And, you're engaged to marry Victoria Snell. You as well as I know that our powers are limited. If your change is related to one of my Corrections, I'd be aware of Olivia and Nathan. I'm sorry, son, but I'm not."

"If you didn't do it, what happened?"

"My guess is twins."

"Twins?"

"You remember the lore where Emily had twins and both children had the power? Each of those twins started their own line, one of which comes down to us. We've been very good about maintaining the record of our lineage. I'm not as sure about the other line. In addition, there probably were other twins along the way, which further muddies the waters."

"In other words, I may never find out."

"I'm afraid that may well be the case. I'm sorry, son."

I couldn't say anything. I was in shock. I may have lost my wife and son forever. My father read my thoughts.

"What are you going to do now?"

"I have to know for sure. I'm going to New York. And then, if things are as I fear they are, I'm going down to Charleston to see if I can get Olivia back."

"What about Victoria? Your wedding?"

"I don't love Victoria. I love Olivia."

"I think you are going to end up in pain going down this road."

"I have to do it, Dad."

He started to offer a counterargument but I hung up the phone before he could finish. I packed my things. I then took a taxi to the train station to take the next train to New York.

22

At Penn Station, I stored my suitcase in a locker, but I kept my encyclopedia sample case with me. I climbed out of the cab in front of my apartment building. I looked up the façade to our apartment, or at least what used to be our apartment. I realized for a fact that Olivia would not be there, but I had to make sure.

I didn't have a key to the building, or to the apartment, so I had to wait for someone else to either show up or leave to gain access. I expected that I wouldn't have access to the building, so I brought my encyclopedia sample case with me. Walking around with a case made me look more official, like I belonged. After ten minutes, Jim England, who lived on our floor, came out. We weren't friends, but we would recognize each other enough to have a nodding acquaintance. Today, I made sure that our eyes met, but there was nothing, not a hint of familiarity. I was just another stranger on the streets of New York.

As he exited, I slipped in behind him. I got on the elevator and hit the button for the seventh floor. I feared my heart was going to pump out of my chest. I got off the elevator and turned right to go to 7E, a route I had made hundreds of times. I rang the doorbell. A slender woman with glasses and graying black hair answered the door. I could sneak a glance into the apartment. It definitely wasn't my place. I asked her if she was interested in purchasing a set of encyclopedias. She politely declined, and I departed.

I walked the few blocks to Nathan's school. My sense of dread was increasing by the second. It hit me hardest as I walked along the hallway where I had last seen Nathan who was running to his classroom, excited about completing his art project.

The school day had ended, so I went to the principal's office and asked to speak with his teacher, Mrs. Dodwell. The receptionist asked my name and then used the intercom to ask Mrs. Dodwell to come to the office to meet me. I figured that she might recognize my name. Olivia and I had recently met with her at a parent-teacher conference. That's where she told us how magnificent a student Nathan was.

When she arrived at the office, her blank expression at seeing me told me everything I needed to know. She was meeting a total stranger. She extended her hand.

"Good afternoon, Mr. Vance. What can I do for you?"

"We just moved to New York and have a young son, Nathan, who will be enrolling here next week. A friend of mine, Ron Harkins, has a boy who is in your class."

"Jeremy Harkins, yes, a wonderful boy!"

"Well, Ron just raves about you and I was hoping Nathan could get you as his teacher."

"That's very nice to hear, but I'm afraid I don't have much say in teacher assignments. We have four teachers who teach first grade, and I can assure you they're all great."

"I don't doubt that. I just wanted to come by and get a feel for the school before Nathan starts."

"That's wise of you. I wish all parents were as committed to their children's education as you are."

"Thank you very much."

I turned away as a tear escaped my eye. The thought that I had lost my son forever was overwhelming me. Mrs. Dodwell called out to me.

"I'll keep an eye out for Nathan's name and make a special request that they assign him to me."

"Thank you," I called out as I exited, knowing full well that his name will never come up in the school.

Why I took the next step, I don't know. I fully realized the only thing I would gain was further self-torture, but I had to do it. I made the six-block walk to Harrington Hospital, where Nathan was born. I headed to the records office and asked if I could get a duplicate copy of Nathan's birth certificate. I lied and said they needed it for enrollment at school. I gave the clerk Olivia and my name and

Nathan's date of birth. She wrote all this down and went to the back where the records were stored.

"I'm sorry but I couldn't find the birth certificate for your son. Perhaps I wrote the information down wrong. Nathan Vance, born December 30, 1948, mother Olivia Vance, father Joseph Vance."

"Yes, that's all correct."

"Well, between you and me, it wouldn't be the first time a record like this had been mislaid. I only started here a year ago, and it's been a full-time job straightening out the files. Your son's birth certificate could very well be here, but stuffed into a different drawer. I'll look some more for it, so maybe if you stop by in a couple days, I may have found it by then. In the meantime, you may want to check with the Borough Clerk's office at City Hall downtown. They get a copy of all our certificates and undoubtedly would have it. Sorry I couldn't be of more help."

"No, you've been very helpful. Thank you."

She was so earnest and conscientious that I had no doubt she would continue to hunt for it. I felt sorry that she was going to waste the time scouring records hoping to discover evidence of Nathan's birth. I couldn't bring myself to tell her she will never find it. My son was never born.

23

I went back home to New Jersey. I would be there for only a day or so. I needed to change clothes and pack some outfits for a warmer climate. I was heading down to Charleston. I had no idea what Olivia was doing now. For all I knew, she happily married a nice man and had a couple kids. She would want nothing to do with me. I wouldn't go down without a fight, though.

I also wanted to see if I could gather any clues as to what happened. Who did this? How was the past changed the way it was? Why was there a connection to Olivia? Was there any way of changing it back? I had little hope of answering any of these questions. I had no choice but to try.

When I got home, Mom and Dad were waiting there for me. Dad had filled Mom in on what had happened to me. She was very soothing, but there was a different tone than when I spoke with day the other day.

"Son," my father started (I knew it would not be good when he started a sentence with 'Son.'), "your mother and I have talked it over. You need to get on with your life. You're engaged to a wonderful woman. Victoria will make a wonderful wife and will help you continue the family. I know you feel awful about, what were their names?"

"Olivia and Nathan."

"Yes, Olivia and Nathan. You must face facts and move on. They seem real to you and perhaps they were, but you can't change the fact that they're gone. Right now, they're a dream. Keep them a dream."

"A dream? They're real! Nathan may be no more, but I'm going to hunt down Olivia. She is the love of my life and I won't give up finding her."

"You're being a sentimental fool. You're thirty-four years old. Men can have children practically forever, but you're getting old to start a family. It's important you continue the tradition. You need an heir."

"The family tradition means more to you than my happiness?"

"It should mean more to you as well."

"Well, it doesn't. If that makes me a terrible person, so be it. The twins, whoever they are, can have the legacy. I'm moving on. If I find Olivia and get her to marry me, you'll have your precious heir. You're not stopping me."

With that, I grabbed my suitcase and turned on them. I lingered long enough to look at Mom, who had tears in her eyes, but then I stormed out as I headed for the train station.

I was taking a trip I had taken six years earlier. Rather, it was a trip that my former self had taken to Charleston where I met my future wife. We were both so sure we were going to marry the other from the first moment we met. Of course, there was a feeling-out period, a courtship, but it was a formality. I was wondering on the train ride whether that magic would still be there when we saw each other. Perhaps that was a once in a lifetime thing and we had our one time.

I couldn't get it out of my head that my parents were so blasé, so cavalier, about my loss. Their only wish was that I perpetuate the family 'gift', even if it meant marrying someone I didn't love. This gift cost me everything that was dear to me. For all I cared, the ability to provide Corrections could die out right now. The world would get along just fine. In fact, given that a Correction directly sparked a world war, I could make a valid argument that the world would be much better off.

My family was, for lack of a better word, selfish. We have prided ourselves on our ability to help others, but I always think we do it as much for ourselves as we do for the people we help. It's the closest thing that anybody can have to being God. We determine who is worthy enough to get help. We don't even give them the choice to go back. Often, we trick them into stating their wishes and that's when we attack. We tell ourselves that we're doing it for the person's own good, but when it comes down to it, we perform the Correction because we can, because we have the power. And like any power, it's addictive. We only want more. We don't feel whole unless we're doing Corrections.

The train arrived in Charleston and, after checking my suitcase into a locker, I headed straight over to the Robinson mansion. I took my encyclopedia case with me. I wanted to recreate the scene as closely as possible to the first time we met. I hoped to press the doorbell, she'd open the door and I would stumble through my usual well-rehearsed sales pitch. She would find my stumbling endearing and she would toy with me. I figured that if I had the power to perform Corrections, why couldn't I have the power to re-enact this scene.

I rang the doorbell, and my anticipation was dashed when Mrs. Robinson opened the door. She was a somewhat plump forty-year-old women with shoulder-length blonde hair. She had a pleasant, kindly appearance.

"Good afternoon, I was wondering if Olivia Wyatt was here. I'm a friend. I've come down from New York to see her."

"I'm afraid Olivia doesn't work for us anymore. She left about a month ago."

"Do you know where she went?"

"No, I'm sorry. I tried reaching out to her to see if we could help her, but she never responded."

"I see. Well, thank you very much."

The nightmare continued. She loved the Robinsons, and they loved her. Why should she leave and then not keep in touch with them? Even when we lived in New York, they remained a part of her life. They came up north for a visit and we showed them the sights.

I walked around Charleston in a morose daze. I was questioning whether perhaps Dad had been correct. My life with Olivia was nothing but a dream, and I should treat it as such. It was the most wonderful dream of my life and I should focus on the joy of that period, but I should move on with my life. I liked Victoria enough, even if I couldn't love her. We could make a nice life together and have a couple kids to carry on the tradition. If I had any sense in my head, I'd return to the train station and catch the first train north. But I had no sense. There was one more stop I had to make.

I arrived about a half hour before the dinner rush. The band was just setting up. The bass player and I were the only white faces in the place. I was hoping one more white face would show up.

Eloise came over to greet me and show me to a table. She gave me a big smile and greeting, but it was the same smile and greeting she gave to every paying patron. There was no recognition. She walked me over to a table. We passed Oscar, who was busy setting a table. He looked up at me, but there was not a glimmer. I noticed a group of loud young guys at the table that was perpetually reserved for Olivia. In a different life, Eloise would have kicked their asses to a different table.

I sat down and Eloise gave me a menu. I was too distracted to look at it. I stared at the band as they were tuning up their instruments and preparing for the night's gig. A cheery voice suddenly tore from my daydream.

"What would you like today?"

I looked up and there she was. Olivia was standing there, waiting to take my order. Like the first time I saw her in a previous life, I was tongue-tied.

When our eyes met, I swear there was a glint of something. It was like she was experiencing a déjà vu. But then any flame that may have been there in her eyes was quickly extinguished. Her face was as beautiful as I remembered, but it displayed a sadness and a weariness I don't ever remember seeing there before.

The wait staff at Eloise's didn't wear matching uniforms, but they were all nicely dressed in a casual sort of way. Olivia was no different. She was wearing a black skirt and a crisp white button-down blouse. The difference between her outfit and the outfits worn by the other staff was that she let hers out to allow for an obvious pregnancy. My heart sank. Then I noticed she didn't have a ring on her finger. Was that why she left the Robinson's? Was she married but couldn't wear her ring because of water buildup? It tore me up that I was looking up at this woman who I knew so much about but was at the same time a stranger to me.

She asked me again what I wanted.

"What's a wombat?" I asked.

Instead of looking at me like I was crazy, a smile curved her lips, which then developed into a full-throated laugh. "It's a marsupial native to Australia."

"Who fought in the Crimean War and when was it?"

"The Crimean War was fought between 1853 and 1856. Russia lost to an alliance made up of the Ottoman Empire, England, Sardinia and France."

"Who was Zoroaster?"

"He was an ancient Iranian prophet who lived in the 6th or 7th century BC. He established Zoroastrianism, the world's oldest continuously practiced religion that, in a nutshell, predicts the ultimate conquest of evil. Any more questions?"

"No, I was just asking you the same questions you asked me when we first met."

"You must have me confused with someone else. I've never met you before."

"I just wanted to make sure the same Olivia was in there somewhere. The way you answered showed me she is in there."

"The same Olivia as what? Wait a minute, how do you know my name is Olivia? I never introduced myself."

"Your name is Olivia Wyatt. I was testing to see if you were the same person I knew and loved."

"But I've never met you before."

"How far along are you?"

"About six months."

"You're going to name the baby either Nathan or Dorothy, after your parents, both of whom died from the influenza when you were two."

Olivia sat down in the seat opposite me, stunned. "How do you know that?"

"Eloise is your mother's sister. She and your Uncle Oscar raised you after your parents died. They sent you to a school funded by the Robinsons to get the education they never received. Mrs. Robinson is very worried about you, by the way. You're allergic to most shellfish. Your favorite color is orange. Your favorite song is 'Someone to Watch Over Me' and you ask the band to play it every night. You have a mole on the inside of your left hip. You can speak a little French and want to learn more so that someday you can go to Paris and talk with the shopkeepers. Your middle name is Emily, which is after your maternal grandmother."

"You're scaring me. How do you know all this? How can you know all this? I don't know you."

Eloise had looked over when Olivia first sat down but didn't say or do anything. Now, however, Olivia was looking distraught and the color had drained from her face. Eloise rushed over to rescue her niece.

"Is this guy bothering you, honey?"

Eloise looked ready to give me a good pummeling.

"No, Auntie, I mean yes, I mean I don't know. He knows all about me, things only my closest friends would know. And even then, he knows things only a husband would know. I don't know how he's doing this. Maybe he's a psychic."

I stood up, if for no other reason than Eloise's standing over me was very imposing.

"Olivia, the one thing I haven't yet said is that you're the most amazing women on earth. You astound anyone who meets you every minute of every single day because you are so amazing. I don't know what your situation is with the father of your child, but if he isn't showering love and attention on you every second of every day, he is an absolute fool.

"Oh, Eloise, keep that table reserved for her like you used to. She should be out in the world, spreading her magic, but have a welcome place when she comes back home.

"My name is Joseph Vance. I'm staying in Room 6 at the Wedgewood Arms Inn on DeCater Street in town. I'll be here for three more days. I'm catching the two o'clock train on Saturday to New York. If you want to find what else I know and why I know about you as much as I do, please come see me. If not, if you can look me in the eye right now and don't believe I'm sincere in everything I say about us being destined for each other, I'll understand. My heart will never heal if I don't get you back, but I'll head back north and you'll never hear from me again."

I turned to go, but before I left I had one more thing to say.

"Please ask your neighbor, Miss Lily, about Hannah Smith and her son, Efrem. They were doctors who came down here to set up the clinic close to your home. Efrem was named after my Great-Great-Grandfather, Efrem Reynolds. He rescued Hannah and her parents from slavery a decade before the Civil War. Good night."

This time, I turned and actually left the bar. As I departed, the band started up by playing *Take the A Train*. I took this as an omen.

I returned to my hotel room and stayed there for the next three days. I would only go out to the restaurant around the corner to get my meals to bring back with me. I bought a newspaper each day, but I couldn't read it. I was too anxious to read or do anything. I simply sat and stared out the window.

When the third day came, I was in total despair. I truly thought she'd come to me. I slowly packed my bags but I would occasionally peek out the window, hoping to see her walking down the street toward the inn. She did not appear. I grabbed my bag. After settling my bill, I trudged the four blocks to the station. I held tears back; there'd be plenty of time for crying over the coming years.

I opened the large ornate front door to station and went in. I stopped in my tracks. Seated on a bench was Olivia. A large suitcase was by her side. She looked up at me as I approached.

"Will you help me with this thing or do I need to call a porter?"

I grabbed her valise and we headed into the heart of the station.

"You're going to have to buy me a ticket. Aunt Eloise gave me some money, but I want to save it."

"I'll be happy to buy you a ticket. Where are you heading?"

"I've always wanted to go to New York. It sounds like an exciting place to live."

"It is an exciting place. I've long wanted to live there myself. It's expensive, so it's wise to save your money."

"I believe we'll do just fine there."

"We'll do just fine? I like the sound of that."

"You better. But you also better treat me like you said the father of my child should treat me. If I remember correctly, you said he should shower love and attention on me every second of every day. If he doesn't, he is an absolute fool."

"I said that, didn't I? I guess I can't back out, can I?"

"No, you can't. I do have a serious question to ask you."

"Shoot."

"You still want me even though I'm carrying some other man's child?"

"Any child that's half yours is going to be special. That's good enough for me."

She took my arm and snuggled up close to me as we walked along.

24

The train ride was full of questions, not all of which had answers. One question that I didn't ask was who the father was. I didn't need to know. She told me that her Aunt Eloise asked her when she first started showing, but Olivia told her she'd rather not say. Eloise didn't pursue it further. I told her I wouldn't either.

I wondered whether the child was going to be white or black. I wasn't sure how that worked, regardless who the father was. Olivia herself of mixed race. It never occurred to me but I guess that our Nathan could have been born black. It really didn't matter to me, but it was something that popped into my mind.

I had to ask her the question I had asked her in our other life.

"Olivia, why?"

"Why what?"

"Why am I so lucky to be sitting beside you, heading to a long life together? Why didn't you just dismiss me as a raving lunatic?"

"You are a raving lunatic, but you're kinda cute."

"Seriously, why did you come with me?"

"I'm curious. How do you know all this about me? About Aunt Eloise and Uncle Oscar? You told me things that are all true, but they are things I can't remember ever telling anyone about. I'm especially curious how you know about that mole on my hip."

I laughed.

"The clincher was when I spoke with Ms. Lily," she continued. "As you obviously know, Ms. Lily is probably over a hundred by now. Her mind has slipped a bit in recent years, but that's more related to recent events. She's still pretty sharp about the past. When I asked her about the man, Efrem Smith, and his namesake, your great-great-grandfather Efrem, she looked at me with annoyance. She said, "Ain't you got a memory, child? I told you and that nice man you were with all about Efrem and Hannah a couple of years ago. He couldn't understand a word I said 'cause he was from up North, so you had to translate as I spoke."

"I told her I didn't remember that at all. She was exasperated but, because she loved me since I was a baby, she patiently told me the story about Dr. Hannah Smith and her son coming down every year to set up a free clinic. Joseph, the man who was with me that time, was that you?"

"Yes, it was."

"What was Ms. Lily's daughter's name?"

"Ethel."

"What plantation was Ms. Lily at when she was a slave?"

"Magnolia Philips."

"What were the names of Ms. Lily's husbands?"

"Nate and Andre."

"What happened to Nate?"

"He was lynched for mouthing off to the wrong white man."

Olivia paused. She looked out the window at the landscape whizzing by.

"James, why can't I remember any of this? Why can't I remember you? When you walked into the restaurant a few days ago, there was a second where I thought I you looked familiar. It was like I was having a, what do you call it, déjà vu. I got over it quickly, thinking you were familiar to someone I knew. Now, you're telling me I knew you?"

"Even more than that."

"I don't understand."

"We were married. We had a six-year-old son named Nathan. You were pregnant with our second child. We lived in New York, in a Manhattan apartment. We were talking about getting a bigger place. I was thinking of a house in Queens or The Bronx, but you so loved Manhattan, we were looking there."

"We had a son, Nathan? Where is he?"

"He was stolen from us, as was our baby."

"Stolen? How?"

"I'm going to tell you a story about me and my family, but you won't believe it."

"I already don't believe what has happened to me over the past three days. What's one more thing?"

I took a deep breath and told her the tale of my family's ability to perform Corrections. I started at the beginning with Francis Wentworth and then worked my way through the centuries. I started telling the story as the train rolled through North Carolina and, by the time I finished, we were pulling into Baltimore. Olivia did not say a word the entire time, not even to ask a question, which I was sure she had plenty. Her eyes opened wide at certain stories such as Sally inadvertently starting the First World War or Efrem saving Andrew from being shot to death, but otherwise she simply took it all in.

Then I described our theory of what happened to her and Nathan. There were obviously other people out there who could perform Corrections, people descended from the twin that we weren't aware of. One of their Corrections misfired. She—and our son and unborn child—were the unintended victims.

"Well, at least I didn't set off a world war," she quipped.

"To me, the result was the same."

She reached over and held my hand and smiled one of her magic smiles at me. Its impact was instantaneous.

"Do you ever think you'll figure out what happened? If you don't, what's to say it won't happen again? I don't think either of us could go through this twice."

"It's going to be nearly impossible to track what happened, but I think I owe it to us and our children to investigate. I need you to remember everything about yourself that you can recall from June 3, 1946 backwards. I don't care how insignificant it is."

"What happened on June 3, 1946?"

"That's the day we met. I rang the bell at the Robinson's mansion and you answered the door."

I noticed a flash of anger and loathing on her face when I mentioned the Robinsons. I had previously gotten the impression that the entire Robinson family was very dear to her. They even came to New York to visit us, and Olivia loved having them visit. When I went hunting for Olivia and the first place I went was to the Robinsons, Mrs. Robinson was concerned about Olivia. She was visibly distressed. The feeling wasn't reciprocated.

"Obviously, the Correction altered something that kept us from meeting on that day. Please try and remember. I remember every detail of meeting you. You had me off-balance from the very beginning and I never recovered. You've always been fairly open about yourself."

"You mean I like to talk about myself," she said with a laugh.

"Well, now that you mention it… but that's okay. I want to hear about you every day for the rest of my life. I recall everything you told me. If you piece together your life as you remember it, I'll be able to highlight any discrepancies from what you told me before."

"You remember everything about me, but you're a complete blank to me."

"We'll just have to create new memories together going forward. The most important thing is to make sure you're comfortable and that your pregnancy proceeds smoothly. We'll go to New Jersey and live in my place until I can get us a place to live in New York and I can find a job there."

"Well, I can tell you exactly where I was on June 3, 1946."

"You can?"

"Yes, I was on St. Thomas in the Virgin Islands."

"Wow, that sounds like a nice trip. Did you save up for a trip like that?"

"No. Out of the blue, Mr. Robinson told me he'd like to pay for a vacation for me and Aunt Eloise to get away. He said he wanted to repay me for all I did. He said it was a post-graduation present, as I had graduated a few years earlier. I was very excited. I didn't realize how beholden I would be to him for taking his gift."

I didn't know what she meant by this, and she didn't explain further. I could tell by the faraway look on her face she didn't want to talk about it. I'd ask her what she meant later.

"When I rang at the Robinsons that day, you were in the Virgin Islands? On a trip that Mr. Robinson suggested and paid for?"

"Uh-huh."

"You're sure of the date?"

"I don't remember the exact days that we left and returned, but I know for sure that it encompassed the first full week of June of that year. I'd never taken a trip like that in my life, and I haven't taken one since, so it really stands out in my mind."

I thought I would have to dig deep into Olivia's two competing pasts to come up with discrepancies. I would set up side-by-side timetables to compare her different histories. I anticipated having to peel back layer after layer to get to the truth, if I ever could get to the truth. I believed that there was some sort of butterfly effect of one minor change that somehow cascaded all the way to Olivia. She would be an inadvertent victim, and so would I. It never would have occurred to me that the discrepancy would become apparent without any probing. I didn't have to go back any further than the day we originally met. In fact, that change did not seem inadvertent or coincidental. It appeared to be a calculated attempt to keep Olivia from meeting me. But who would do such a thing, and why?

25

Before I left Charleston, I had called my parents from my hotel room. I asked them to pick me up at Trenton when the train got in. My father asked whether I tracked down Olivia. I told him I had, but it didn't go well. She didn't know who I was and had no interest in getting to know me. I was coming home alone. This was before I went to the station and found her sitting there, waiting for me. We had to catch our train. Thus, I didn't have time to call them with what I thought to be good news. It would be a surprise.

When we pulled into Trenton, Mom and Dad were waiting on the platform for me. I got off the train and waved to them. I reached back, grabbed our bags and put them on the platform beside me. Then, I helped Olivia down the steps to the platform. Her back was hurting her after the long train ride and she needed my help. My parents were aghast when this obviously very pregnant woman came into view. We walked over to them.

"Mom, Dad, this is Olivia, the woman I told you about."

"I thought you were coming home alone," Dad intoned.

"I thought I was as well, but she was waiting for me at the train station. She believed me, or at least she believed that I believed everything I was saying. Anyway, she came with me."

My parents cordially shook hands with her, but they were icy. I hoped they'd come around, but my primary concern was Olivia. I wanted to get her comfortable. The drive south was relatively quiet. Mom and Dad dropped us off at my place. As we climbed out of the car, my father said to me in a low voice, "We'll talk." I wished them a good night as we walked in.

Over the next few days, I was very busy. I settled Olivia into our place. Then I took trips into the City for our big move. I went to the building where we lived previously. Our apartment was occupied—that much would have been too much to hope for—but there were several available in the building. I selected what I thought was the best one and put a deposit down to hold it for forty-eight hours, during which time I could bring Olivia to check it out. I had a feeling she would love it, but I didn't want to make that assumption.

I went to my former employer, Askin's Oldsmobile, for a job. They advised me they weren't hiring. Then I described the virtues of each of the models: the Olds 88, the Olds 98, the Olds Super 88, the Olds Fiesta Convertible. I told how each of these models would appeal to various demographics: single men, families, the social climbers or whatever. I could see that Frank, the manager, was wavering but still not convinced to hire me. Then I went through the new models planned for the upcoming year: the Starfire and the Holiday series. His eyes nearly popped out of his head when I mentioned these. This information hadn't been released to the public. He asked how I knew all this. I just said I had connections. I don't think he would have believed it if I told him I was his top salesman a mere week and a half ago. I also could have told him that his wife was Misty, his two kids were Eva and Bonnie Jean, and he had season tickets at the Polo Grounds right behind the Giants dugout, but that would have been pushing things a little too far and would make me suspicious. He offered me a job. I was to start in a week's time.

My last stop in Manhattan was at Rosenberg's Jewelry in the Diamond District on 47th Street. This was where I had purchased Olivia's engagement ring, and I wanted to see if they still had that model. I was in luck. I walked in and the exact same ring was displayed right up front in the display counter. When the clerk walked over, he was a bit surprised that I'd selected the one I wanted without even asking the price. It was a moderately priced ring, and the salesman tried to steer me towards a couple more expensive models. I stood firm and walked out of the jewelers with the box in my pocket. I headed back to New Jersey.

When I arrived home, Olivia gave me a big hug and a greeting. I never felt as alive as when I was in her arms. Once we let go, I pulled out the box, got down on my knee and held it up to her.

"Will you make me the happiest and luckiest man on earth and marry me?"

"Don't I already have one of these?" she said as she took the box from my hand and opened it.

"I thought so, but I don't know what happened to it."

"I'll try not to lose this one. And my answer is yes, I will marry you. I know this is a lot to ask of you, but could we get married immediately?"

"Of course. We can marry whenever you want."

"It's just that," she paused to find the correct words. "It's just that, even though you're not the baby's father, you said that you're willing to take on that responsibility. I'd like our baby to be born with a father, not as a bastard. Am I being foolish? My head tells me it doesn't really matter, but my heart tells me otherwise."

"Then let's follow your heart. I'll make whatever arrangements you want."

"In my condition, perhaps a big white dress church wedding is not the most practical approach. Maybe we should go with a justice of the peace or some other private affair."

I was friendly with a local Methodist minister who I thought would perform the ceremony with no judgment. I would reach out to him the following day. Now that things were falling into place, there were two unpleasant conversations that I'd avoiding having but could not put off any longer. The first was with Victoria.

I'd known Victoria Snell since we were children. She lived a block away from our house. Her father and my father worked together at the shipyard. Our families would occasionally get together for barbecues and such. Once I entered adulthood, my mother would occasionally mention that Victoria would make an ideal wife. There was nothing I could say to refute my mother's assertion.

Victoria was a stunning blonde with a sunny disposition. Intelligent and well-read, she was even athletic and shared a love of sports that I had. Everything a man could ask for. She had confided to people that she wanted to be a mother and consensus was that she would make a very good one. In this other reality where Olivia did not exist as a possible mate, I succumbed to my parents' pressure and asked Victoria to marry me. Now that both realities had caught up with each other and I knew Olivia was the one, I had to break off our engagement.

I had no desire to harm Victoria. She was genuinely a sweet, wonderful, beautiful person. Any man would be lucky beyond their wildest dreams to marry a woman like her. That we were friends from an early age and that our families were close made it all the tougher to deliver the news that I was about to give her I wanted to break off our engagement.

I arrived at the Snell's house. Victoria and I sat in the living room. I dove right in, giving her the bad news. The conversation went as bad as I thought it would. In later years, I would think back on Victoria's reactions and think of the five stages of grief put forward by Dr. Elizabeth Kubler Ross: denial, anger, bargaining, depression and acceptance. The differences were that she shuttled back and forth between denial, anger, bargaining and depression and she never got to the acceptance stage. It was in her first bout of anger that her mother came in and they joined forces. She went through the same process. I was lucky that Mr. Snell was not home. Otherwise, you might have added murder as a new stage.

At one point, I announced that my mind was made up and that I was going to marry Olivia. I apologized profusely for hurting her and told her that was not my intention. In fact, it was the last thing on earth that I wanted. I said my piece and I left. Expecting my parents would get an immediate call, I headed over there for a fresh round of punishment.

As expected, when I got there, my mother had just gotten off the phone with Mrs. Snell. She was livid. She said a little of her piece but said she'd wait for Dad, who was on his way home that minute to talk some sense into me. That was preferable, actually. I'd rather get it over in one sitting with both of them rather than rehashing it first with her and then with him.

"What the hell are you doing?" Dad screamed as he walked through the front door. "How dare you do this to your mother and me?"

"I didn't do anything to you," I calmly stated. "I did something for myself, so that I can be with the woman I love."

"The woman you love? That slut? She's pregnant by another man, for God's sake!"

"Don't you ever, ever call her a name like that in my presence." I remained calm but I said this with such menace, he dialed it back a bit.

"Joey, what about your gift? What about passing it on to your first-born? It's your duty—your obligation—to select a proper wife who can give you a child who can carry on."

"What do you mean a "proper" wife?"

"Victoria is what I meant."

"No, you made a statement directly against Olivia. This is the second time you've said it. You said the exact same thing when we were married."

"What I'm saying is that she's having a baby by another man. That will be her first-born. It may keep any child you have together from having the gift."

"And if it does, I don't care. We had a first-born together. His name was Nathan. He was torn from us. We may have another, or we may not. I'm not losing her again."

"That may not be under your control."

"What do you mean?"

"I mean, she was sent on a trip that kept you from meeting, wasn't she?. Who's to say it can't happen again?"

"Wait a minute. How do you know she was on a trip when we were first supposed to meet?"

"You must have told me."

"No, I didn't. I only found out myself on the train ride north. I haven't told anyone. What did you do, Dad?"

"I didn't do anything."

"Are you responsible for killing off my son? Did you kill my baby before it was born? Tell me, Dad."

"James, what did you do?" my mother asked.

"I did nothing, I tell you."

"Wait a minute. The day Olivia disappeared, the Robinsons were in for a visit. I had to work and Olivia was feeling low with her pregnancy. You came in to show them around."

"Who are the Robinsons?" Mom asked.

"Olivia was the nanny to their children. You wouldn't know them because with the Correction, they never would have come to the City because Olivia and I never met. Dad, what did you say to the Robinsons? Did you get him to wish something? Did you convince him to send her on that trip? Please tell me you didn't do that. Please, Dad."

My father didn't say a word as he looked out the window. Then he spoke softly.

"She isn't our people."

"Olivia? Are you saying she isn't our people because her mother was black?" His silence indicated consent.

"So that means your grandchild wasn't 'your people' either."

"Sometimes we have to do what we have to for the family."

"How dare you play God? How dare you play with my life?"

"Everything I did was for you, for this family. You have a duty to carry on the line and to carry it on properly."

"There's that word 'proper' again. First off, this isn't the twelfth century. You have no right to select my bride. Second, regarding my duty, I didn't select this gift. I'm having serious doubts whether it's a gift or a curse. If you remember correctly, I didn't have it until you killed off Luis."

The mention of the name set my father off in anger. My mother looked perplexed. "Who's Luis?" she asked. The way she asked it, I could tell she was nervous about what the answer would be."

"He's nobody. I don't know any Luis. Joe doesn't know what he's talking about."

"I think I've heard enough and I think I've said enough. I'm going home to the woman who will be my wife. Within the next couple of days, we're moving into New York City. You won't hear from me again. Don't even think of playing any games, Dad. I'll know if you do anything. Olivia is my wife. Get used to that fact. Also, get used to the fact that you're responsible for the demise of our family's contribution to the world through Corrections. If Olivia and I have a child, I will never tell him or her of the gift. Maybe you can come back as a ghost like Grandpa Michael did in the old days and start the string again. Goodbye."

"Joey!" My mother called out to me as I departed, but I did not stop. Dad said nothing. Perhaps he was figuring out what to say to Mom to save their marriage. She had almost left him before when she found out about Lydia and Luis. She hadn't left him because of his infidelity but because he did the unpardonable sin of erasing a life. Now she not only knows about Luis, but she also knows about Nathan. I had no idea how he was going to Self-Correct himself out of this one. I didn't care.

I hurried home and ran into Olivia's arms. I burst into tears. She was my entire world now. I would never let her go.

26

I sat down with Olivia and walked her through my encounter with my parents. When I mentioned how my father betrayed us by tricking Mr. Robinson into wishing that he had given a trip to her on the date we met, she displayed the same anger and disgust every time I mentioned their name. I stopped.

"Okay, what is it with the Robinsons? You used to be so close. What changed?"

She would not answer immediately. I sensed she was going to tell me, but had to screw up the courage. I patiently waited for her. Finally, she spoke.

"Arthur Robinson is the father of my baby."

I couldn't say that I was entirely shocked by the news.

"I had just finished sitting for the kids when he got home. Mrs. Robinson was in Savannah visiting her sister. I was about ready to head out when Mr. Robinson asked me if I'd like a drink. He'd never asked me before to join him, so I felt really special. We went into his study. He always kept the door closed so I'd never been in there. The room had rich wood paneling that matched his ornate desk. There were so many books in cases all around the room. It was incredible.

"As he prepared our drinks, we chatted about my studies. He told me how proud he was of me. I'd never felt so special in my life. We had a couple drinks and I was feeling more lightheaded than I thought I should. I've never drunk all that much, but I spent much of my life at Eloise's bar and restaurant. I could take a couple drinks but I was getting more and more lightheaded after one drink. I mentioned to him how dizzy I was feeling and he moved over to sit beside me.

The last thing I remembered was him kissing me. I was powerless to fight him off. Then I passed out.

"When I woke up, it was morning. I was still on the couch in his study, but I had a light blanket over me. My clothes were all on me, but they were disheveled, like they had been put back on me while I was lying there. I felt a bit sore. My head was splitting and my brain was fuzzy. Arthur Robinson walked in with a cup of coffee for me. He said I had dozed off, and he didn't have the heart to wake me. He said he called Aunt Eloise to let her know I was okay and would stay the night. I thanked him for not making her worry. He then drove me home.

"I thought nothing more about it as I went about my life like before, but then about a month later, I started feeling nauseous. It continued morning after morning until finally Aunt Eloise looked at me and asked, "You pregnant, chile?" I told her I couldn't be, but the baby was definitely growing inside me. A month later, I was showing. I thought back to that night. It had to have been then. He raped me; I had no doubt about it.

"A week later, I screwed up enough courage to confront him. At first he denied it. Then he turned on me and told me I had no proof. Then he said, 'I'd keep my mouth shut, if I were you. Who do you think people are going to believe, a prominent attorney, a pillar of the community or a nigger whore?'

"I walked out the door and never went back. I thought about going and telling Mrs. Robinson, but then I decided against it. Either she wouldn't believe me or, if she did, I'd hurt her beyond repair. She was always nice to me. I couldn't do that to her."

"Why did you not think you couldn't tell me?"

"I was ashamed."

"You have nothing to be ashamed of. You didn't do anything."

She smiled, but it was a sad smile. "You're very sweet to say that, but you're also a man. As a woman, I know it doesn't work that way. I bear the mark, the burden, of an out-of-marriage pregnancy. But there's another reason I didn't confide in you."

"And that is?"

"You were a stranger, and a strange stranger at that. Remember, you knew me for years, but I had never heard of you until a little over a week ago. You were telling me unbelievable things. It really wasn't until I met Ms. Lily that I decided you weren't totally a crackpot. She was a big part of the reason I went with you, but I also saw you as a way out. I had nowhere to go. Being mixed race, I always felt like I straddled two worlds, but never fully a part of either. Being an unwed mother would only exacerbate my predicament.

"Aunt Eloise would always support me, but that wasn't the way I wanted to live the rest of my life. I was waiting tables at her restaurant with no plans for my future. I jumped at the chance to go with you to get out of there. I'm sorry I used you like I did, but I was desperate."

"If your using me results in us spending the rest of my lives together, you can use me any time you like."

"You always know the right thing to say."

"That's funny because the first thing that appealed to you was how I stumbled over my sales pitch when we first met in another lifetime."

She laughed. "Do you really think this life can be as wonderful as the life we had before?"

"I have absolutely no doubt. I know how much it hurt to lose you and the absolute joy I felt when I got you back. I'm going to keep that feeling of joy as long as I can."

The next day we took a train into the city to look at the apartment. As I predicted, Olivia loved it. I also watched her face as we walked along the streets of Manhattan. Like I remembered, she had a look of wonderment at the bustle and sounds of the city. We moved into our apartment that weekend, but not until after we got married. My minister friend performed the ceremony with his wife in attendance. We all went out for a nice Italian lunch afterwards.

On that Monday, I started back at my old/new job selling Oldsmobiles. My first day, I sold three cars. I amazed dealership management. They said I did the job like a veteran. I told them my encyclopedia experience had trained me well.

A week after we moved in, Olivia asked me what we should name the baby. She said she would have liked to name a boy Nathan after her father, but she thought that might be too weird. I thought the same thing. It might bring back too many memories. But if she had her heart set on naming him Nathan, I wouldn't object. I was therefore privately relieved that she said something first. I was also pleased that she was including me in the naming process. She knew full well that I was going to be the child's father, regardless of where he came from.

I considered for a second and then I said, "If it's a girl, how about we name her Sally? My great-grandmother Sally is my connection to you. She was Efrem's daughter and Hannah's best friend. If it weren't for them, I probably never would have gone to Charleston in the first place."

"That would be fine. I've always liked the name Sally. And if it's a boy?"

"If it's a boy, how about Oscar?"

"Are you sure?"

"Of course. Oscar's the one who raised you. He's partially responsible for forming you into you and should be rewarded for doing such a fine job."

That evening, Olivia called her aunt and uncle to tell them of their choices. She made it clear that I was the one who suggested the name. She said she could hear her Uncle Oscar bawling in the background at the honor. Then I overheard her tell Eloise that his middle name was going to be Joseph. She wanted to name her baby after the two men who had saved her in her life. Before too long, we surrounded Olivia with stereo bawling.

After she hung up, Olivia asked me a question. "What kind of boy was Nathan like?"

"He was such a wonderful kid. Smart as a whip. How could he be anything but smart with us as parents? There was one time when he was not even four years old that you were out with him on a winter's day. It was icy out and, as you were walking, you slipped on the ice and fell. You hit your head, knocking yourself out cold. A lot of kids would have panicked or would have stood beside you and cried. He didn't do either of these things. He knew he was about five blocks from Askin's and he ran there. I was showing a young couple the latest Olds when I looked out the front door and saw him walking through the front door. He told me what happened and together we went back to you. You were just coming to and were frantic that he wasn't there. When we explained what he did, you were as proud of him as I.

"Anyway, he was a joy. My last memory of him was telling me about an art project he was working on at school. He was so proud of it. When I asked him if I could see it, he very sternly told me I couldn't see it until he finished it. I told him, fair enough. I watched after him as he hung up his jacket on his peg and then ran down the hallway at school to get to his classroom. I can still see him running down the hallway. I guess I'll never know what the art project was, will I?"

27

Despite her pregnancy, Olivia worked full time to make a home of our apartment. I told her she should slow down some, but she told me she was having too much fun. She promised me she'd be careful. I knew she would, but I was still worried. After what I'd gone through, I could be forgiven for being a bit over-protective.

Oldsmobiles were flying out the door. I'd only been there a few weeks, and I was already one of the top salesmen in the dealership. I guess I was having fun, too. I missed my parents, however. Since our fight, I hadn't called them nor had they called me. I thought my mother would have called at some point, but she didn't. I didn't know if she was following Dad's lead or whether she was angry at me for her own reasons.

I really felt I was the more aggrieved party. My father erased the memory of my son, for God's sake. I shouldn't be the one to extend the olive branch, and yet a part of me felt like I wanted to. Relationships can be strange, can't they? I wouldn't waste a lot of time and effort thinking about it. I had other things on my mind, like Olivia's rapidly approaching delivery and my new job.

I no longer performed Corrections. My father's use of our unique gift for his own purposes left a foul taste in my mouth. I didn't have the drive to help people like I did before. I told myself that I was helping plenty of people by putting them in safe, affordable automobiles. If people made mistakes in the past, that was their problem. Cozying up to people to sell them a car gave me lots of opportunities to hear about people's problems. There were numerous times when I could have reached out a hand and put it on someone's shoulder to make their troubles evaporate away. But I took the stance that their problems certainly weren't mine.

Sometimes I thought that certain people spilled out how hard their lives were thinking they could get a better deal out of me. One man related to me how he had mistakenly backed over his wife, killing her. He could no longer bring himself to drive that car. He wanted to trade it in for a new Olds. His old car was fine; it had plenty of miles left in it. He could not bring himself to drive that car any longer.

This was a not case where someone was using a sob story to get a better deal. He was just explaining why he needed a new car. Probably that was the reason I gave him a tremendous deal, both on the new purchase and on the trade-in. I knew the pain he was feeling. Losing Olivia was still fresh in my mind. I could have performed a Correction for him to restore his wife to him. In fact, I should have done so. It would have been the right thing to do. I just couldn't bring myself to do it.

Even though I had sworn off performing Corrections there was one Correction that I still wanted to do. In fact, it preoccupied my mind for months. One of the longstanding rules of our trade was that Corrections weren't for revenge, but I couldn't help it. I wanted to figure out some way to make Arthur Robinson suffer for what he did to Olivia.

The situation turned out well, but he scarred Olivia for the rest of her life. Sometimes I'm holding her and I suddenly feel her sobbing. She'll tell me they are tears of thankfulness. I don't contradict her, but I'm never entirely convinced. She endured a rape and an unwanted pregnancy, after all. That's not anything one gets over easily.

I've done my best to ensure that she not live the rest of her life in shame. However, I could have just as easily followed my parent's advice and settled for a marriage to Victoria instead of dropping everything to search for Olivia. Seeing Olivia pregnant with someone else's baby could have repulsed me and forced me to depart Charleston empty-handed..

Eloise and Oscar were accepting and loving, but they weren't the same as having a husband to look after and care for her. My happening to come along to turning things around for Olivia didn't expunge Arthur Robinson's record. He would be guilty until the day he died. I had to figure out a way to make him pay for his sins, but I had to do it in a way that didn't have any unintended repercussions. I couldn't do anything that could jeopardize Olivia or my relationship with her.

I had plenty of time to think over my options. I couldn't leave Olivia until after she had delivered the baby and was comfortable taking care of him or her. In addition, even though I'd quickly established myself as a star salesman, I'd only just started my new job. I'd have to wait until I'd been there at least six months before I could ask for a few days off to go down to Charleston and come back. One thing I have is patience. It would happen, but my revenge would have to wait a little.

A few months later, I was showing a young couple the latest Oldsmobile Holiday Ninety-Eight when Tracy, one of our secretaries, came up to me and told me that Olivia was on the phone. I excused myself and went to the phone.

"Hi, hon."

"Joe, I think it's time."

"I'll be there in ten minutes. You want to meet me downstairs?"

I gave my apologies to the couple and then turned them over to Stanley, one of our other salesmen, as I grabbed my jacket and ran out the door. When I got to our building, I hailed a cab and asked him to wait while I went to gather Olivia. As expected, she was in the lobby with her suitcase we had pre-packed in anticipation.

Five hours later, Oscar Joseph Vance was born. I walked into her room to find Olivia looking down on the baby. She had that same look of love I remembered when I walked past her room with Nathan. I walked in and noticed that Oscar had darker skin and curlier hair than Olivia. I supposed it was her mother's/Eloise's family coming through.

"What do you think?" she asked.

"He's beautiful. He looks just like me. Why shouldn't he? He's my son."

She smiled. I leaned down and kissed them both.

28

Olivia and Oscar stayed an extra day in the hospital because she had an irregular heartbeat. She didn't feel especially bad but when she tried to stand up, the world spun around. The doctors were sure it was a temporary condition that would shortly level off. She experienced a similar condition when she had Nathan, which the doctors had likewise dismissed as a minor transitory issue. Still, I was petrified at the thought of anything that hinted of ever losing my wife. As ever, she was my touchstone and assured me that nothing was going to happen to her.

It was a big day when I brought them home. I had a banner made up. Oscar was unimpressed, but it brought a tear to Olivia's eye. She was still weak but was gaining strength all the time.

My life entered what I considered a surreal stage. For the first time in my memory, Corrections weren't the absolute center of my life. I was refusing to do them and I had a son who I knew was incapable of ever performing them. Throughout my life, Dad was doing Corrections and then I was expected to carry on the family tradition. Even when I couldn't deliver because of my father's extramarital dalliance, there was intense pressure on me. Now, there was no pressure on me to perform.

There was no pressure to perform, that is, until Olivia pressured me. She asked me how long I could stay out of work.

"Frank told me to take as long as I needed. He's devoted to his wife, Misty. One of her pregnancies was very tough. He almost lost her. He remembered being on pins and needles the entire time, so he knew what I was going through. Perhaps in a couple days I'll go back."

"I'll probably be sick of you by then and kick you out of here!"

"I don't doubt it."

"I've been so into myself that I haven't asked you anything about how you're doing."

"Quite understandable."

"So, tell me something. Any interesting people you've dealt with?"

"There was this one guy who wanted a new car because he couldn't drive his old one."

"What was wrong with the car?"

"There wasn't anything wrong with it. It had years left on it, but he couldn't drive it because he backed over and killed his wife with it. He wanted a new car because of the memories."

"And you did nothing?"

"I couldn't. I've sworn off doing Corrections. After losing you and seeing you put through hell, I can't bring myself to do them anymore."

"That's bull and you know it! This man, he's the one who is going through hell! You have a gift to help people and then you use me as the excuse not to use it? That makes me very mad."

I'd never seen her this mad before, and her anger was aimed at me. I was immediately chastised, but her passion was intoxicating. She was setting me straight, and I deserved it.

I want you to go down to Askin's right now and call this man. I know it will cost you a sale, but you have to make this right. Reunite this poor man with his wife! Get out of here. Oscar and I will be fine.

I did as she told me. I surprised Frank when I walked in, but when I told him Olivia had kicked me out and told me to go to work, he shrugged his shoulders and said, "Women, I know I'll never figure them out."

I dug out my Rolodex and looked up the man's name and number.

"Mr. Pruitt? This is Joseph Vance from Askin's Oldsmobile. We've been contacted by Oldsmobile about an adjustment that we need to do to the steering in your particular model. It's nothing that is immediately dangerous, but it could become so if not addressed. It's only a half-hour fix. Could you bring the car in over the next day or so? Tomorrow at nine? That would be perfect. I'll see you then"

The next day arrived and promptly at nine in the morning, Ted Pruitt walked up to my desk. I took his keys and told him I'd bring them to the service department for them to fix the car. I said I'd be right back. I disappeared for a few minutes and then returned. Of course, there was nothing wrong with his car and I didn't hand his keys over to anyone. If things went as planned, in a few minutes he'd disappear from the dealership, his wife would be alive, the keys would disappear from my pocket and the car would either be in its spot looking to be sold, or it would be owned by someone else.

"Can I get you a cup of coffee, Mr. Pruitt?"

"No, I'm okay, thank you."

"How have you been holding up since losing your wife?"

"Not well. Not well at all. I thought that giving up the car would have been cathartic, that it would have allowed me to move on. It didn't."

"I bet you're wishing you never backed out of your driveway that day."

His eyes blazed as he stared at me.

"Of course, why are you bringing this up? I'm tormented every minute of every day knowing that I killed her. I don't need an asshole like you reminding me of the biggest mistake of my life."

"So, you wish you never backed out of your driveway that day."

"Are you deaf?" He was screaming at me at this point. All eyes in the dealership were on us. Undeterred, I continued on.

"Tell me. Tell me you wish you never backed out of the driveway that day."

"Damn you. If it will shut you up then yes, I wish I never backed out of the driveway that day."

I reached over and put my hand on his shoulder. He disappeared. My world spun a little as I closed my eyes. When I opened them, I was sitting in my apartment. Olivia was nursing Oscar, singing softly to him. She looked at me.

"You seemed far away. Did you do a Correction?"

"Yes, I did. You may not remember it, but you browbeat me into it."

"Well, you always do the right thing. I'm sure you would have done whatever was right on your own, eventually. What did I make you do?"

"Hold on one minute and I'll tell you."

I walked over and picked up the phone. I dialed the number I remembered. After two rings, I heard a woman's voice.

"Hello, is this Mrs. Pruitt?"

"Yes, it is. Who is this?"

"My name is Joseph Vance. I'm a salesman at Askin's Oldsmobile in Manhattan. Are you in the market for a new car?"

"No, I don't believe so. Our car is perfectly fine and has plenty of miles left on it, I'm sure."

"You have a Buick, correct?"

"Yes, a Buick."

"I could give you a nice deal on a brand new Oldsmobile."

"I don't think so. I'll talk it over with my husband, but I think he'll agree."

"Oh well, it was worth a try. If you change your mind, keep Askin's Oldsmobile in mind."

"We will. Thank you."

I hung up, content I'd done a good thing.

"Well, you made me save a woman's life. I just spoke with her and she sounds just fine, not even realizing she'd been dead for a while."

"Saving a life is always a good thing. How did I do this?"

I explained to her about Mr. Pruitt backing over his wife and buying a new car to help erase the memory of what he had done. I had petulantly refused to help him because I was mad at my father. She, however, read me the riot act and told me to do something, to help this family. It was my duty.

"Like I said, you would have gotten there, eventually. We all need an occasional kick in the butt to point us in the right direction."

"Well, I'm pretty black and blue back there right now."

"Later on, I'll kiss it and make it all better."

"You are feeling better, aren't you? It looks like he's all done. Why don't you let me hold him while you get yourself cleaned up?"

She handed Oscar over and I took over lightly patting his back to help his digestion. I closed my eyes as I enjoyed holding him. When I opened them, Olivia was standing at the doorway, looking at us with a loving smile on her face.

"Just a couple months ago, my life was in disarray. I felt so lost and so afraid. Now I feel like I have everything I could ever want. I feel like the luckiest women on the face of the earth. Any idea what the difference could be?"

"I haven't a clue. It must be New York. This city has a magical effect on some people."

"Yeah, that must be it."

A couple days later, I went back to work. Olivia and Oscar were both doing fine now, and I had to get back to making some money to support my family. I was in an ebullient mood. I was even looking forward to doing Corrections once again. I decided that it was time to reach out to my parents.

I couldn't ever forgive my father for what he had done, but perhaps we could salvage somewhat of a relationship to move ahead. Perhaps forgiveness could come in time. I gave them a call. My mother answered.

She told me they wanted nothing to do with me. I had crossed a line. I brought up the past that was better off left dead and forgotten. When I tried to plead my case, she cut me off.

"Joseph, I have made a choice, and the choice is your father. To him, you have turned your back on him and on the family. You have forsaken the tradition of eight hundred years. He feels like he has failed you and himself and all his ancestors. He cannot forgive you for that. Nor can I."

With that, she hung up. I was stunned. I was the aggrieved party. His racism killed off my son. Despite all that, I was willing to hand over an olive branch and work towards reconciliation. In response, he, through my mother, took that branch and repeatedly struck me across the face with it. I was right to be indignant. I would not make the mistake of reaching out again.

I was going to immerse myself in Olivia and Oscar, the people I loved more than anything, in my work and in my life here in Manhattan. Olivia had convinced me that Corrections, even though they could be used for selfish and even evil reasons, were still a good thing. I reunited Ted Pruitt with the woman he loved most in the world through a Correction. She'd revived my passion for my calling.

I was eager to pass my knowledge on to my child, if Olivia and I were to have one. It would be interesting to pass the gift of to a child who was not my first-born. If you think about it, he or she would be the fourth-born. Nathan and our unborn child were one and two. Oscar, even though he's not my biological son, would be three.

I never tried to communicate with my parents again. They had cut me off, permanently. It didn't affect me as much as I thought it would. I was going to live my life.

29

Over the next few years, Oscar grew by leaps and bounds. He was going to be a big kid. I thought maybe he'd be a basketball or football player, so I started to take an interest in sports that maybe we could share. He was a bright inquisitive boy. He reminded me of Nathan that way. I pushed that thought from my mind. It wasn't healthy to dwell on the past or to compare one child with another.

I was back to performing Corrections on a regular basis. I sometimes had to slow myself down to make sure I wasn't doing any that may have foreseeable adverse consequences. Of course, it's impossible to fully anticipate the dominos that may fall once the past is changed, but I proceeded as if the ancillary effects were minimal. Otherwise, I'd drive myself crazy or do nothing at all.

It was two years after I had helped Ted Pruitt when he walked into the dealership. I went up to greet him and ask him if I could help him. It took everything I had to keep from greeting him by name, asking him how his wife, Esther, was and asking him if his Buick had finally given up the ghost. I had to play dumb and act like I'd never met him before. That's the way he was with me.

Mr. Pruitt said his car was finally showing its age. He needed a new one and something inside him told him to try out an Oldsmobile. He laughed when I told him it's always wise to listen to such a smart voice. It felt good to sell him a car, not because the old car had run over his wife but because it had simply worn out.

I was with another client when Olivia called. She'd just been to the doctor, and he told her the news, which she was now relaying to me. She was expecting. I must have whooped or something like that because everyone in the entire dealership gave me funny looks. I apologized to the customers after which I explained the news I just heard. They were somewhat humorless and couldn't understand why I was making a fuss in the middle of a sale. I didn't mind. We were going to have another baby.

Olivia delivered a baby girl, whose name would be Sally. Olivia's heart rate plummeted after the birth. This time, the doctors were extremely concerned. They were having trouble getting her pulse and blood pressure back to normal. After three days, Olivia passed away. There was nothing anyone could have done. The doctors theorized that she had a congenital heart defect—a ticking time bomb they called it—that could have been triggered any time. The rigors of childbirth just happened to be that trigger.

I was in absolute shock. I couldn't believe it. It had to be a mistake. There had to be a way to reverse this. There had to be a Correction I could do. I should be able to figure out the day we had sex that conceived Sally, and then gone back and not have sex that night. That was the level at which I was thinking. But every time I devised a scheme like this, I had to think what Olivia would want. If I went back and saved her life but in the process deprived Sally of hers, Olivia would never forgive me. I wouldn't blame her. I'd be as guilty as my father.

I had to accept the fact that she was gone. It was nobody's fault. It was just that it was Olivia's time.

I've heard of cases where a mother dies in childbirth and the father is resentful of the child for the rest of his life, as if the child were to blame. I could never understand this. I could never hate Oscar or Sally; they have Olivia in them.

I sat with Olivia until they brought the gurney in to bring her down to the morgue. I sat for a few moments longer, staring at the empty bed. I had to pull myself together. I had the two lives of my kids to look out for. They had to come first in all of this. The nurse had placed Sally in a crib in the nursery. Oscar was staying with a friend. I did not relish having to explain to a three-year-old that his mother would not be coming home.

As the kids grew, it became obvious they'd each need their own rooms. We'd have to find ourselves a bigger place. When it came time to move, I know I should have thrown out this old love seat that Olivia had brought north with her. It was threadbare and stained. I definitely should have replaced it, but I couldn't bring myself to get rid of it. Every time I looked at it, I could see her sitting there, curled up in her pajamas, reading a book or sipping some hot chocolate. It had her imbedded in it throughout. How could I get rid of it?

Olivia had occasionally hired a nanny to come in and watch Oscar. Her name was Emma. I asked her if she could continue to help. She was a little nervous about caring for a baby, but she had been very fond of Olivia, so she agreed. This allowed me to go back to work, at least on a limited basis, but my heart wasn't in it. I couldn't bring myself to be enthusiastic about selling cars when Olivia wasn't at home to come back to.

Being an effective car salesman often requires flexibility. Sometimes, selling a car involves coming to the dealership in the evening or on weekends. Your schedule isn't always yours. You must adapt to the clients' timetables, not make them adjust to yours. If you're not flexible, the client will just move on to the next salesman or the next dealer.

When Olivia was at home, I could have this flexibility. I knew she would take care of Oscar. Now that she was gone, I couldn't count on Emma to stay late while I tried to seal a deal. I had to consider something else to bring in some money. But what could I do? I knew how to sell, but most of those jobs either had the same time requirements or were jobs where I'd be bored out of my skull. I wanted something where lots of money would fall into my lap. It goes without saying that this job had to be one that didn't land me in prison.

I'd just finished closing the deal on an Olds Fiesta Convertible and I went over to the coffee machine for a break. A fellow salesman, Ernie Withers, was regaling some of his colleagues about how well he did out at Belmont Park the previous day. He bet on the winners of two races and won the Exacta in another. A lot of what he said was in a foreign language to me. I'd never been to the races, nor had I ever bet on a horse. It didn't really interest me either, but listening to him, an idea came into my head of a legal, but probably not entirely ethical, way to earn money.

I was friendly on a 'good morning' basis with Ernie, but nothing more. Like all the other salespeople, he had come up to me to offer sincere condolences at Olivia's passing, but we weren't friends or anything like that. If nothing else, Ernie wasn't that great of a salesman. I got the sense that he didn't put in the work to learn everything there was to know about the cars, about the new models that were coming out, about all the extra features that could excite a buyer. He sold enough cars to stay employed, but not any more than that.

Like most ventures in life, the dealership was comprised of cliques. In high school, the popular kids flocked together; at the dealer, the cliques were based on sales success. Since I was the biggest seller at Askin's, I hung around with other more successful salesmen. I didn't like to think of myself as snobby, but you never know how others view you.

Later that day, I approached Ernie. He seemed a little wary when I came up to him. I guess my question on whether I was in fact snobby was being answered. I immediately tried to make him ease by entering his sphere of expertise.

"Hi, Ernie. I heard you talking earlier about Belmont Park. I've always been interested in going to the races, but frankly I don't know squat about it. I'd be too intimidated to go alone to the races. Could I tag along next you go?"

His face beamed. "That would be great, Joe. I'm heading down to Monmouth Park in Jersey next Saturday. They have their big stakes race. There should be some pretty big payouts. How does that sound?"

I had no idea what a stakes race was, but it sounded impressive.

"Can you guarantee I'll win?" I asked.

It took him a second to realize I was joking, and then he laughed. "Can't say I can guarantee that, but I think I'll be pretty safe in saying you'll have a good time."

"Sounds great then!"

I got Emma to sit for the kids. I think she thought me a little selfish running off to the horse races. I hoped she just passed it off as part of an unorthodox grieving process. I didn't think I could come up with a way to tell her I was doing this for the kids, to provide for them. I didn't entirely believe it myself.

Ernie showed up at ten and we headed off to New Jersey. During the ride, Ernie explained some terms to me. Like any field of endeavor, horse racing had its own language. I didn't need an in-depth understanding, just enough to catch on and place bets. He also started describing some of the horses that would compete during the afternoon. He told me of their various characteristics that increased their chances of winning. I didn't want to clog my mind with these details, so I didn't pay as much attention to what he was saying.

Ernie also told some hilarious stories and was a very likeable guy. I was kind of sorry that I never got to know him better. I also felt somewhat guilty that I was only with him now to use him and his expertise, but I pushed that guilt to the back of my mind.

We got to the track relatively early. We found our seats, but Ernie noted that we probably wouldn't be in them all that much since we'd wander a fair amount, occasionally venturing down to the rail. Ernie was correct. There is quite a thrill to be down there when the horses thunder around the curve and head down the homestretch toward the finish line.

He brought me up to the betting window and explained the types of bets he was placing. He put a small bet on the Daily Triple. This was a bet on the winners of the first three races. People rarely win this, he explained, but if you do, the payoff is incredibly large. He only put a few bucks down on this, but he said he'd kick himself if he didn't and his horses won. He did get it once, and that was enough to suck him in for life.

He said another bet that he stays away from were trifectas and superfectas. The trifecta was when you bet on three horses to finish first, second and third. The superfecta was when you bet on four horses to finish in the exact order of first, second, third and fourth. The odds, he said, are just too astronomical. Even if you had the best system in the world, there were too many variables for that many horses. You might as well just throw your money away as place this bet.

Other than that, he just placed straight bets on horses to win. By the end of the day, he had made a little money, not as much as he did at Belmont, but he was in the plus column. I broke even. When I bet with Ernie, I did better than I thought I would. On the few times I ventured out on my own, I did very poorly. This was not unexpected, nor did I worry about it. My main objective was to learn, and that's what I did.

Ernie drove me back to my apartment. I told him I had a great time, and I meant it. It was a lot of fun and it allowed me to escape my world for a couple hours. It was worth it. Emma was angry that I came home as late as I did, but when I explained what I got out of the day, she softened somewhat. The extra hundred dollars I paid her as she departed evaporated any animosity she may have held against me.

The next day I sat down to review my notes from the day before. I approximated the amount I could have won had I bet the correct way. It would have been close to one hundred thousand dollars instead of the couple hundred dollars I lost. I appreciated Ernie's system, but I can guarantee that my system would be even better.

I didn't think it wise to go back and correct yesterday's performance. It would have been suspicious to have such beginner's luck. If nothing else, it would have been an insult to Ernie, who was playing by the rules. He was proud of his earnings and I would have robbed him of that. I really enjoyed the time I spent with him and wanted to do it again. My plan was to do Corrections when I was on my own.

Belmont and Aqueduct were the most convenient racetracks for me to get to, but there were a number of racetracks I could go to in the New York metropolitan area. I figured I would spread my attendance around. I didn't want to attract attention to myself.

My plan was simple. I would go to the racetrack, place a few bets, hang around for an hour, place a few more bets, and then head home. Emma would not have to wait hours for me. The next day, or the day after that, I would review the race results in the Daily Racing Form and then do a Self-Correction. The Self-Correction would involve reciting the races, the horses I bet on and the type of bet I placed, but this time I'd place the bets on the horses that actually won. After making this wish, I'd place my hand on my shoulder. Things would go black for a second and then I would wake up in the exact same place I was. In fact, nothing seemed different, except I would have memories of winning.

The first time I did this, I went to Belmont with $15,000 in my pocket. Two hours later, when I returned home, I had only $213 left. Most racing patrons who did this would be advised to get professional help for their gambling problem. I didn't have any such person to give me such warnings, nor did I need them. The next day I got the racing form results and took copious notes of the winners. Then, I put together my wish for a superfecta, a quinella and a daily double. I performed my Self-Correction and I went back to Belmont to place these bets instead of the ones I did. When I came to, I still didn't quite believe I did it. I went to my desk and pulled the deposit slip out of the drawer where I kept them. There on top was a deposit for $45,623. That means I netted a profit of $30,623. Not a bad payout for a couple hours of work.

For the first couple of weeks, I did this process two days per week to build up a surplus. After I raked in $82,000 at Aqueduct, I had over $325,000 in the bank. The only racetrack I had gone to twice was Belmont. I knew these places did not like to lose money. My picture might have been on display with instructions to deny me the right to place bets. I needed to be creative about how, when and where I placed my bets. After that, my attendance was sporadic and spread out over several racetracks.

After four months, my bank account balance had ballooned to $827,000. I lost a little when I would go with Ernie once a month, but I wanted to maintain my friendship with him. I simply liked the guy. I wouldn't do any Corrections on the days I was with him.

I now felt financially secure enough to go Frank and advise him I leaving Askin's. The loss of Olivia was too much for me to bear. It was obvious my heart wasn't in sales anymore and, as a result, my standing as the dealer's star was tarnished. While Frank said he was sorry to see me go, he did little to convince me to stay. I entirely understood. I had had a good run with them—two good runs, actually—so I was not leaving with any ill feelings or animosity.

By this time, I'd settled into a pattern. I would go to the races twice a month. I'd go once with Ernie for fun and once to run my Self-Correction scam. I'd gotten to where I would occasionally win some money when I was with Ernie. It wasn't as much as when I was on my own but it was still nice to know I had learned something. I was earning between twenty and fifty thousand per month, enough for my kids and me to live very well. Then two interrelated things happened.

First, police arrived at my door one day. I was playing with Oscar when they arrived. They'd been dispatched to question me about a profitable day I had at the harness racetrack in New Jersey. The track wasn't too far from where I used to live and where Mom and Dad still lived. I contemplated dropping in for a visit, but I didn't believe I'd be welcomed. Nor did I want to see them. I still hurt with Olivia's passing and could not forgive what they did to Olivia and me.

I won about $70,000 that day, and the track owners were not pleased. They suspected I did something illegal and filed a complaint. They had no specific evidence that they could use to charge me, but the track had connections to the police so they filed a complaint. When you win that much at a racetrack, for tax purposes you have to fill out a form with your name and address and other information. They knew exactly where to find me.

I knew there was nothing they could do because they had no evidence of a crime, but I didn't need the hassle of answering questions and raised suspicions. I also didn't want the cops doing a thorough investigation of the other tracks in the region. That would raise further suspicions. So, I did a Correcting Self-Correction and wished I hadn't placed those bets on that day. I put my hand on my shoulder and the police officers disappeared. Oscar and I were alone again, playing on the floor.

The second thing that happened was a call from Dad. I hadn't told them where I lived or my new telephone number, so it surprised me when I heard from him. I was going to ask him how he got my number, but he launched into a tirade.

"How dare you perform Corrections for your own gain?" he screamed.

How did he know? He would have felt a sensation whenever I performed a Correction the same way I do whenever he performs one, but he wouldn't know the details of what I did. I thought it over for a few seconds and then it dawned on me: police radio. Dad often listened in on the police bands to see if there were any people out there in need of a Correction. When the warrant was issued for my arrest, a call must have gone out for the local cops to start the process of working with New York City police to come and get me. Dad did some research when he heard my name and found out what I'd been doing. He probably got my number from my former employer.

"Hi Dad, nice to hear from you," I lied.

"Don't 'Hi Dad' me. How dare you use our gift for your personal profit? I knew that woman would convince you to do something like this someday."

"Dad, Olivia is dead. She died after giving death to your granddaughter."

I did not wait for him to respond. I hung up. Before he mentioned Olivia, I was eager to engage him. I was ready to point out his hypocrisy. What was erasing his firstborn son to save his marriage other than for his personal benefit? He was very selective in how he applied his Corrections.

I was also going to tell him I was doing this so I could make us financially secure. These were also going to be the last Corrections I ever did. Neither was I ever going to let Sally know that she had the power to perform Corrections. The gift may not stop with me, but unless something extraordinary happens like the ghost of Great-great grandfather Efrem appears to her and tells her of her gift, she will never know. I will never tell her.

30

I realized immediately that I'd made a mistake. My father was a zealot, a Correction zealot. He would do anything to ensure that the power to perform Corrections be passed along to future generations. Prior to my conversation with him, he didn't even know there was a future generation. I never should have let it slip that Olivia and I had a child. He would make it his sacred duty to track Sally down, tell her of her power and teach her how to use it.

He had obviously gotten my name and address from my old employer, Askin's Oldsmobiles. I didn't blame them. When somebody's father calls and says they can't get in touch with one of their children, the tendency is to help with contact information. But now he knew where I lived and where his granddaughter lived. I had to move the kids away and not let him know where we are.

I was actually thinking that maybe we should move out of the City. There were too many reminders of Olivia for me here. She so loved it and thrived in it. Maybe we should resettle somewhere. I was thinking of a town up the Hudson, perhaps a town like Rhinebeck.

Oscar hadn't yet started school, so this would be the perfect opportunity to move. There was plenty of money in the bank and I could always go back to the racetrack to replenish. I packed the kids up and we headed up the Taconic Parkway. I'd never been to Rhinebeck, but I always heard nice things about it. It lived up to its reputation. We all fell in love with it. It was early fall, and the leaves were just turning.

We walked around the village and there was a house for sale in the center of town on Market Street. The sign out front said it had three bedrooms, which would be perfect. We walked around the house and Oscar fell in love with the large backyard with several enormous maple trees. He said he wanted a swing. I said that could be arranged. I asked him if he'd like to help me build a treehouse for him to play in. He nodded vigorously.

We walked up the street to the realtor listed on the sign and we spoke with the agent, Michael Haley, about seeing the inside. He grabbed the keys, and we were off. The inside needed a little work, but it was move-in ready. I told him we would take it. He hadn't even told me the price yet, but I saw it was a good fit for us. He told me the price, and it was reasonable, so I told him we'd be back the following day with a check.

I ended up spending the rest of my life in Rhinebeck. The kids grew up and went to school there. Upon graduating high school, Oscar applied to Cornell University in Ithaca and the college accepted him. He would become a pediatrician. Sally followed him there a few years later. I was so thrilled the kids went to Cornell. It was a short three-hour drive away. It was far enough away for them to feel they were getting away from home, but close enough for them to come back and see me on a regular basis.

Sally would become a veterinarian. When she told me that's what she wanted to do with her life, a smile came to my face as I thought back to Mary Calabrese. She was one of my biggest victories. My Correction transformed her from being a depressed, downcast paraplegic with no past or future to a vital and active wife, mother and veterinarian.

Cornell was not a cheap place to send two children. Without a source of income, I was steadily depleting the amount I had in the bank. I probably should have gotten myself a job, something to occupy my time each day and bring in some honestly earned money. I'm not sure if it was laziness or depression or some other reason I couldn't get back into the work world, but I just couldn't bring myself to do it. It was depression. Some days were a real battle for me to go on without Olivia. When the kids were growing up, I let them occupy my time. Now that they were gone, it had gotten harder and harder for me to carry on.

It was then that I heard of a new state lottery that New York had started up. It was almost as if the state had answered my call. I bought a ticket each week. I'd track whether there was a winner. If there was no winner, I'd buy a ticket the following week as the jackpot rose. Over the course of five weeks, there had been no winner, and the jackpot had risen to three and a half million dollars. I wished I had played the winning numbers for that fifth week, touched myself on the shoulder. When I regained my senses, two and a half million additional dollars, the jackpot amount less withheld taxes, were in my bank account.

I knew this was wrong. It was stealing, but I didn't care. So much had been taken from me, things that money could never replace. I thought I deserved to get some of my own back. I was entitled.

I also thought that this was a shot at my father, only doing Corrections for this purpose. I thought he was still alive since I could feel one of his Corrections every now and then. It didn't concern me one way or another.

After I won the lottery, I became a bit of a local celebrity. I achieved what Andy Warhol had once called my fifteen minutes of fame. It felt nice to have people recognize me when I walked down the street. It didn't last long, though. Before I knew it, my fifteen minutes were over and I returned to obscurity. I was fine with that.

Both while they were in school and afterwards, neither Oscar nor Sally were too far away. They visited regularly. They both met their respective spouses at Cornell and, as soon as they graduated, they married and started their families, I got to see my grandkids on a recurring basis, which was very nice.

When Sally told me she was pregnant with her first child, my first thought was that the tradition was being carried on. I had too many years of Correction tradition to not make that my initial reaction, but I had to hold myself in check. The tradition was stopping with me.

I missed a lot of things. Mostly, I missed Olivia. Despite how much they hurt me, I missed my parents. I missed helping people like Mary Calabrese through Corrections, but I couldn't go back to that life. There was too much water under the bridge and too many terrible memories. I felt pretty sorry for myself and I drank, perhaps a bit too much.

There was an old-time tavern in the middle of Rhinebeck Village called The Rusty Bull. There was a plaque on the front of the building noting that there'd been a tavern on this spot since the Revolutionary War. In twenty years of living here, I'd never gone in. I gave it a try.

It had a colonial look to it with rich oak paneling throughout and a matching oak bar that ran the length of the tavern. Even the beer spigots looked old-fashioned. The place was quite packed for a Wednesday. I was one of the older people, so I wasn't sure how long I'd last. It might be too young a crowd for me, but I'd give it one beer.

Over in one corner was a small raised stage on which were a stool and a guitar sitting on a stand. That probably explained the crowd. Again, I wasn't sure if the music would be my cup of tea.

I searched around for a seat and at first couldn't find one. Then someone got up from a stool at the bar just as I was passing by, so I took it. To the right of me was a young couple. They were obviously in love and probably hadn't taken their eyes off of each other in days if not months. To the left was a woman who looked about my age, or around sixty. She had short blond hair and a pretty roundish face. She had the look like she'd put on a few pounds in recent years but was otherwise fit. The year was 1980, but she wore a long denim dress that was more reminiscent of the 1960s. She was nursing a white wine. She looked at me like she was sizing me up when I sat down. A radiant smile lit up her face as she addressed me.

"Can't say I've seen you in here before."

"First time. Just happened to be walking by and thought I'd come in for a beer. I'm Joseph Vance."

"And I'm Hallie James. Pleasure to meet you." She called over to the bartender, "Marco, give my friend here whatever he wants. It's on me."

She turned back to me. "Now that I bought you a beer, it's your job to hold my seat for me until I get back. Okay?"

Even in the dim light, I could see how lovely her blue eyes were.

"Will do," I responded. I ordered my beer, going with a local brew. I expected her to head for the bathroom and then return in a few minutes. Instead, she walked over to the stage and climbed up on the stool. She reached over and grabbed the guitar, putting the strap over her head and pulling the pick out of the strings. She strummed the guitar a few times, adjusted the tuning knob on a couple strings, and strummed it a couple more times. Satisfied that the guitar was in tune, she leaned forward and spoke into the microphone.

"How is everybody tonight?" Not waiting for a response, she continued. "I'd like to dedicate my first song for my new friend, Joe Vance." She looked over at me and smiled. I returned the smile. She then performed a heartfelt rendition of *If Ever I Saw Your Face*. She had a lovely medium-range soprano voice that easily complimented her flawless guitar work. After that, her repertoire included folk classics by Bob Dylan, Pete Seeger, Woody Guthrie, Tom Paxton and others. After forty-five minutes of solid singing and playing, she took a break. She came back to resume sitting on her stool beside me.

"That was absolutely lovely," I told her. "I can't remember having a better time in many years. Why haven't you put out a record?"

She beamed at my compliments. "I could never perform like that. The chorus of Harry Chapin's song, *Mr. Tanner*, sums it up for me. *But music was his life, it was not his livelihood; And it made him feel so happy and it made him feel so good; And he sang from his heart and he sang from his soul; He did not know how well he sang, it just made him whole.*"

"Well, I'm just ecstatic that I stumbled in here to hear you sing and play. Your singing from your soul touched my soul. It's just what I needed."

"Thank you. What do you do, Mr. Vance?"

"I'm retired now. I used to sell cars, Oldsmobiles, to be exact."

"Ooh," she said with a look on her face that betrayed a revulsion to automobile salesmen.

"Would it improve your opinion of me if I told you that, before I sold cars, I sold encyclopedias?"

"Now that's an occupation I can have respect for. You must know lots of things, just by osmosis."

"I know that a definition of osmosis is the process of gradual or unconscious assimilation of ideas and knowledge."

She laughed. "I was only kidding."

"The first time I met my wife, I knocked on her door looking to sell her a set of encyclopedias. She asked me was what a wombat is. I answered that and then she asked when the Crimean War was and who fought in. After a series of questions, she said if she was going to buy a car, she'd expect the salesman to know all about the vehicle he was selling. She expected the same from somebody who wanted to sell her encyclopedias. Luckily, I killed time in hotel rooms reading through the books. She was impressed, and we were married less than a year later. I must sound quite dull to you, reading encyclopedias."

"You have a wife?" It was obvious she hadn't listened to much of what I said after the word wife.

"Had. She died over twenty years ago."

"I'm sorry, it's obviously still painful for you after all that time. I only just met you and here I am, prying into your life."

"That's okay. It's nice to have someone to talk to. My kids are grown and moved away with families of their own, so it's kind of lonely. You have kids?"

The sorrowful, far-away look on her face showed that now I was the one who was prying into her life. "I'm sorry," I said. She brightened up. "It's okay. No kids. I just wasn't lucky on that score. Well, I have to go back on for another set. Have I depressed you too much for you to consider sticking around?"

"I'm glued to this seat. I have to make sure nobody steals your seat here, don't I?"

She smiled and kissed me on the cheek before going back to the stage. I ended up staying until the tavern closed down at one in the morning. Marco was a little angry because I wasn't drinking that much, but he brightened up when I left him an overly generous tip.

I was saying my goodbyes to Hallie when she asked me if I'd mind walking her home. She said she was always nervous walking home so late. I later learned that she walked home alone all the time, but I didn't mind. It would be nice talking with her without having to speak and listen over the constant din of a noisy bar.

When we got to her house, she leaned over to kiss me, but I gently warded her off. I said I liked her but I wasn't quite ready. She understood. We said our goodbyes, and I walked away. Neither of us had asked if we could see the other again. I feared that I had ruined the evening. I wanted to see her again, but perhaps because of my rebuff she wouldn't want to see me.

31

The following Wednesday I went back to The Rusty Bull. I had my trepidations about what her reaction to seeing me again might be. As it was the previous Wednesday, the tavern was filled with a crowd that was younger than I. I took that as a testament to Hallie's talent and song selection. Folk songs from the 60s and 70s were still very popular, even with a younger crowd.

I looked over to where I'd sat the previous week, and the stool was open. And in her same spot was Hallie, smiling away at me.

"I was wondering if I scared you off." She remarked. "I can sometimes be a little too pushy."

"And sometimes I need a little push. So, are you buying me a beer again this week or am I on my own?"

"Marco, anything he wants. On me."

Many of the songs she sang were the same as the week before, but she threw in a couple new ones to mix things up. After her evening concluded, I walked her back home again.

"I'm sorry about last week. One would think that twenty-plus years would be enough to get over someone."

"We all have to process our grief in our own time."

"That was in one of the songs you sang, wasn't it?"

"I think you're right!" she said with a laugh. "Anyway, you came back. That's what counts."

She reached over and took my hand. We held hands as we walked along. When we got to her place, she looked up at me. This time I kissed her. We embraced for a few minutes, and then she took my hand and led me up the stairs.

Afterwards, we lay in bed cuddling. "I was afraid I'd be so out of practice that I wouldn't know what to do."

"You did quite fine. Then again, it's been a long time for me as well. Who knows if I remember either?"

We fell asleep in each other's arms. I hadn't felt this blissful in a long, long time. From then on we were inseparable. Besides her weekly gig at the tavern, she also worked part time doing administrative and bookkeeping duties for a local church. Besides that, her time was her own. I was not doing any work, so I was perpetually available.

She wanted to know everything about me there was to know. I was willing to tell everything, everything except about the Corrections. How does one explain them? Since I wasn't doing them anymore—except to raise a few dollars now and then—there wouldn't be any need to tell her.

The first order of business was therefore for her to meet my children and their respective families. I hadn't yet told either of them about Hallie. Sally was visiting me one weekend when I suggested we go to church. I wanted to surprise her because Hallie was singing a solo that morning and I'd introduce her then.

"Church? You? Us?" she asked. She had a point. When Olivia was alive, we weren't frequent churchgoers, but we would attend every once in a while. We would definitely go on Christmas and Easter. Since her death, I took Sally there when she was an infant to get her baptized because Olivia would have wanted it. That was the last time I stepped inside a church.

"Yes, us. It wouldn't kill us to go to church one Sunday, would it?"

"I guess not," she replied, but she did very little to hide her suspicions I was up to something. She knew me well enough to believe I'd suddenly found religion. Something else was up.

She and I walked to the First Methodist Church, which was on the other side of town but still only about a fifteen-minute walk, while her husband, Fred, stayed at home with the kids. When we approached the church, the front door was open and we could hear Hallie singing and playing guitar to welcome the congregation. She was singing *Come to the Church in the Wildwood* as we took our seats. We were enjoying listening to her when out of the corner of my eye I saw Sally looking at Hallie, who had noticed our arrival and was looking at me. Sally then looked at me and then back at her. She leaned close to me and whispered in my ear.

"Dad, you old fox. You have a girlfriend. It's about time."

After the service, there was a small coffee reception where we got together with Hallie. She and my daughter hit it off immediately as we talked about how we met. Sally was especially taken when Hallie said how intrigued she was when I told her that I used to sell encyclopedias. Sally knew how taken her mother with my occupation at the time we met.

When we left the church, the two women gave a heartfelt embrace. Sally and I talked on the walk back home.

"Dad, I thought there was something different about you. You're like a new person!" Sally exclaimed.

"Is that good or bad?"

"Good. Definitely good. Is this how you were with Mom?"

"Your mother was one of a kind, but so is Hallie and so are you. I won't spend the rest of my life comparing one with the other. I'm just going to enjoy."

"Rest of your life, is it?"

"Don't go analyzing me now. That may work on the dogs and cats you work with but not your father."

She laughed. "Okay, okay, one day at a time."

"Absolutely. Have you spoken with your brother?"

"Yeah."

"He's coming next week and I'm going to introduce him to Hallie. I don't think I'll be able to drag him to church, however."

"Oscar, no way you're dragging him to a church."

"I hope he's okay with Hallie and me."

"Why wouldn't he be?"

"Your brother has some memories of your mother. They're very faint, but they're there. I hope he doesn't think I'm sullying her memory."

"Oscar will be fine. He wants you to be happy. He'll see the look of happiness on your face and he'll think it's the best thing ever."

"I hope you're right."

"And if he isn't fine about him, I'll beat him up."

"You do remember he was all-State in wrestling, don't you?"

"You've never seen me in full-fury!"

"You are so much like your mother. I could hear her mouthing those exact words."

"Hey, don't get maudlin on me. We're looking to the future here. One day at a time, remember?"

"How d'you get so wise?"

"That trait I'm sure I got from my mother."

I grabbed her in a headlock and tousled her hair, just like when she was a kid.

32

Hallie really wanted to find out everything about me, so I told her. When I was sure I was being totally boring, going on and on talking about myself, she pressed me for more. It wasn't until she began telling me about herself that I understood. Her history with men was, in a word, tragic. Her grilling me was a defense mechanism; she didn't want to go through another heartache.

For context—and also to help explain the act I ultimately took—let me recount the history of Hallie's life, as best as I can recall it.

Hallie Siebert was born on April 8, 1923, in a hospital in Yonkers, New York, the daughter of Armand and Marilyn Siebert. She was the fifth of six children. The Sieberts lived in Yonkers until Hallie was six years old when the family moved to Rhinebeck. Armand was in the construction trade and he tired of working for someone else, so he set up his own business in Rhinebeck. Besides overseeing construction projects throughout the region, Armand Siebert began building a house for his family on the outskirts of town. The Sieberts rented a house in the middle of town while Mr. Siebert built their new home.

Although Armand had two teenaged sons to help him build the house, Hallie would rush to the construction site to help. Marilyn Siebert was terrified that her daughter would get hurt, but Armand was very careful. He gave her specific assignments that made her feel involved and helpful, but he kept her away from the actual hammering and sawing and other activities that could expose her to danger.

During this time, Hallie got especially close to her oldest brother, Armand, Jr. Despite a twelve year difference in age, they had an especially strong rapport.

He took her under his wing and taught her many carpentry skills. He could coax the best out of a piece of wood, an ability he passed on to her.

When she wasn't in school or working at the house site, she was learning guitar from her sister, Allison, and learning to cook from her mother. How she found time for everything was anyone's guess.

During the Great Depression, the Sieberts could withstand the downturn. There wasn't as much building as before, but there was enough to put food on the table. Hallie entered high school and was a fine student. She was also turning into a fine, attractive young woman who could have her pick of any boy she wanted.

There was one boy, Alan Parker, whom she had known since second grade when she moved to town. His family belonged to the same church and attended many of the same functions the Sieberts did. Marilyn had become very fond of the boy. Even though the Parkers had little in the way of money, she not-so-secretly wished that Hallie and he would become involved. Marilyn could see how infatuated Alan had become with her daughter. Marilyn would observe how Alan couldn't take his eyes off of Hallie when she sang in choir. Marilyn wished her daughter would notice it, too. He would be a perfect match for her daughter.

Hallie had often told her mother that the one thing she wanted in life was a marriage like her parents. Marilyn and Armand had been classmates in high school, and it was practically love at first sight. Six kids later, they were still the apple of each other's eye. That's what Hallie wanted, and Marilyn believed Alan would make that wish come true.

One day the phone rang and, when Marilyn answered it, it was Alan asking to speak with Hallie. She handed the phone over and crossed her fingers as she left the room to give her daughter some privacy. A few minutes later, Hallie emerged. "Well?" Marilyn asked. "That was Alan. He asked me if I wanted to go out on Friday. I told him I had to babysit." "You didn't offer him another time or give him any encouragement?" "No, why should I?" was Hallie's response as she went up to her room. Marilyn could only sigh as she looked at her daughter's back as she went up the stairs. Marilyn knew how painfully shy Alan was. It had taken everything in his being to screw up his courage to make that call; it probably wouldn't happen again.

A few weeks later Hallie started dating Michael Monson. Michael was one of the most popular boys in school. He was captain of the basketball team. He was a top student. His family owned and operated the local Chrysler-Plymouth dealership. He was a nice, polite kid. Marilyn should have been ecstatic for her daughter landing such a catch, but she wasn't. She hoped for the best, but wasn't entirely optimistic about the ultimate prospects. For one thing, everyone suspected his father to be a philanderer, and kids learned by example. She so wanted to be wrong, but she had a feeling the match would not last. Since Hallie seemed so happy, Marilyn was reluctant to say anything.

Hallie and Mike had been going out for a few months when she came home from a dance one Friday night. Marilyn and Armand were in the living room listening to the radio when Hallie walked in.

"Hi honey," Marilyn called out. "How was the dance?"

"It was good. They had a great band this time. You know what happened? Alan Parker asked me to dance. What a jerk! He knows Mike and I are going steady. I danced with him to be polite, but still."

Marilyn was about to berate her daughter, but then thought better of it. She just remained silent as Hallie went up to bed.

Mike was ahead of Hallie by one year. When he got accepted at New York University, Hallie was sad he was going to be away, but she said she would also apply to NYU. They'd see each other during school breaks and then in a year, they'd be together full-time. Hallie could hardly wait for her senior year to finish. During the year, she applied to NYU and was accepted. She would start in the fall of 1941.

Three months into her starting college, Mike told her he was seeing someone else. He hadn't meant for it to happen. It just did. He was sorry and the last thing he ever wanted to do was to hurt her. After he departed, she broke down in tears. She called home. Even though she knew her mother had a feeling the relationship would end this way, Hallie knew she wouldn't get an 'I told you so'. Her mother would say all the right, comforting things.

Hallie was in the common room of her dorm ostensibly studying, but what she was doing was sitting there feeling sorry for herself. At one point, a tear rolled down her cheek. A young man on the other side of the room noticed the tear and came over to see if she was alright. He assumed she had gotten the news about the bombing of Pearl Harbor. She responded that she hadn't had the news on all day. Neither had she spoken with anybody because she was so depressed. She told him about splitting up with Mike and he told her he had recently broken up with his girlfriend. He sat down and they talked into the night.

His name was Sam Madigan. He was an engineering student with hopes of someday becoming an architect. He came from the upstate New York town of Coxsackie. Hallie exclaimed that she was from Rhinebeck, just south of there. Sam said he played basketball against Rhinebeck a few years back. The more they talked, the more they discovered they had in common. They started dating.

Hallie was fully aware of how perilous it could be to go with someone on the rebound, a time when she's most vulnerable. Being with Sam felt so right, though. She chalked them hooking up as fate. It was meant to be. Within six months they realized they were in love and wanted to get married. They had hoped to wait until after they graduated before they married, but it was wartime and everything was accelerated. Both her brothers had enlisted, and they were waiting for their call-up. Sam had been declared eligible for the draft but had not yet received the call to report.

The wedding took place in a vast park in the Adirondacks. It was a beautiful spot amongst thousands of pine trees. Hallie and Marilyn sent a general invitation to all the church congregation. Hallie observed that Mr. and Mrs. Parker attended, but Alan was not there. She knew he was in town, so she was a little hurt he did not come. She considered him a friend. When she mentioned her thoughts to her mother, Marilyn responded, "You know, you can be rather dense sometimes."

Sam had landed a job with an architectural firm in New Rochelle, so that's where they rented a house with plans to purchase a house of their own once they saved enough money. Hallie got a job working in a bank to bring in some extra money. Six months after getting married, Hallie announced that she was expecting her first child. Her goal of having one man to love her for her entire life may no longer be achievable, but in a matter of months, she would have a baby. That would take care of everything.

In her eighth month, she started feeling pain. She initially passed it off as normal, but the pain only got worse. Finally, she was so doubled over that Sam drove her to the hospital. The doctor determined that the fetus was in trouble. He rushed Hallie into surgery for an emergency Caesarian delivery. It was too late. The baby was stillborn. Moreover, Hallie and Sam were advised that there was significant damage to her uterus. She may never be able to have children again.

Three days later, Sam drove a despondent Hallie home. She asked God what she did to deserve this fate. She got no answer.

32

Hallie stayed home from work for over a month. Her mother watched over her for one week and two of her sisters for two other weeks. Hallie could barely bring herself to even get out of bed. Sam would leave early in the morning and return later and later each night. He said that work was very busy, but Hallie suspected he did not want to be around her. Her mother and sisters agreed.

Hallie needed to start living again. She would go back to work. The bank had been very understanding, but they were asking when she thought she'd return. She appreciated their flexibility but understood their increasing impatience. They had work that needed to be done. If she could not do it, they had a right to bring in someone who could.

She got out of bed that day when Sam did. She showered, got dressed, had her coffee, kissed Sam and headed off to the bank. It felt good to be back doing something productive again. She reacquainted herself with her coworkers and got to see some of her regular customers. She put in a full day and felt exhausted but exhilarated.

When she walked in the kitchen, an envelope with her name scribbled on the front was on the kitchen table. Recognizing Sam's handwriting, she opened it and started reading the letter inside. Her attitude of curiosity changed to one of horror and outrage. It read:

My dearest Hallie,

I write this in sadness and sorrow. The last thing I would ever want to do is to hurt you, especially during this time when you have been so vulnerable. Now that you're healthy again, I have to tell you this bitter truth. To continue on like we have will only perpetuate a lie, and that's not healthy for either of us. I know how deeply wounded you were when we lost our child. I was likewise deeply wounded, but I don't think I can continue on in our marriage if I cannot have an offspring. Again, I am truly sorry. I will be in touch regarding our separation.

With love,

Sam

"With love?" she screamed, "with love?" She fell to the floor, not knowing if she could go on. She had no idea how long she laid there. Eventually, she pulled herself up and went to the phone. She dialed and her mother answered. Marilyn could hardly understand what her daughter was saying, but her daughter was in trouble. Marilyn told Hallie to stay where she was; they'd be there as soon as they could. Marilyn called Armand. He dropped what he was doing, and they made the two hour trip from Rhinebeck to New Rochelle. They walked in the kitchen and found Hallie where she had been since she called, sitting in a chair, staring off into space.

Armand got down on his knees in front of his daughter and looked into her face. "Honey, what's wrong?"

Hallie lifelessly handed Sam's note over to him. Armand and Marilyn read the note together.

"Why that bastard! If I ever get my hands on him!"

Marilyn gently put her hand on Armand's shoulder. While she agreed with her husband, Hallie didn't need that right now. Armand understood and bent down to give her daughter a big hug. While Marilyn stayed with her, Armand went to Hallie's bedroom and filled a suitcase with clothes and other necessities. They then led her out to the car and made the trip back to Rhinebeck.

Armand made a couple of trips back to New Rochelle to retrieve the rest of Hallie's belongings. On his last trip, Sam was there. Armand used all the self-control he could muster not to carry out his original threat. As he was exiting the house, Sam called out to him. "Tell Hallie I'm sorry," he said. Without even turning to acknowledge him, Armand replied, "You pathetic asshole."

Over the next couple of weeks, being in familiar surroundings and under the watchful care of her mother and the occasional sister who could get away from their family responsibilities, Hallie improved. She appeared to be getting her old spark back, but then one day two telegrams arrived in one day.

The first was not unexpected. It was a message from a lawyer Sam had retained advising her that Sam was proceeding with the divorce. There would be additional correspondences and meetings in the near future. It was not unexpected, but it still dealt a blow to Hallie as she read this on paper. Still, she held on, though, but her stability didn't last.

The coup de grâce came two hours later. It was from the Department of the Navy and addressed to Mr. and Mrs. Armand Siebert. It read:

Dear Mr. and Mrs. Siebert:

We regret to inform you that on Monday, November 22, 1943, your son, Sgt. Armand Edward Siebert, Jr., was killed in action on the island of Tarawa in the Gilbert Islands in the South Pacific.

Sgt. Siebert was killed by Japanese gunfire in the course of an intense battle during which your son was rescuing his wounded men. He had already evacuated two wounded soldiers and was mortally wounded while evacuating a third. You can be very proud of your son and his heroism.

Our deepest condolences on your loss.

Sincerely,

Rear Adm. Alvin Escot

Marilyn screamed and burst into uncontrollable sobbing. Armand maintained his usual stoic demeanor while fighting back tears. Hallie ran into the kitchen, asking what was wrong. Armand sat her down and gently told her the news. Hallie gasped, but she didn't cry. Instead, she closed down completely. The cumulative impact of everything that had happened finally caught up to her.

She neither said anything nor ate or drank anything for days. Unable to get her to do anything for herself, Marilyn and Armand became concerned about her survival, never mind her mental condition. They took her to the hospital. After an initial evaluation finding nothing physically wrong with her, they recommended placing her in a mental rehabilitation ward where she could get the therapy she needed. Her parents reluctantly agreed.

Hallie wouldn't talk or even interact with anyone. A therapist came in to meet with her twice a week, but it was always the same. The therapist would carry on a monologue for a half-hour and then leave.

She was in the ward for three days when one of the staff, a young man who was a physical therapist, walked by her room and looked in to see her sitting in a chair, staring off into space. She wasn't a patient of his, so he had no excuse to come into her room. Whether he was attracted by her beauty or took pity on her condition or some other reason, he walked in to speak with her. Similar to the therapist, she wouldn't respond. The man smiled and said he'd be back the following day. Just before exiting the room he turned around and said, "What did the duck say when she bought a lipstick? Put it on my bill!" He got no response.

Every day after that, he'd stop by. He'd chat a little and then leave, but before leaving he'd tell her a joke, usually a bad joke. His repertoire of bad jokes was endless. "What do you give to a sick lemon? Lemon aid!" "When's the best time to go to the dentist? Tooth-hurtie!" "Why do seagulls fly over the sea? Because if they flew over the bay, they're bagels!" "What kind of dogs love car racing? Lap dogs!" He often laughed at his own jokes, but Hallie never reacted.

Despite her lack of response, he was undeterred. He did this every day for three weeks. He even came in just to go to her room on his days off. Then, on the Saturday as she started the third week of her therapy, he was leaving the room and he turned around. "Why do mice have such small balls? Because only ten percent of them know how to dance." As he headed to the door, he heard what sounded like a laugh. He turned around one more time and Hallie was looking up at him. "What's your name?" she asked.

"Joshua James."

The alliteration of his name struck her funny as she burst into full laughter.

"Hey, I didn't choose it. Blame my parents."

She continued laughing. Her laughter was contagious as he joined in.

"You're beautiful, but you're especially beautiful when you laugh. I must do my best to keep you laughing."

"And you think your jokes will do it?"

He just smiled in return.

Three days later, the hospital released Hallie. Marilyn and Armand were in her room, gathering her stuff and sitting her in the wheelchair when Josh walked in.

"Mom, Dad, this is Joshua. He saved me when nobody else could."

Armand walked over to Josh and extended his hand. "Thank you, son, for giving us our daughter back. We'll forever be in your debt."

Josh became a regular at the Siebert household. He had a knack for showing up just when Hallie showed signs that she might slip into her despondency. He'd talk with her and any observer could literally see her anxiety evaporate away. Soon she'd be laughing and carrying on like the Hallie of old.

One time Josh was over and he and Hallie were in the family room. Marilyn was in the kitchen preparing dinner and could hear them laughing and carrying on. A minute later, everything was quiet. Marilyn knew full well what was going on and smiled. She knew that all you had to do was spend ten minutes with Josh and you could tell he was no Sam. He was a good man who would stand by Hallie through anything.

As they got serious about each other, Hallie knew she had to be upfront with Josh.

"Josh, I have to let you know that I can't have children. I had a stillborn child a few years ago and there was damage to my insides. I just thought you should know before we get more involved."

He just shrugged. "I'm child enough for any family. What thrilled me just now was you talking about 'getting more involved' with me. Getting involved with you was my intention from the first moment I looked into your room and saw you sitting there. I don't know about you, but my plan for the rest of my life is to be involved with you. I was hoping you'd have similar intentions, but I didn't want to push you too hard."

Three months later, Hallie and Josh were married in an intimate service at the church. The speed with which they married was similar to Hallie's and Sam's engagement, but this one was far different. This marriage was meant to be. When she had mentioned about Josh being her stable rock who would provide her refuge when she was adrift in a sea of anxiety, she wasn't kidding. He was her rock; he would remain so for the next fifteen years.

Then, one day Josh came home from work early because he was experiencing excruciating stomach pains. He tried taking an antacid, but that did nothing. The pain only increased exponentially. They went to the doctor and he came back with the diagnosis they most dreaded. He had cancer. The doctors predicted he had only months to live.

True to form, Josh was the rock. He sat down with Hallie and took both her hands. "You can't let yourself go when I'm gone. You have to live for both of us. I've had the best fifteen years any man could ever imagine. I want you to remember all the great times we had, not the fact that I'm gone. I'll never leave you, not really. I want you to promise me that you'll never despair. In case you do." Josh reached into a bag he had by his side and pulled out a book, which he handed to her.

She read the title out loud. "*Really Bad Jokes That Are Really Very Funny.*" She laughed. "I thought you wanted me to think of you. Shouldn't it be *Really Bad Jokes That Aren't Really Very Funny?*"

Josh laughed, but that made him double over in pain. The pain subsided and he sat back up. "I want you to miss me, of course, but I want you to move on. Keep living your life. Keep doing your music. Look to date again. Don't close down. Promise me."

"Oh, Josh. You saved me once. Now you're looking to save me again. How can I go on without you?"

"You will. Promise me."

"I promise."

33

"Now that you know how damaged I am, I'd understand if you want nothing to do with me."

"Damaged? You're amazing! The first image I have of you is singing and playing your guitar. After all you've been through in your life, you still can sing? If that isn't amazing, I don't know what is."

"Thank you for that, Joe."

"You still have the book of bad jokes?"

She rummaged through her bag and pulled it out. It was pretty worn from obvious use in the ten years since Josh passed away. She handed it over to me. I leafed through it casually. "I like this one: *My new thesaurus is terrible. Not only that, but it's also terrible.*" I handed it back to her as we both moaned.

"Hallie, what you said about Josh saving you, you did that for me. I was in mourning for twenty years. It wasn't until I met you that it became obvious to me how much of a fool I've been. Olivia didn't have a chance to have the same conversation with me before she died that Josh had with you, but she would have told me the same thing. If she came back today, she'd be so disappointed in me for wasting all those years. Thank you for bringing me back and for being my rock."

We held each other for a long time. I know I was crying tears of joy. I sensed she was doing the same.

We talked more about our stories over the next few days. I never felt so free about confiding in somebody as I did her.

"What ever happened to Alan?"

"He lives down in Yonkers."

"Yonkers? Isn't that where you were born?"

"Yeah, weird, isn't it? I see his sister around town occasionally and she fills me in on him. He's okay, but from what I understand, he's not in a permanent relationship. He had a girlfriend for many years, but they never married."

"What's he do?"

"You won't believe this. He sells cars. He works at the Chrysler-Plymouth dealership in Yonkers. I think he's a manager there. He should have retired by now, but I guess he's pretty good at his job because they still keep him around at his age. His sister says he's married to the job. That's his life. It's funny, I always saw him going further in his life."

"Yeah, car salesmen are a lower life form. Gee, thanks."

"Oops, I didn't mean it that way. I just saw him more as a doctor or lawyer with a wife and kids and picket fence."

"You ever regret blowing him off when he called to ask you for a date?"

"Yeah, I actually do. I really hurt him. I don't think he ever got over it. Looking back on this and many other things, I often marvel at how right my mother was on so many things. She kept pushing me to give him a chance, but I was too stubborn. I was easily taken in by charm and money. As a result, I ended up being hurt by Mike and then Sam. Who knows? It's all water under the bridge, isn't it? I'm just thankful that I'm in the place I am now because of Josh and now you."

We moved in together to make our relationship official. We talked about getting married, but neither of us felt a burning desire to rush into it. My kids and grandkids were all comfortable with Hallie, and I thought they were growing to love her. Hallie's music captivated the grandkids. She'd sit in the middle of the living room and start strumming her guitar. The kids would hear the music and then start gravitating towards her. They'd be mesmerized as she started singing. Just like when she sang at the tavern and at church, she could appear like she's singing just to you, even in a packed crowd.

Both Oscar and Sally and their respective children were visiting one time. There were five kids in all, ranging from five to twelve years old. It was raining, so everyone was in the house. The place was joyous bedlam with the kids running all over. At one point, I was wrestling with the three youngest. For an old guy, I wasn't doing badly.

They were getting a bit out of control. I didn't want the parents to come down hard on them and ruin their fun. They were just being kids. I thought maybe it might be time for Hallie to work her musical magic to reel them back in. I looked for her around the house, but I couldn't find her. I looked up in our bedroom, in the study, everywhere. I thought maybe she stepped outside for a breath of fresh air, but I didn't see her. I finally went into the garage and there she was, sitting in the car. She was looking through her joke book. It was obvious she'd been crying. I climbed into the passenger seat beside her.

"Hi, hon. Noise getting to you in there?"

"No, that's not it."

I said nothing. I figured she'd tell me in her own time and in her own way.

"I saw you wrestling with the kids and I realized I'd never have that. Don't get me wrong; I love your kids. They're a joy. But I grew up in a large family with loving parents. Growing up, I wanted to recreate that, what do you call it, joyful bedlam. I was robbed of that. You and your family do a wonderful job of giving me a taste of it, but it's just not mine. It's a woman thing, I guess. I'm sorry. I don't want to ruin your party."

"There's nothing to apologize for. You could never ruin anything. Your welfare is paramount to me."

"I know that. You go back in. I'll just be a little longer."

"You better. Things are deteriorating in there. We need your music and we need it quick."

She squeezed my hand. "I love you," she said.

"I love you, too."

I left her as I went back inside. I went back to playing with the kids, but my thoughts were definitely elsewhere.

My mind was in Yonkers.

34

Over the next month, I rolled our garage conversation around and around in my mind. I knew there was something I could do to help Hallie, but should I? I was selfish; I did not want to lose her. She meant the world to me. But if I loved her as much as I said I did, I should be willing to give her up if it meant she'd get a lifetime of happiness. Then again, I was only guessing that I would give her happiness. What if my actions gave her the same sadness and heartache she'd known, but then her alternative path wouldn't match her up with Josh? Who would be there to bring her back from the brink? But, perhaps she could have a life with children and grandchildren of her own. She could have a husband who would love her unconditionally throughout her life. Weren't these the unclaimed dreams she always professed to have?

Perhaps I was misreading what could happen. Maybe she and Alan wouldn't hit it off and she'd move on to Mike, anyway. Perhaps she and Alan would hit it off, get married but then get divorced in a few years. I could only control the Correction, the one change, but I couldn't control any subsequent events that happened after the Correction.

Something in me—and something in my family's history of performing Corrections—told me this was the right thing to do. Hallie always talked about her parents being high school sweethearts that she wanted to emulate. She really thought she could get that with Mike and then, when he didn't pan out, with Sam. By the time Josh came around, the dream had been totally extinguished. Luckily, he was the rock that she could grab onto in her storm.

After a month of wracking my brain, I was still up in the air. I needed some research, some additional data. I did not want to make an uninformed decision.

The next day I made a call to Sampson's Chrysler/Plymouth in Yonkers. "Hello, I'd like to speak to Alan Parker. He's not in? Does he work on Wednesday? He does. I'm in the market for a car and a friend of mine said Alan's the guy to see. I was wondering if I'd be able to make an appointment to see him Wednesday afternoon? You'd be able to help me with that? That would be wonderful. Would three-thirty work? Great. My name is Joseph Vance. And your name is? Abby, well thank you very much, Abby. You've been most kind. I'll see you on Wednesday."

I chose Wednesday because Hallie sang at the tavern on that day. I'd tell her one of my old colleagues from my Askin's Oldsmobile days called me and wanted to get together to reminisce. He lived in the City so we'd meet halfway at a bar near West Point. She always arrived at the tavern by four-thirty to set up. Because of the timing of my get-together, she wouldn't be tempted to want to join me. I told her I'd only be gone a few hours, so I'd be back in plenty of time to catch most of her show. I hated lying to her, but I was meeting with a person from a car dealership, so I could rationalize that I was only telling her a white lie.

I walked into the dealership and told the receptionist I had an appointment with Alan Parker. She walked me back to his office. Walking along past the cars, past the rows of desks with dealers, to the fully windowed office brought back a flood of memories. Man, I was a good car salesman.

Alan got up to greet me. He wasn't what I had expected. Hallie had always described him as tall and thin, but this man was pudgy. No, he was obese. His face was jowly, but at least it sat below a mane of thick gray hair. I imagined he wasn't bad looking when he was younger but he had let himself go over the years.

I looked around the office. There were no pictures of a spouse or children. The office was devoid of any personal touches except for a guitar sitting on a stand similar to the one that held Hallie's guitar at the tavern.

"Mr. Vance, it's a pleasure."

"It's my pleasure. I'm an old car salesman myself. Oldsmobiles. I've been out of the game for a while though."

"We have some nice Chryslers that might help you forget those Oldsmobiles."

"I don't know about that, but I'm always willing for to you to convince me." I looked around his office. "No pics of your wife and kids?"

"I'm in between women at this point and no kids, I'm afraid."

"How long have you played guitar?"

"Since I was eight. I play it at lunch break, sometimes off in a corner of the lot, sometimes in our breakroom, if my co-workers ask me to."

"Do they often ask you?"

"All the time. I guess I'm not too bad. I hate to be rude, but I have another appointment in a half hour. How can I help you?"

"I'm interested in a reliable, affordable car. I'd heard good things about the Reliant."

"Oh, it's one of our best-selling models, and deservedly so."

He rattled off all the features of the Reliant. Going back to Olivia's line about 'if I were going to buy a car, the salesman should know his product', this man obviously knew his product. In my book, that was a mark in his favor.

He walked me out to the lot to look at a Reliant for me to see and perhaps test-drive. As we walked along he said, "My assistant said that a friend referred you to me. May I ask who that friend is? Just curious, that's all."

"Hallie Siebert."

He stopped in his tracks. "Hallie? How is she? She's alright, isn't she?"

In that one moment, he told me everything I needed to know. His eyes told me everything I needed to know. The man still loved her after all these years.

"Wait a minute," he added. "Why did you refer to her by her maiden name? She hasn't been Siebert in well over thirty years. Her name is James now."

Every word out of his mouth advanced his cause without him even knowing it.

"Why did you say Hallie Siebert?" he repeated.

"If I told you, you wouldn't believe me."

"Try me." He was getting defiant.

"Let me just say that I'm a man of second chances. I assure you that Hallie is fine and will remain fine. I love her, but I'm not the man for her. You are. Don't blow this. Be devoted to her. That's what she deserves."

I turned and walked away. He called after me. "What are you talking about? Are you crazy? You better not harm Hallie!"

I turned around.

"I'd never dream of hurting her. Be sure to tell her you play guitar on your date. I think it will seal the deal."

He called after me, but I walked on. I got in my car and hurried back to Rhinebeck. I fully expected Alan to call Hallie to tell her about our conversation. He'd call to warn her about me, that I was insane. The thing I had in my favor was that Hallie had moved in with me and we shared my phone. She wasn't listed. He'd have to work through his sister who, as far I knew, didn't have our number. By the time either of them tracked her down, she'd be at the tavern setting up.

He would eventually track her down. I knew he would. He'd do everything in his power to protect her, which further affirmed that I was doing the right thing. I just had to get to Hallie before he did. I could never explain why I went to see him or why I lied to her.

I arrived at the tavern just as she was starting her first set. She smiled sweetly as I walked in. I went over to my usual seat. Before I sat down, Marco handed me my usual beer. I settled back to hear Hallie sing, perhaps for the last time. She was in the middle of *Blowing in the Wind* when I sat down. Then she launched into a spirited version of *Thirsty Boots*.

After she finished that song, she spoke into the microphone, but she looked directly at me. "I'm going to do one more song before I take a break. I'm going to stray from my usual fare of folk songs to do an old standard, but let me explain where this song is coming from. I have needed saving a couple times in my life. Luckily, I've had good men—and I mean really, really good men—willing to save me, to bring me back from the abyss. I want to dedicate this song to one of those men, Joe Vance. I love you so much, Joe."

She put her guitar down and sang this song *a cappella*. Her beautiful voice filled the tavern as she sang George and Ira Gershwin's *Someone to Watch Over Me*.

There's a somebody I'm longing to see
I hope that she turns out to be
Someone who'll watch over me
I'm a little lamb who's lost in the wood
I know I could always be good
To one who'll watch over me

Although I may not be the man some
Girls think of as handsome
To her heart I'll carry the key
Won't you tell her please to put on some speed
Follow my lead, oh, how I need
Someone to watch over me.

By the time she finished, I was bawling. She was making what I had to do very hard, but I was undeterred. I loved her so much that I had to give her up.

She finished the song and came over to me. "You know, you breaking down like that made it difficult for me to finish the song."

"You soldiered through it, though. I'd expect no less."

She smiled at me.

"I love you."

"I love you, too."

We talked about our days. I told her about how much weight my friend had gained. We had a nice get together. I was glad I hooked up with him. She mentioned a few things she had done. Then she told me that, as she was leaving the house, the phone rang. She was in a hurry so she let the answering machine take it. In case I was calling, however, she hung around long enough to listen to the message. It was Kathy Gaines, Alan's sister, who said she got a weird call from Alan and needed to talk. Hallie figured she'd call her back in the morning.

"Hallie, do you wish you had gone on that date with Alan?"

"We went over this, didn't we? Yeah, I wish I did."

"I need you to say it."

"Say what?"

"Say that you wish you went on that date with Alan when he called?"

"You're acting very strange. I have to go on for my next set."

"Just humor me. Say it."

"Okay. I wish that when Alan called me for a date, I said yes."

I reached over and put my hand on her shoulder. I blacked out for a second. When I came to, I was in my house. I looked around. All traces of Hallie were gone. I put my head in my hands and sobbed.

35

The following Sunday was my birthday. Both Oscar and Sally were bringing their respective families over in the afternoon to celebrate. It promised to be another rambunctious day. I acutely missed Hallie, so I was looking forward to a houseful of kids to distract me. I had asked Sally to come by an hour earlier than Oscar. There was something private I needed to discuss with her.

Sally thought she would surprise me by coming even earlier than I asked. She would come alone with Jeff and the kids arriving later. She thought she'd spring a surprise by meeting me at church where we could hear Hallie sing. As she was walking up the church steps she could hear Hallie singing and playing her guitar, but there was another guitar playing with her.

She entered the sanctuary and saw Hallie and a tall, thin man with a shock of gray hair on his head playing and singing. The two musicians sounded perfect together. He was dressed like he was the minister, but this was a different minister than the one who there the last time she attended a service a couple months ago.

Sally looked around for me. Seeing that I wasn't there, she chose a seat in the pew near where we sat the times she came with me. There was a young couple around her age with two young kids, a boy and a girl, in the front pew right in front of her. They all seemed enraptured by the music.

Sally kept looking around for me, but I never arrived. She knew I attended every Sunday, leastwise every Sunday that Hallie was singing. Maybe I wasn't feeling well, but wouldn't I have called to tell her not to come today if I were sick? She was somewhat concerned but not overly worried. There was probably a very logical explanation. She'd sit through the service and then hook up with Hallie and they'd come to the house together.

After Hallie and the man finished singing, he gave her a kiss before he headed up to the pulpit. It was a kiss that was appropriate for the place and occasion, but it was still on the lips, which Sally found strange. She may have thought the kiss odd given that Hallie was in a relationship with her father, but she found the next series of events even odder.

Instead of going to sit with the choir, Hallie went to sit with the young couple and the kids in the front pew. As she approached, the kids squealed "Hi Nanna!" Hallie put a finger to her lips but was smiling and obviously didn't mind the reaction. The congregation laughed, and then Hallie kissed both the kids and sat between them. She would remain there until she joined the choir to sing the anthem. After the anthem, Hallie returned to the kids.

Sally was extremely confused. Hi Nanna? Dad had said she couldn't have kids. What was going on? She looked at the bulletin and saw the name listed was Hallie Parker, not Hallie James. She also noticed that the minister's name was Alan Parker. What on earth was going on?

After the service was completed, Hallie had just finished chatting with a few parishioners when Sally walked up to her. Hallie extended her hand in welcome.

"Good morning, I don't recall seeing you here before. Welcome to our church. We hope you will be a regular here."

"Excuse me, but aren't you Hallie James?"

"My name's Hallie, but my last name has been Parker for over thirty years now. Before that it was Siebert. I'm afraid you must have me mixed up with someone else."

"Do you know Joseph Vance?"

"I don't think so. The name doesn't ring a bell. I'm sorry."

"Are those your grandkids?"

"Two of them, anyway. That's my son Armand and his wife Eva."

"Those kids are adorable."

"Thank you. They're a handful, but so worth it."

"I hear you. I have two kids around their age. Anyway, I have to go now. It was nice talking to you."

"You're always welcome whenever you like. Bring Mr. Vance with you."

"I will. Goodbye."

Sally headed straight over to my house. She found me sitting in the kitchen sipping a cup of coffee.

"Dad, I just came from the church. I don't know what her deal is, but I don't think Hallie's been truthful to you. She has a husband. He's the new minister at the church. She has kids and grandchildren. I spoke to her after the service. She claims to have never met you. I assume you know all this, and that's why you weren't at the service. I wish you had told me so I wouldn't have made a fool of myself."

"I didn't think about you going to the church, nor did I know that Hallie would still be with the church. I thought you'd come here, and that's why I wanted you to come an hour before Oscar. Pour yourself some coffee and sit down. I have something to explain to you. It's going to be unbelievable and will take some time."

Sally looked utterly confused and somewhat defiant, but she complied with my request.

"Before we begin, I have a couple questions. First, did Hallie look happy?"

"Yes, extremely happy. She absolutely glowed when she was with her grandchildren, that was when she was at her happiest. I hate to say this, but whenever I saw her with you, she looked happy, but there was an underlying sorrow about her. It was like she was world weary. I'm sorry, Dad. I'm just giving you my honest opinion of what I saw."

"No apologies are necessary. In fact, what you just told me makes me deliriously happy. The second question I have is, you said she married a minister. What's his name?"

"Parker, Reverend Alan Parker."

"What did he look like?"

"He was tall and thin. He had a mane of grey hair on his head."

"The hair sounds the same, but when I saw him last week, he was a plump car salesman. Happiness and love did wonders for him. How did Hallie look?"

"Great. Her hair had more style than the last time I saw her and she lost some weight."

"This is all exceeding my wildest dreams."

"Dad, what the hell is going on? Are you happy the woman with whom you've fallen in love is with another man?"

"Yes, I am. It's because I love her I'm so happy."

"Can you start explaining? I'm totally lost and, quite frankly, I'm afraid you're losing it."

I sighed. There was no way but to dive right in.

"Sal, I have a special gift, a power, that's been handed down from generation to generation. You have this gift, too. That's what I wanted to talk to you about today. I thought I'd be able to break it to you slowly and gently to reduce the shock, but now that you've run into Hallie, I better get to the point."

"Which you're not doing. What power do we have?"

"We call it The Correction. We can allow people to go back and reverse or change a decision they made in their lives."

"You're kidding, right?"

"No, I'm not kidding."

"How do you do it?"

"Someone says they wish they did something instead of what they actually did. I put my hand on his or her shoulder and the person corrects the past. After that, they lead their normal life, which may or may not be changed by the altered decision. We pick the person up again in the present, but they will have lived the new life. They'll have no memory of the previous life. Neither will anyone else. The only people who are aware of both realities are those with the power to perform Corrections, namely you and me. She doesn't realize it yet, but Hannah has the power, too."

"I believe that you believe this, Dad, but I'm having trouble wrapping my head around this."

"That's exactly what your mother told me when I told her about Corrections, although I doubt that 'wrapping one's head around something' was an expression of her day. Hold on one second." I got up and went into my study. When I came back, I was carrying a shoebox. I put the box between us on the table and opened it up. It contained at least a hundred pieces of paper.

"What are these?"

"Betting slips. Growing up did you ever wonder why I never had to work? Before your mother passed, I used to be a very hard worker. I sold encyclopedias for years and then I sold cars. I was good at both. After your mother died, I was so down on life that I used my power for my gain. It's strictly against the rules, but I didn't care. What you have here are winning betting stubs. I'd go to the racetrack, I'd bet ten thousand dollars on a bunch of races, and I'd lose it all. The next day, I'd look up the winning horses and make a wish that I bet on them instead. I'd touch my shoulder and the next thing I knew, our bank account had fifty to eighty thousand more dollars in it. I was winning so often that the police visited me, so I changed targets. I'd buy lottery tickets and the next day I'd look up the winning numbers and play those. One lottery, I won over three million dollars. Look through these. Nobody is that lucky. I wouldn't know the front end of a horse from its ass. It's not the proudest time of my life, but I did what I had to do."

Sally leafed through the box, looking at all the winnings. It was amazing. While not ironclad proof, the box gave ample evidence of what I was talking about. Sally had to admit that the odds of winning that much and that often were impossible.

"What happened with Hallie?"

"She and your mother are the two most amazing women I ever knew and loved. Hallie's life was one tragedy after another, but she had such strength she could come through it. If she had stayed with me, those tragedies would have scarred the rest of her days. I had it in my power to erase a lot of that tragedy away. I knew I would lose her by doing a Correction, but I could never say I truly loved her if I selfishly held on to her instead of helping her. What I did was to allow her to go back and say yes to the man she's now with, the minister, when he asked her for a date. They obviously hit it off."

"But now you're alone."

"Not really. Hallie saved me. She gave me my will to live back. For twenty years since your mother died, I wasn't living. Now I am, and I'll always be grateful to Hallie for that. I remember seeing one of those joke signs that read: 'Some people live alone and like it. Other people live alone and look it.' Before Hallie, I was the type who looked it. Now, I live alone and like it.

"I have no regrets she has no memory of me. That comes with the territory. I do regret that she has no memories of her second husband, Josh. It sounds like he was a wonderful man. If it weren't for him, she may have been dead long before I met her. Unfortunately, he died of cancer. Another one of her tragedies."

"You say I have this power?"

"Yes, I'll help you do something easy to get used to it. My first Correction was a neighbor who had backed over his son's bicycle. I got him to wish he hadn't backed the car out that day and, voila, it happened. We'll find an easy one for you."

"Can Oscar do these, what did you call them, Corrections?"

"No." I had to figure out how to phrase the next thing I said. "What I'm about to tell you can never get back to your brother. Promise me."

"I promise."

"The gift has been around for eight-hundred years and has been passed down generation-to-generation through the first-born child."

"Now I'm really confused. Isn't Oscar first-born?"

"I'm not Oscar's biological parent."

"You're not his father?"

"Oh, yes, I am one hundred percent his father! Just because I didn't contribute any DNA doesn't mean I'm not his father!"

The vehemence with which I made this statement startled Sally and even frightened her a little.

"I'm sorry. I didn't mean to scare you. Your mother was raped and Oscar was the result. As far as I'm concerned, and as far as Oscar is concerned, I'm his father."

"Yes, you are, Dad. I'll never tell. I promise."

"I know you won't. I look into your eyes and I see your mother. She was such a fine woman, and she passed that on to you. She was such an honest woman. If she told you something, you believed it. You have that quality. I, unfortunately, can be a bit more duplicitous. In addition to Corrections, that's something I inherited from my father."

I looked at my watch. "Oscar and everybody will be here soon. I have so much to tell you, including the reason I never told you all this before or why I haven't done real Corrections in years, but that will have to wait. Let's put on our party faces. Oh, remember that as far as Oscar is concerned right now, he has never met Hallie. I know it's confusing keeping realities straight, but you'll get used to it."

"Thanks, Dad. Oh, by the way, I have a sure tip on a horse at Saratoga on Saturday."

"Do I really have to put you in a headlock again?"

36

We had a wonderful party. Sally's husband, Jeff, arrived with their kids, Hannah and Frank. They were shortly followed by Oscar and his wife, Jen, and their three kids, Billy, Connor and Heather. The house was soon filled with joyful noise.

As I predicted to Sally, Oscar had no recollection of Hallie. He didn't wonder why she wasn't there. He didn't ask where she was or when she would arrive. At one point, I caught Sally looking at her brother. Then Oscar noticed it, too. "What?" he asked.

In true sister-brother fashion, she responded, "I was just wondering how such a jerk like you turned out to be such a nice guy."

"Good genes, I guess," was his response.

She looked over at me, "Yeah, that explains it."

Later in the afternoon, I was sitting alone. I needed the break. I'd been playing with the kids for hours. The adults were cleaning up or chatting and the kids were off playing. Hannah and Heather were playing on the floor in another room, but I could see them. They were both such beautiful girls. Hannah had short blond hair while Heather had long brown hair kept back in a ponytail.

I once asked Sally how she came by the names for her kids. She and Jeff honored their respective deceased parents with middle names, Olivia and Walter, but the first names, Hannah and Francis, were chosen at random. Sally said they liked the names. Could it be pure coincidence that they chose names that were significant in our family lore well before she knew there was a family lore? I wonder.

I was dozing off for a second when I heard footsteps. I looked up and seven-year-old Hannah was running towards me. I opened my arms and she jumped into them to give me a big hug. She then sat on my lap while we talked.

"Grampa, I had a dream last night."

"Was it a good dream?"

"It was…weird."

"Weird how?"

"This old man with a beard was there. He knew my name and Mommy's name and your name. Then he said he was my Grandpa. I told him I already had two Grandpas. I didn't think I could have any more. He said I was right, but he was a Grandpa from many, many years ago. Was he your Grandpa, Grandpa?"

"In a way, yes, he was."

"He said he was known as Grandpa Michael. He knew I was going to see you today and when I saw you I should tell you that Holly was doing well. You did a good job."

"Hallie, her name is Hallie. Do you remember her at all?"

"Is she the nice lady who used to be here?"

"Yes, she is. Hannah, I'd like you to do something for me. Think you can help me out?"

"Yes, Grandpa."

"The only people I want you to tell about Grandpa Michael and Hallie are your mommy and me. You can't tell your brother or teachers or cousins or anybody else, not even your daddy. Tell only mommy and me. It will be our little secret. Do you think you can do that?"

Her eyes widened. "We'll have a secret?"

I gave her a big hug. "Yes, we will, my darling little girl. We're going to have lots of secrets together. This is only the first."

"Okay, Grandpa."

She jumped off my lap to go play. She got two steps away when she turned around. "Grandpa Michael wanted me to tell you, welcome back. He said you would understand."

"I do, honey, I do." She ran off to play. I fondly looked after her. The Correction was going to be in excellent hands.

37

A month later, I went to church. As much as I was at peace with what I did, I put off going to see Hallie again as long as I could. It would be painful seeing her, knowing that she wasn't mine or even that I was a memory—good, bad or indifferent—for her. Going to the church would be a reminder of all that I lost, but I couldn't keep myself away. I had to see her happy. Despite Hannah's transmission of Grandpa Michael's assurances about Hallie, I had to witness it myself. It's in our nature to want to see the results of our handiwork, I guess.

I wasn't planning on talking to her or interacting with her. I just wanted to sit in the back of the church and look at her and hear her sing and play. I might not even stay the entire service once I did this.

As Sally had described, I could hear Hallie's and Alan's beautiful guitar work as I mounted the steps to the front door. I walked in and could not take my eyes off of her as I found a seat in the last pew. This would not be easy. I thought about leaving right then, but that would have been too noticeable, so I stayed.

Hallie and Alan finished their song, and they retreated to their respective spots. None of Hallie's kids or grandkids were in attendance, so she sat with choir. Alan started with an opening prayer and then invited everyone to join in the first hymn, *O for a Thousand Tongues to Sing*. We all stood as the organ gave a brief introduction. It was during the second verse that Hallie looked around the congregation and she saw me. She stopped singing. For an instant, our eyes locked. She looked back at her hymnal and resumed singing. The rest of the service she would make glances in my direction, but when I looked at her, she would look down or away.

During the organ processional as the service concluded, Alan, or rather Reverend Parker, made his way to the front door to shake hands with the congregation as they left. He invited each person to join him for coffee and pastries in the community hall at the back of the church.

If I had just seen her happy, I would have been happy, too. But the look on her face bespoke recognition, and I thought that perhaps The Correction wasn't as foolproof in wiping clean the memories as my father had taught me. The last thing on earth I ever wanted was to create doubt in Hallie's mind, to plant a seed in her mind that her life with Alan hadn't been real. I wanted to get out of there as quickly as I could before I caused any more damage.

Although I was in the last pew, departing was not to be quick or easy. The man beside me wanted to introduce himself. His name was Hank Simon. Mr. Simon was on the membership committee and I was a new face, so he pounced. I didn't want to be rude, but I had to leave. He asked if I'd like to come back for the social hour. I said yes, so he left me alone and went off to talk with someone else. Because of him, five people had lined up in front of me before I could shake Alan's hand and then freedom.

I looked out of the corner of my eye and Hallie was trying to make her way over to me, but a matronly woman that Hallie could not avoid had waylaid her. She was talking with this woman but her concentration was on me. I could feel her eyes boring into the back of my head. Finally, I got up to Alan.

"Reverend, that was a nice service."

"Are you new to our church?"

"Yes, I go by here all the time and thought I'd stop in."

"Oh, you live here in Rhinebeck? I'm glad you joined us, Mr."

"Vance, Joseph Vance."

"Would you like to join us for our social hour? We'd love to get to know you and for you to get to know us."

"I'd love to, but I can't today. Maybe some other time."

Just then, Hallie appeared at her husband's side.

"Hallie, let me introduce you to Joseph Vance. Mr. Vance, this is my wife, Hallie Parker."

"Joseph Vance? A month ago, a young woman asked me if I knew a Joseph Vance."

"That was my daughter, Sally. You have a lovely voice and your guitar work is superb."

"Thank you, Mr. Vance. I was wondering if I could have a word with you, in private?"

This was only getting worse by the moment, but there was no way I could tell her no.

"Of course, if you'd like."

She leaned over and whispered something in her husband's ear. His expression was one of disbelief as he looked over at me while hearing what Hallie.

"Why don't you go use my office."

Hallie led me through the sanctuary and into the community room in back. Hank Simon noticed me and motioned for me to join him, but I kept close on Hallie's heels as she brought me to The Reverend's office in the back. I walked in and Hallie closed the door. She motioned to me to have a seat, which I did. She sat down across from me.

"Mr. Vance, I don't know if you saw me looking at you during the service. At times, I admit I was staring at you."

"I noticed, but I took no offense."

"Have we met before?"

"Not in this lifetime, anyway."

"I'm not sure what you mean by that, but I'll take it as a no. I don't recall ever meeting you, but when I first saw you, you looked very familiar. The more I looked, the more familiar you looked. Then finally I realized where I saw you."

"I live here in town, so you probably ran into me at a store or in a restaurant."

"No, that wasn't it."

"Then where was it?"

"A dream."

"A dream?"

"A dream I've had a couple times over the past few weeks. They started shortly after I met your daughter. The dream was so real, and then when I saw you, I couldn't believe it. Can I describe this dream to you?"

"Yes, perhaps you should."

"I'm on an island. I'm playing my guitar. I can hear Alan—Reverend Parker—playing the same song, but I can't see him. He picks up the pace and I stay with him, but his playing is getting fainter and fainter until I can't hear it anymore. I hear someone call to me. It's Mike Monson, a guy I went to high school with. He's in a boat and tells me to get in. I do, and he rows away. He charms me as we talk but as time goes on, he gets nastier and then he angrily tells me to get off at the next island. I'm crying, but I get off. Another woman passes me and climbs into the boat. I'm all by myself but soon another boat shows up. The man rowing the boat says he'll rescue me and asks me to get in. I like him and I get in, but it's exactly the same thing. He kicks me off, but there's no island. He throws me into the water. I'm drowning, but then a hand reaches down to me as a third man pulls me into his boat. He brings me to another island and we both get off together. We stay on that island together and are very happy, but then he fades away. He's very sorry he has to leave, but he has no choice. Then he's gone. I'm by myself but then you show up. You take care of me but you see I'm not happy, so you get into a boat with me. You row until I recognize that I'm approaching the first island. As we get closer, I see Alan. He's playing his guitar. I look down and there's a guitar in my hands. I play the same song as he's playing. As the boat docks, he reaches out his hand. I look to you. You smile and nod your agreement that I should go. I kiss your cheek and take Alan's hand as I step off the boat. Then I wake up."

"That's quite a dream."

"Yes, it is. It's a very disturbing but ultimately satisfying dream. What does it mean? Why are you there?"

"I'd take it to mean that you are destined to be with Alan."

"That's a given. What about the second question?"

I contemplated playing the game through to the end, saying things like: "I have no idea why I would be in your dreams." or "The mind can be a very tricky thing. You may have thought I was the one in that dream. Perhaps my face was transposed onto someone else's body." I couldn't lie to her.

"This was all a mistake, a big selfish mistake. I never should have come to see you. I should have accepted that you were happy and then be happy myself. Everything worked out exactly the way I hoped it would. You have one man to love throughout your life, just like your parents and grandparents before you. You have kids and grandkids to love. I bet you even pursued a line of work that not only satisfied you but allowed you to help others, right?"

"I was a social worker at a State developmental center."

"In my mind, that's far more noble than working in a bank. And Alan's a minister instead of a car salesman. There's nothing wrong with being a car salesman, but a minister is a much higher calling, isn't it? It was you that did this for him."

"What are you talking about? I never worked in a bank and Alan never sold cars."

I smiled fondly at her. "No, you never did, did you? I better go now."

"But you never told me who you are and how you know me."

"It doesn't matter. I'm satisfied knowing that I have a place in your dreams. That will carry me for the rest of my life."

"But what about me? How am I supposed to carry on with these questions in my mind? I've obviously not only met you before, but I knew you well. In fact, you allude to a relationship we had, but I know nothing of this. I have no memory of you. Am I going crazy? How can I just go on?"

"Before you saw me today, it was just a fascinating but non-threatening dream you had, right?"

"Well, yes, but I can't just forget today, can I? I can't forget meeting you, can I?"

"Actually, you can. Be well, my love. Love Alan and your kids and grandkids. Keep playing your music. You're a beautiful person and you spread beauty wherever you go."

"Thank you, Joe."

"One last thing before I go. Why do mice have small balls?"

Hallie burst out laughing. It was an uncontrollable, unrestrained laugh. When she composed herself somewhat she responded, "Because only ten percent of them know how to dance."

"Goodbye, Hallie. I wish I didn't go to church this morning." I put my right hand on my left shoulder and all went dark. When I woke, I was sitting in my living room.

38

The next day, I confided in Sally, telling her everything about my encounter at the church with Hallie.

"I thought I felt something, I guess it was when you did your Correction. How can you explain her dream?"

"I don't know. Sometimes the various streams of history have a way of seeping in. I still can't explain how Miss Lily could tell your mother that she remembered me. She was about one hundred years old at the time, so perhaps her mind wasn't the sharpest, but I wonder. Maybe she was given a glimpse into our world, just like Hallie was. It's beyond me."

"So, are you going to get back in the saddle again? Are you going to see women or even going out with the guys once in a while?"

"I don't know."

"Dad, you were a great father to Oscar and me. You still are, and you're a great grandfather for the kids. But that's about all you were. For most of my life, you shut down to the outside world. It was so great seeing you with Hallie. She brought you to life. I don't want you shutting down again."

"I won't, honey. The situations are worlds different. Your mother was stolen from me, twice. The first time I did something about it. The second, I was helpless. I gave up Hallie freely because I loved her and I wanted her to have unvarnished happiness. I have no regrets and you're right. She brought me back to life. If I become a solitary, misanthropic curmudgeon, it'll be because I want to be, not because I lost something."

"That works for me. Oscar and I and the kids will do our best to make sure you're not solitary. However, there's not much we can do to keep you from being a misanthropic curmudgeon."

"Don't even try. So, where were we when we stopped last week?"

"You'd just started telling me about Efrem rescuing Andrew, Eliza and Hannah from slavery."

"Ah yes, Efrem. Well, sit back. This is a great story. It's one of our family's crowning achievements and a case where we put a Correction to its highest purpose."

39

Rhinebeck is a small town, so it's hard not to run into someone else who lives here. I had to be careful whenever I was out to either not run into Hallie or make sure she didn't recognize me if she did. For the first time in my life, I grew a beard. I also started wearing glasses full-time. Oscar said he liked the beard. He said I should have gone for this look years ago.

Sally said she wasn't crazy about the new me, but she understood why I was changing my appearance. She was actually happy I was doing this because it meant that I wasn't shutting down or shutting in. I was altering my appearance for the sake of getting out of the house.

My beard and glasses got their first test a few months later. I was in line at Brewed Awakening, the town's coffee bar, when Hallie walked in with two of her granddaughters, who were obviously twins. They got in line behind me. Hallie was having an animated conversation with them. She wasn't sure the place could make a fruit smoothie for them, but she would find out.

"I believe they can whip up strawberry and banana smoothies," I said to them. The girls cheered.

"Thanks," Hallie replied. "This is the third place we've tried. The diner couldn't accommodate us, and the ice cream shop was inexplicably closed. I was ready to give up, but when two seven-year-olds get something on their mind, it's hard to move on to anything else. Anyway, it's my job as their Nanna to spoil them, isn't it?"

"It absolutely is. I'm the same way when my grandkids are around."

"I've lived in this town practically my entire life, but I've never come in here. I've always preferred to prepare my own coffee, I guess."

Which you take light with two sugars, I thought to myself. I had once approached the owner of this shop to see if Hallie could play and sing here. He was interested, and we were about to set it up when I performed the Correction.

"I'm a regular. My doctor told me I should cut back on the caffeine, but it's hard giving up some addictions."

"Isn't that the truth."

We got up to the front of the line. The young barista called out to me. "The usual, Mr. V?"

I turned to Hallie. "See? A regular."

"How are you, Sandi. Yeah, the usual. And give my new friends here whatever they want. It's on me. I think the girls here want smoothies. Let me guess. This one wants banana, and this one wants strawberry."

"I think it will be the other way around, actually," Hallie corrected.

"It's obvious I've never had to deal with twins. And what will you have, Mrs.?"

"Parker, Hallie Parker. And this is Wendy and that's Carly. I'll have a regular coffee." Sandi retreated to prepare the order. "Thank you so much, Mr.?"

"Varnum, Efrem Varnum." I said it soft enough to make sure that Sandi couldn't hear me. She knew my name was Vance. Sandi soon came back with our drinks, which I paid for.

"It's been a pleasure meeting you, Mrs. Parker, and you too, Wendy and Carly." I turned to leave when Hallie spoke up.

"Please, join us. I don't dare walk with these girls while they drink their smoothies. One or both of them—or me—will probably wear it if we do."

I knew I was pushing my luck. Something I said or a certain look might seep through her consciousness, but I couldn't resist. "Sure, I can sit for a few minutes."

We sat down at a table. The girls slurped their smoothies while we talked. Hallie noticed the small stage over in the corner.

"Do they have music here?"

"Occasionally the local talent come here to play and sing. The owner put that stage up years ago."

"I wish I knew about this place. I would have liked some place to come and play my guitar."

"Oh, you play guitar."

"Yeah, my husband and I play at church, but I've always wanted another outlet."

"Nanna's real good," Carly piped up. "Yeah, she's good!" Wendy concurred.

"There, you have those unbiased testimonials to go on," she laughed.

"I know the owner. I'd be glad to speak with him on your behalf."

"You're very sweet, and maybe if I'd learned about this place earlier I might take you up on it, but we're leaving town in a month or two. My husband's retiring and we'll be moving to the Schenectady area. That's where both kids and our grandchildren are. I don't want to miss a moment with these two monkeys."

Both girls gave her a look at being called 'monkeys' but the prospect of having Nanna permanently nearby clearly thrilled them. I knew in my heart that this is what Hallie should do, but it grieved me that she would move away from me forever.

"What's your husband retiring from, if I may ask?"

"He's a minister at the Wesley United Methodist Church here in town. He had wanted to retire a couple years ago, but they were slow in finding a replacement for him. Now it's time."

"You've got a month or two left? I must make my way over there one of these Sundays."

"Please do. It would be great to see you again before we go. Thank Mr. Varnum again, girls, before we head back home."

They left the coffeehouse. It was the last I ever saw of her. I never did make it over to the church.

40

I was afraid of wallowing in my despair and bitterness like I did when I lost Olivia so, immediately after Hallie moved, I immersed myself in doing what I do best. I performed Corrections. Instead of doing them for people I randomly met, I went to a place filled with people in dire need of second chances. I volunteered at a halfway house.

Since Rhinebeck is such a small town, there's not much need for such facilities there so I traveled an hour south twice a week to Ossining. Ossining is small by city standards, but its size dwarfed Rhinebeck. The principal thing that drew me to the halfway house in that town was its proximity to one of the more famous prisons in the country. When I first started working at the halfway house, the prison was known as the Ossining Correctional Facility, but its name has since reverted back to its original name, Sing Sing.

The Irving Van Dressen Halfway House, so named for a philanthropist who financed the center in the 1950s, acted as the transitional home for former male prison inmates. It can handle up to thirty men at a time. They stay there an average of three months, but no longer than six months. While at the halfway house, they learn skills and coping mechanisms for life outside prison. Sometimes, the training takes hold and the man lives a fruitful life without resorting to criminal activity that would put him back in prison. However, the recidivism rate is very high and these men have difficulty coping. Eventually, their criminal proclivities land them back in prison, or worse.

I applied to volunteer there as a "life therapist" using my work experience as examples of skills that I could apply in any setting. Places like these are always desperate for willing employees, so even though what I offered could be viewed as a pile of horse manure, they accepted me. I worked every Tuesday and Friday and reported to Dr. Ellis Maxwell, a behavioral psychologist assigned to the house.

Dr. Maxwell was an affable man and an extremely competent psychologist. His evaluations and diagnoses of individual residents were, at least from my layman's perspective, on the mark. Maxwell's problem was his attitude. To the residents, he was caring and helpful, but when we would meet to talk about them with me, his tone was mocking and contemptuous. I think it was that he saw these men so briefly—a half-hour per week for three to six months—that he knew he couldn't do much with them.

Like I said, however, his evaluations were accurate, and that's what was most useful to me. His evaluation was the first thing I would consider when determining whether that person would receive a Correction. If Maxwell's conclusion was that a man was almost certain to revert to a life of crime, I most likely would not help him. It could be a waste since I would return the man back in time and there would be a strong probability that he would simply start up anew as a criminal. I would also rely on Maxwell's determination whether the man's behavior was the result of environmental factors—an abusive parent, for example—that the man could not overcome. It would likewise be a waste to do a Correction for him since there would be too many variables that would put the man back on the route of criminality.

The men I would look to help would be those who can trace their current situations back to a single decision they made. They knew the exact moment that they fell in with the wrong crowd, for example. Perhaps he went for a joyride with guys he thought were his friends and, the next thing he knew, he was in a car fleeing from a bank after a robbery. His life went totally awry after that, but there was a point when he could have said no. That's what I was looking for.

My job was to talk to the residents before Dr. Maxwell did. I would put together notes for the doctor of our conversation so he would not go in cold. Given that he had limited time to work with each patient, this allowed him to dive right in without wasting precious time getting acquainted. This approach was also beneficial for the resident who could be intimidated if he were to sit down with the doctor with no warmup. Instead, he would open up with me, a nobody without a 'Doctor' in front of my name or a string of initials after it.

I would talk with them about the crimes they committed, the time they served, and other basic information. I would ask them if they had kids or any other family waiting for them when they were released. Then I would delve into their upbringing and what led them into a life of crime. During my first week, there was only one candidate for a Correction, and then I backed off. Something about his story didn't ring true, so I decided not to proceed.

I was wondering if I was going to help anyone or whether the guys who come to this place were too damaged and couldn't be redeemed. Then I met Eddie McKinnon. I read his file prior to our meeting. He'd just been released from Sing Sing after serving ten years of an eighteen year sentence for armed robbery. He was a quiet, unassuming twenty-eight-year-old Black man. Happy to be out, he was anxious about his future. As an ex-con, the deck was stacked against him. He wanted to go back to school, but he had no idea about how to make that happen.

"So, what happened? How did you end up in prison?"

"My own stupidity. My Mom always said that Gene Franklin was bad news, that he'd end up either dead or in prison. She told me to steer clear of him. She said I was smart and could make something of myself, perhaps even go to college. But I was a cocky young kid. I knew better. I went with Gene one night. We stopped at a convenience store and he pulled out a forty-five to get some quick cash. I told him I didn't want any part of that. "Suit yourself," he said. Gene went in, but the store owner was ready for him. He pulled out his shotgun and shot Gene square in the chest. He was dead before he hit the floor.

"The owner called 911 and then ran out to the car and aimed the gun at me until the cops arrived. I got extra time because Gene died during the commission of a crime. My mom wanted to visit me in prison, but I told her not to. I didn't want her to see me like that. Now that I'm out, I don't know if I can see her, not until I can make her proud of me again. Do you think you guys can help me straighten myself out?"

"We'll see what we can do. You don't have any kids, do you?"

"No, what's that have to do with anything?"

"Just a routine question. Do you remember the date you were arrested?"

"I'll never forget it, June 5, 1974."

"Good. Repeat after me. I wish I listened to my mother and didn't go with Gene Franklin on June 5, 1974."

"I already said that, didn't I?"

"Just humor me."

"Okay. I wish I listened to my mother and didn't go with Gene Franklin on June 5, 1974."

I reached over and put my hand on his shoulder. He disappeared. I found myself sitting in the same chair at the conference table, but across the table from me was a different halfway house resident, Charlie Anderson.

"You okay, man?" Charlie asked. "You zoned out on me there. It's like you was somewhere else."

"Sorry about that, Charlie. Just give me one minute."

I pulled out a pen and wrote everything I could remember about Eddie. I would no longer have his file here, but I had memorized information such as his mother's address and phone number. I wanted to write it down before I forgot it.

I knew I wasn't being fair to Charlie, taking some of his time to write notes about somebody else, but I'd already determined Charlie was too damaged by an abusive father and a drug-addicted mother for a Correction to do any good. I needed to find out if my work had done any good with Eddie. I finished my writing and turned my attention back to Charlie.

"So, Charlie, you were telling me about your dad."

I finished my interview with Charlie, and I was done for the day. I hit the road for home. The next day I called Eddie's mother.

"Hello, is this Mrs. McKinnon?"

"Yes, it is."

"I'm trying to reach your son, Eddie."

"He doesn't live here. He hasn't lived here in five years. You can probably reach him at his office."

His office? That was encouraging.

"Do you have the number there?" I asked.

"Yes, it's 718-555-2641."

"Thank you."

I dialed the number she gave me. A young woman answered.

"Councilman McKinnon's office. How can I help you?"

"Councilman? Eddie McKinnon?"

"Yes, that's who you called, isn't it?"

"Yes, yes it is. Thank you."

I did this job for ten years. I averaged about a Correction per month during this time. None of them approached the success of Eddie McKinnon. The majority didn't work out at all. They may have gone back and changed their behavior for this one instance, but then got in trouble with the law in another. A couple men over that ten years showed up again at the halfway house a couple years after I had originally seen them.

The few who actually took advantage of this second chance to make something of their lives made the entire venture worthwhile for me. Hell, Eddie alone would have done it. There were a few times when I wished I could have gotten credit for my efforts, but I got over that quickly. I just had to tell myself: "We do this to help people, not for credit."

41

That's my life. After the halfway house, I rarely performed Corrections. I hadn't soured on them like I had in the past, I just wasn't encountering many people. I settled into a quiet, solitary existence to live out my days, but it was a content existence. The kids and the grandkids would come by occasionally, and that was enough. Eventually, there were great-grandkids.

I tried looking up Hallie and Alan about ten years ago, when they would have been about ninety. However, both had passed the previous year. They did that thing where long and happily married couples die within days of each other. Hallie had said many, many years ago when she was briefly mine that she grew up dreaming of loving one man throughout her life. Another part of that dream was that she would have children and grandchildren. If I'd never done another Correction in my life, providing her with the opportunity to live her dreams was enough for me to die in peace.

Sally was performing Corrections on a regular basis, as was Hannah. Then Hannah called me to tell me she was expecting twins. That would be two more to perform Corrections. I hoped the world could take it.

If someone ever comes up to you and asks you if there's anything in your life you'd like to go back and change, don't automatically think it's a rhetorical question. There are people who can make dreams come true.

About the Author

John Hazen, the author of seven acclaimed suspense novels, lives with his wife, Lynn, and dog, Castle. He spends his days writing, playing tennis, playing his clarinet and trying out new recipes in the kitchen. He has adopted the Beatles' song "I'll Follow the Sun", as his mantra: he grew up in Massachusetts, lived most of his life in New Jersey and now has retired to Florida.

Special thanks go to Mary Ellen Bramwell, Christy Cooper-Burnett,
Ricky Ginsburg, Cory Swanson, Sue Tokuyama and
Scarlet Sparkuhl Delia for their vital, editorial insights.

Note from the Author

Word-of-mouth is crucial for any author to succeed. If you enjoyed *The Correction*, please leave a review online—anywhere you are able. Even if it's just a sentence or two. It would make all the difference and would be very much appreciated.

Thanks!
John Hazen

Thank you so much for reading one of **John Hazen's** novels. If you enjoyed the experience, please check out our recommended title for your next great read!

Fava by John Hazen

Best Thrillers "18 Best FBI Thrillers Books" of All-Time

View other Black Rose Writing titles at www.blackrosewriting.com/books and use promo code **PRINT** to receive a **20% discount** when purchasing.

www.ingramcontent.com/pod-product-compliance
Lightning Source LLC
Chambersburg PA
CBHW010734100726
47899CB00009B/3040